MISSING

Also by Shelley Shepard Gray

MISSING

The Secrets of Crittenden County
BOOK ONE

SHELLEY SHEPARD GRAY

AVON
INSPIRE

An Imprint of HarperCollins*Publishers*

HarperCollins books may be purchased for educational, business, or sales promotional use. For information please write: Special Markets Department, HarperCollins Publishers, 10 East 53rd Street, New York, NY 10022.

FIRST EDITION

Library of Congress Cataloging-in-Publication Data has been applied for.

ISBN 978-0-06-208970-0

12 13 14 15 16   OV/RRD   10 9 8 7 6 5 4 3 2

To Cindy. Thank you for believing in me.

I will call to you whenever I'm in trouble, and
you will answer me.

Psalm 86:7

It's better to make new mistakes than to repeat
old ones.

Amish Proverb

Chapter 1

"Perry was the sort to say one thing and do the exact opposite. But surely most boys are like that?"

BETH ANNE BORNTRAGER

Despite her reservations, Abby Anderson cut through the Millers' land. Crooked Creek was rising, which meant the low-lying areas were at risk for flooding. But the Amish family's property was right in between the high school and her house, and crossing the Millers' fields instead of going around saved a lot of time. Besides, it wasn't like she had much of a choice. If she wanted to hang out with Jessica and Emily, she needed to get over her fear of trespassing.

"Hurry, Abby! If we don't get to the thicket of trees fast, someone from school is going to see us," Jessica called over her shoulder.

Abby bit her tongue so she wouldn't blurt out that they shouldn't have been there in the first place. Especially not so they could sit around and smoke. With every step, she felt worse about her decision.

But she couldn't change her mind now.

Right as they got near the thicket, a light rain started falling, soaking her sweatshirt and making her hair frizz. Well, of course it was raining. Did it ever *not* rain in March in Kentucky?

They tromped on. Deeper into the woods, closer to the swollen creek—following Jessica, who was heading toward what looked like a pile of logs and rocks. Abby tried not to look as nervous as she felt. But with every step, she half expected to hear Mr. Miller yell at them in Pennsylvania Dutch.

Everyone knew he didn't like people trespassing on his property.

"Hey, you think we should maybe turn around?"

"No." Jessica said as she pulled out her pack of cigarettes and popped one in between her lips. "Your problem, Abby, is that you need to learn to relax."

As she approached the pile of rubble, Abby knew relaxing wasn't her problem. Her problem was that she was trying too hard to fit in, to make friends with girls she had nothing in common with.

"Come on, Abby. Sit down," Emily said as she perched on one of the biggest rocks, her feet balancing on a nearby pile of wood. After lighting up, she leaned back on her elbows. "This is the perfect hiding spot. I bet a lot of kids have hung out here, doing stuff they shouldn't." She waggled her brows. "I bet even *Amish* ones."

Jessica tossed a stub down before lighting up another Marlboro. "Well, I don't know what they'd be doing. Singing Amish songs?"

Emily giggled. "That's what they do, right? Sing when they date?"

Abby rolled her eyes as her two girlfriends started singing off key. She knew "singings" were when Amish teenagers got together on Sunday nights. Sure, they sang—but they goofed off, too. And just hung out.

But she knew her girlfriends could care less about that.

What she really wished was that they'd stop singing so no one would hear them. Or that they'd want to stop smoking and get out of the rain.

Or that she was brave enough to just go home.

She sighed as Emily passed over the Marlboros and lighter. Nervously, she took a cigarette and lit it. But after two experimental puffs, Abby started to feel sick. She didn't want to smoke, and she didn't want to get in trouble.

"Look, I'm just going to go home. If my parents find out that I didn't come straight home from school, I'm going to get grounded again."

But instead of waving her off, Jessica gave her a look, then grabbed Abby's backpack. "Nope," she said coldly. "You've got to stay here."

"Jess, I've got to go."

"Stay. Relax."

"Come on. Hand it over."

"How about you come get it?" Jessica said with a grin.

Tired of the game, Abby reached out. But as soon as she did, Jessica turned and threw the backpack behind her. Hard.

Abby watched as it sailed through the air and disappeared into the brush about twenty feet away. "Jess, c'mon. I can't believe you threw it in the dirt."

"It's no big deal. Just get it and go home."

Too upset to speak, Abby stomped over to where she saw the bag land. As the rain fell, she swiped the wet hair from her eyes and started searching through the brush.

But she didn't see her backpack anywhere.

Bending down, she pulled some brush away, uncovering a gaping hole. Great. That was so her luck. Only *her* backpack would get tossed down some ditch on the Millers' land.

She got on her hands and knees to see how deep the hole went and whether her bag was at the bottom. Leaning over, she spotted the orange knapsack . . . on top of a crumpled body.

When she screamed, the other girls came running.

And then the three of them just stood there. Staring at her orange backpack and a dead Amish guy in a hole.

Under a pile of brush. In the middle of the Millers' farm.

Where they never should have been in the first place.

Deputy Sheriff Mose Kramer wearily pulled off of Turkey Knob Road and made a left onto Fords Ferry. He'd already surveyed most of the surrounding area around where Perry Borntrager's body had been discovered but wasn't any closer to understanding what had happened to the guy.

It looked like someone had bashed him on the head with a brick or rock and tossed him down the abandoned well. Later, the medical examiner confirmed that Perry had died from an injury to the head, and that his body had been in that hole for quite a while before Abby Anderson discovered him.

Perhaps two months.

That was all he knew thus far. Very little evidence had been found near and around the body. To make matters worse, the rain didn't seem to have any interest in stopping, which had made the creek swell. Well, guess that's what you get with springtime in Kentucky.

In addition, after months of speculation that the boy had jumped the fence and was living in the city, his friends and neighbors had suddenly become closemouthed. No one was talking, not even the Millers, on whose property the body had been found.

His truck slid a little on a patch of gravel and he rode the brake, slowing the truck just in time to see a wild turkey pecking at the ground to his right. There was no one around, an abandoned trailer beside the road, and no cars behind him, so he stopped completely and, for a spell, watched the turkey through the constant drizzle of rain.

The turkey's appearance, so out of place yet hopelessly familiar, felt like his own in the county. He'd grown up Amish off of Highway 91, and had lived barefoot for most of his life, until he was fourteen. He'd gone to school, helped at his parents' farm—but had always wanted to be someone different.

Now he was. He'd gone to the University of Cincinnati, studied criminal justice, and graduated with a degree and his certification. Got a job in Clermont County, then saw the posting for the sheriff's department in Crittenden County. On a whim, he applied for the job. When he was called out to interview, he'd been delighted.

Getting offered the job felt right.

But he soon learned there were complications in becoming the sheriff in the county you grew up in. He knew too many people. Knew too many stories. Was too entrenched with the rhythms of life around the town of Marion. It was obvious they were counting on that, too. People were keeping secrets. Maybe they felt guilty. They'd all assumed the worst when Perry first disappeared, jumping to the conclusion that'd he'd given up their way of life.

All Mose knew was he needed help. The sheriff's office was short-handed—and, besides, none of his staff had had to deal with this kind of investigation before.

As he turned back to the road and started the drive back to Marion, Mose knew it was time to pick up the phone and give an old buddy a call. Luke Reynolds had just made detective in the Cincinnati Police Department. As luck would have it, he was also on leave, recovering from a gunshot wound.

If Mose played his cards right, he was going to get Luke to come help him out. For free.

Two Days Later

"Lydia?" her mother called out softly. "Lydia, won't you please join us for breakfast?"

Caught in the middle of pinning the front of her dress, she spat out the remaining pins she'd been holding between her lips so she could speak. "I'll be down soon, Mamm."

"When will that be? It's already after six, daughter."

Reality set in. Six in the morning might as well have been noon at their house. Since they owned a thriving farm and greenhouse nursery, each one of them got up before dawn in order to tend to the many chores that awaited.

Lydia had done just that for as long as she could remember. It was her way of life, and it was all that mattered.

Well, until she'd heard that Perry's body had been found in an abandoned well.

Now it felt like nothing mattered at all.

Just as she was neatly tying her black apron over her violet dress, her little sister, Becky, knocked on the door. "Lydia, you want eggs and sausages?"

"I do," she said as she opened the door. "Tell Mamm I'll be right there. All I need to do now is put on my *kapp*."

Becky looked doubtful. "And then you'll finally come downstairs?"

"Yep." When Becky turned away, Lydia carefully picked up her pressed *kapp* and pinned it over her hair. Now she was ready for the day. Even if she didn't feel that way inside. Blinking hard, Lydia tried her best to calm herself before descending the stairs. If she cried anymore, she was going to get sick.

But knowing Perry was dead was still such a shock. He'd been her first boyfriend. He'd given her her very first kiss. And though she'd broken things off with him in November, she still felt like part of her heart was missing.

Her family stilled as she entered the kitchen. All five of them were sitting around the large oak table like they always had. But their worried expressions were new.

Though she hadn't thought it was possible, she felt even more ill at ease. "I'm sorry I'm late."

"Will you be fit to work today?" her father asked.

The plants and the work always came first. "*Jah.* As soon as I eat, I'll head out to the greenhouse. I can put in a full day's work, for sure."

A long moment passed as both her parents studied her closely. "*Gut,*" her father said finally. "That is *gut.*"

Lydia supposed it *was* good that she was getting back to her normal routine. But she knew that inside, she felt anything but normal.

Two hours later, she was on her hands and knees under one of the long tables in the greenhouse, her arms elbow deep in potting soil. As the rich, dark dirt surrounded her skin, she breathed deeply. This was familiar. The dirt and the plants and the earthy smell were what she knew.

"Excuse me? Are you Lydia Plank?" an *Englischer* asked from the doorway.

"I am." Carefully, she pulled her hands out of the bin and shook off the remaining dirt that stuck between her fingers. "But we're not open yet. We don't open until nine."

His expression set, the dark-haired man stepped inside with a bit of a limp. He looked at her carefully. "I'm not here for plants. I came to speak to you, if I may."

Foreboding churned in her belly as she slowly got to her feet. "Yes?"

"My name is Luke Reynolds, Lydia. I'm a detective from Cincinnati."

"From Ohio?" Brushing off the last crumbs of dirt from her apron, she straightened. "What do you want with me?"

"I'm a friend of one of the county's deputies," he said.

She shook her head. "I'm afraid I don't know too many of the English."

"His name is Mose Kramer." He smiled slightly. "Ring a bell now? He grew up off of 91." Before she could comment, he continued: "Mose and I are old friends, and given that you don't have too many suspicious deaths around here, he asked me to help out with the investigation. I'm on leave at my job due to this bum leg." Because she still must have looked confused, he added bluntly. "I'm here to look into Perry Borntrager's death."

Her mouth went dry. "I . . . I don't understand."

The *Englischer*'s mouth tightened, as if it was paining him to speak. "The county coroner determined Perry Borntrager's death wasn't accidental."

"You're saying he's been murdered?"

"Yeah," he said with a nod, his eyes grave. "Perry died when he was hit on the back of his head with a rock."

She felt herself struggling to breathe. "I canna talk now."

"I'm sorry if I shocked you but we need to continue."

Her heart was racing. This was a true nightmare. As tears pricked her eyes, she found herself begging. "Please? May I, I mean, may we do this tomorrow?"

"I'm sorry, but no." He pulled out a pad of paper. "Lydia, since the two of you used to date, I'm hoping you can answer some questions."

"I don't know if I can." Looking around, she searched for

her parents. Or her brother, or even customers. But instead of finding support, she found she was alone.

The man stepped forward, his cheeks already turning red from the warm, humid air of the greenhouse. "Is there somewhere outside where we can talk?" He smiled slightly as he waved a hand in front of his face. "Some place where it's a little cooler? It shouldn't take too long."

Her hands began to tremble as she nodded. "We can go to our bench by the oak, if that's all right?"

"Sure. You lead the way."

Her heart sinking, Lydia led the man outside, wondering how much he knew . . . and how much she could keep secret.

Though he was only three years older than his sister Abby, Walker Anderson felt like he was double that. Ever since his little sister had been found with two other girls screaming and crying in the middle of the Millers' land, she'd been in a daze.

There didn't seem to be anything he could say to her that would make her feel better.

But still, he had to try. "You really should go to school today. It will be easier in the long run."

"Walker, all anyone's going to do is ask me about Perry. Plus, I'm a senior, it's not like anything matters now, anyway." Eyes almost identical to his own sparkled with pain. "I wish I was you. I wish I was in college instead of high school."

"I know. But you can't change how things are."

"I wish you were going to be the one questioned instead of me. You knew Perry. You knew him really well."

Walker swallowed hard. He and Perry had met when they'd both taken part-time jobs at the Schrock's Variety Store. Even though Perry was Amish, they'd clicked and become fast friends.

Perry had a reserved manner but a dry sense of humor. His dark hair and hazel eyes had attracted girls like bees to honey. And for a time, Walker and the Schrocks' son Jacob had been with him constantly. But then Perry had started dating Lydia Plank. Then had started keeping secrets. As the weeks passed, he'd become more serious, more short-tempered. Developed a short fuse.

When Lydia broke up with Perry, Walker hadn't blamed her. He'd told her that, too. She was too good for Perry.

But then the downward spiral began in earnest. Perry began skipping work and started hanging out with a lot of new people, new people Walker didn't trust. Some of these people were from the county, but others were new faces, people he'd never seen before in their small community.

Finally, when Walker learned some of Perry's secrets, he'd quit working at Schrock's and vowed never to associate with the guy again. A lump formed in his throat as he remembered how he'd stopped by Schrock's at the end of December and had seen Perry, Jacob, and Lydia for the first time in months. He hadn't been able to get out of there fast enough.

"Walker?" Abby said. "You okay?"

Walker shook his head and turned toward his sister. "Sure."

She bit her lip. "I heard the police are questioning people about Perry. All they asked me was how I found him." She blinked hard. "You don't think they'll come talk to me anymore, do you?"

"No." Walker figured if the police started digging around Perry's past, there was only one person in the Anderson family who they would seek out. And that would be him.

He was going to have to figure out how to keep that from happening.

Chapter 2

"When we all heard that Perry was gone, I thought he'd left town. And you know what? I was relieved. I wasn't the only one to feel that way, either."

WALKER ANDERSON

Lydia's hands were shaking by the time the *Englischer* rose from the bench.

"I am sorry I've frightened you," he said. "I promise, that wasn't my intent."

Lydia looked down at her hands instead of replying. They still trembled, so much so that she was having a difficult time grasping the edge of her apron like she always did when she felt agitated.

The detective stepped forward, obviously uneasy. "I don't want to leave you alone like this. Is there someone who I could take you to?"

His voice, so terribly kind, made her finally lift her head and meet his gaze. She noticed for the first time that he had green eyes and a scar above his left eyebrow. "I will be perfectly fine here." By herself.

He blinked at her cool tone. "All right, then. I'll be going."

She said nothing as he awkwardly turned and limped

toward the parking lot. The uneven ground was doing him no favors. It was obvious he was finding the journey painful.

Well, now they were both in pain, she thought uncharitably. She hadn't liked his questions about Perry one bit. Nor had she appreciated the way he'd talked to her.

Or how he'd looked at her like she knew more than she was saying.

Both his voice and his manner conveyed that he thought she was worldly, that she knew more about what happened outside of the quiet comfort of her home and her town than she let on. As if she was hiding things. Information.

"Have you ever taken drugs, Lydia?"

She'd been so taken aback by the question she had hardly done more than shaken her head in dismay.

"Are you positive? You won't be in trouble if you've tried a couple of things. Pot? Meth?" He waited a moment. "Pills, maybe?"

"Nee."

"You sure? I'm not lookin' to get you in trouble here . . . I just need to know."

Of course, she'd finally found her voice and had told him in no uncertain terms that she had most certainly not taken drugs. Ever.

But instead of looking at her with a new respect, the detective had only seemed more troubled. Like she'd given him the wrong answer.

How could that be? Hands still shaking, she tucked them under her black apron. She needed to get control of herself. Had to. If she didn't, more questions would be asked that she didn't want to answer.

"Lydia, you need to get back to work, child. We are open now."

Startled, she turned to see her father watching her at the

edge of the slate walkway leading to the greenhouses. "*Jah,* Daed."

Work came first. Always.

Standing up, she went back into the greenhouse and hastily cleaned up the soil she'd scattered on the floor when the detective had shown up. After claiming the broom hanging on the wall, she deftly took care of the crumbs and went ahead and cleaned off the steppingstones that ran through the middle of the greenhouse as well.

Lydia had always found it silly to pay so much attention to dirt in the greenhouse when their whole business was dirt and plants. But her mother was a stickler for organization and order. She didn't want any dirt to settle where it didn't belong.

She'd just put up the broom when the door opened and customers entered. "*Wilkum,*" she said. "May I help you?"

"Hello, Lydia. We're looking for some tomato and pepper seedlings," Mrs. Brown, one of their best customers, replied. "What do you have?"

"Several varieties of both," she said with a shaky smile. "The seedlings are over here. I'll show you."

And so it began. Another day of pretending that nothing was wrong.

Even though Perry was gone forever.

Luke Reynolds knew it did no good to continually blame the pair of teens whose shenanigans had injured his leg. During all his years on the police force, he'd never had to do much more than look like he was about to draw his weapon, and no matter how misguided, the teens had backed off—and none had *ever* gone on to cause so much damage in such a short amount of time. They'd stolen a Camry, led him on an eighteen-mile chase through the streets of Cincinnati, caused a four-car pileup, and then accidently shot him in the leg.

But it didn't help to hold a grudge.

He was trying to rely on faith to get him through this hard stretch. He believed that everything happened for a reason— even the difficult, painful things. It wasn't the Lord's job to explain things in detail.

And here in Kentucky, away from Renee, his on-again, off-again girlfriend, his mind felt clearer. Maybe it was breathing the humid, thick, woodsy-smelling air instead of city smog and exhaust fumes. Maybe it was the slower pace. Here in Crittenden County, no one seemed to be in much of a hurry.

No matter what it was, he was healing, his mind was clearer, and his outlook on life was improving.

But on a day like today, when the weather was cool, and the damp rain made the bones in his leg feel like they were breaking apart instead of fusing together, Luke was tempted to blame someone for his troubles.

Otherwise, he was going to descend even deeper into depression.

And that depression was the only reason he'd taken Mose's call a week ago. That, and the fact that he genuinely liked the guy. He was plainspoken and easy to get along with, and had a great sense of humor. The darker the situation, the more morbid the guy's jokes became. And though most people would find his quips off-putting, Luke knew the jokes were part of the territory.

If you didn't try to find some humor in the difficult things seen or heard while on the force, the job would be just too much.

Like his conversation with Lydia Plank.

The girl was as pretty as a picture and had been as wary and nervous around him as anyone he'd ever interviewed.

Actually, she'd been so innocent-seeming, he realized that he'd forgotten that there were people out in the world who weren't actively trying to take advantage of him or the system.

It was really too bad she was a suspect in Perry Borntrager's death.

Luke had just pulled out of the greenhouse's gravel driveway and was negotiating his way down the narrow road, past another Amish farm and a rundown, rusting single-wide, when his cell phone rang.

"How's it goin', Luke?" Mose's voice boomed in his ear.

As he stopped for a buggy to pass in front of him, and as he thought about the mess of questions he had about the case, he chuckled softly. "It's going."

"Finding your way around the county?"

"Pretty much."

"You're using my directions, not that Garmin contraption, right?"

"I'm sticking to your directions like glue," Luke quipped, remembering how he'd gotten lost on a long stretch of windy road with no signs for miles, the Garmin squawking "Recalculating" every ten feet. "Just got done visiting with Lydia Plank for a bit. Off to go see Walker Anderson now."

"That Lydia's a sweetie, ain't she?"

"You know her, Mose?" She'd made it seem like they were strangers.

"Oh, sure." Mose's voice turned fond as he continued on. "I remember when she was just a little thing. Back when Lydia was only four or five, why, she used to hang on to Ann's, her momma's, sleeve when she worked . . . why sometimes I even went to the Planks' nursery just to get a peek of her. She had a smile that would light up the sky, she did."

Luke drummed his fingers on the steering wheel. He was both amused and slightly disturbed by his friend's reminiscing. The investigation needed to come first, not the guy's reflections on the past.

And though he'd at first let his buddy tell stories, Luke felt it was time to remind Mose which of them had a uniform full of medals and commendations and who was wasting away on the back roads of Kentucky. Speaking his mind, he said, "It's comments like that that make me real glad you called me, Mose. You're too close to the community. Lydia's a suspect."

"I know but, shoot, I just can't imagine her doing anything so evil."

"Everyone has the propensity for evil, Mose. Even the Bible states that."

As Mose grumbled, Luke stopped at a four-way, waited a bit for another horse and buggy to cross the intersection, then glanced at Mose's hand-drawn map. He needed to get off of Fords Ferry Road and head into Marion. Crittenden County seemed to be made up of the most winding, hilly roads he'd ever seen in his life.

"So . . . where do you plan to go after you visit with Walker?"

Luke could just imagine his friend eyeing a map and practically charting his progress, mile by mile. "Mose, are you going to be making this a habit? Because I didn't expect you to be checking up on me like I was a new recruit."

"I'm not checkin'," he grumbled. "Just interested."

"Just *really* interested."

"Hey, you know I wanted to go with you today."

"And you know why I asked you to stay back. I'll find out

a whole lot more if I act new and dumb. I can ask questions about all this better than you." Luke paused. "And you know I'm right, Mose. That's why you called me on the case."

"I know. But these are my people."

Something about that phrase struck Luke in his heart. Had he ever felt like that in Cincinnati? That the people he'd sworn to serve and protect were his responsibility, not just a job?

"So, Luke, do ya need any information about Walker Anderson?"

His friend sounded so hopeful, Luke couldn't help but grin as he clicked on his turn signal. "I think you've told me all I need to know. Walker's working at Schrock's Variety, right?"

"He is." His voice warmed. "He's a good kid, Luke. Hardworking. Handsome. You're going to be quite taken with the boy, mark my words."

"I don't want to date him, Mose. I'm looking for information, right?"

"Of course, right. Well, I'm sure you'll soon find out plenty about Walker." After a pause, he added, "Now, something that you might not know is that Walker quit that job a while back and only recently got back on board. I'd be curious as to why he did that."

After glancing at Mose's directions again, and taking two quick right turns, he focused on his friend's comment. "Isn't he in college? Maybe he decided doing both was too much and then got a handle on things."

"Maybe, but that don't seem likely. I'd bet money that there's a story there."

"I'll do some asking, then."

"And I'd also be curious about how well he knows Lydia. And maybe I'd even try to ask him about—"

"Thanks, Mose," he said quickly, cutting him off. "I'll check in with you later."

"You sure you don't—"

"Positive." He chuckled and disconnected, cutting off Mose's comments. Taking a breath, he put both hands on the wheel and concentrated more fully as he turned right onto South Main Street, the main thoroughfare of Marion.

He passed the Marion Café and the courthouse. Noticed a spring flower display in one of the small gift shops that lined the street. Stopped and smiled at a mother and her two children at a crosswalk.

The streets were by no means crowded by city standards and he felt his mind drifting back to Lydia Plank. She was a pretty young woman, graced with wide-set eyes and a slim, willowy figure. Her manner had been sweet. Until he'd rattled her good. Then she'd become far more quiet and withdrawn. And far less talkative.

He pulled into the parking lot in front of Schrock's Variety and walked in, prepared for anything.

Except for what he found.

"Duck!" a voice called out the moment he opened the front door.

Obediently, Luke ducked, but was taken aback by the next order.

"Close the door behind you, man!"

"Huh?"

"Hurry, English, or you're going to let the chicken out!"

He shut the door just as a squawk erupted right by his ear. Like the city boy he was, Luke ducked down again and attempted to crouch lower.

"Crouch" being all a matter of opinion. His leg hurt like the dickens and he was becoming more afraid of either getting embarrassingly stuck on the floor or being pecked by an angry bird. "What's that bird doing in here?" he called out as he heard another angry squawk and the crashing of cans.

"It's a hen, English. And we're sellin' her, of course."

As the Amish man darted and grabbed, a younger voice entered into the conversation. "The latch on the cage got loose, mister. And don't worry. This doesn't happen all that often."

The "all that often" comment sounded foreboding. "I hope not." Finally brave enough to lift his head, he saw a pair of men looking at him with humor shining in their eyes. The younger one was dressed like any other kid his age, in a T-shirt, jeans, and boots. Beside him was an Amish man with a graying beard, wire-rimmed glasses, and an irritated chicken in his arms.

"Listen. I'm going to stand up now. There aren't any more birds on the loose, are there?"

"Not presently."

As gracefully as he could, Luke attempted to get to his feet. But he needed something to grip in order to take the weight off his right leg as he straightened and, of course, there was nothing around.

"Need a hand?" the boy asked.

"Yeah. If you don't mind, I could literally use your hand," he admitted, swallowing his pride. "My leg's busted."

The boy looked at his black and stainless steel brace attached with Velcro over his khakis and grimaced. "That stinks. Did you break it?"

"Gunshot."

The look of grimace turned to fascination as he strode forward. "Really? Wow. Were you in Afghanistan?"

"No. Cincinnati," Luke said dryly as he gripped the kid's

well-built, thick arm and carefully pulled himself up to his feet. "I'm a cop. I was chasing some kids who didn't want to be caught. Turns out one kid's gun was faster than my feet."

"Wow." The boy looked like he wanted to ask more questions, but he stepped away the moment Luke was steady on his feet.

"I'm better now, it's just a little stiff."

"What are you doing here in Kentucky? Just visiting?"

There was an edge to the boy's voice that set Luke's sensors on alert. "No. I'm helping a friend out."

"Must be some friend."

"He's the best. I went to the police academy with Mose Kramer," he explained, taking a stab in the dark that the boy knew the county's deputy sheriff.

As he'd expected, the boy froze.

Luke was just about to explain his purpose for visiting when the Amish man's voice cut through the space.

"Enough with the questions, Walker. Customers don't come in here to be pestered."

Before Luke could jump in and say that the boy was no trouble, the older man puffed up his chest a bit and stepped forward. "What can we help you with? Need a chicken?" He grinned good-naturedly. "This one's cheap."

"I'll pass," Luke said with a laugh. "I like my chicken sealed in plastic containers or, better yet, fully cooked and on a plate." He walked forward. "I'm actually here to speak with Walker."

The older man's eyes darted to the kid and they exchanged a look.

Luke could tell the older man was not only the boy's boss, but a good friend of his. For a split-second, he debated whether to tell the complete truth. In the end, he decided to keep things open and honest. "I'm investigating Perry's death."

The elderly man sucked in his breath while the kid stilled. "But we've all talked to Sheriff Kramer," the man said. "Don't think there's anything more to tell ya."

"I know. I'm just going to ask a couple more questions." Turning to the older man, he said, "I assume you're Mr. Schrock?"

"I am."

"I'm sorry about Perry's death. I understand he worked for you for several years."

Something flashed in the man's eyes before he nodded. "Perry, his going missing, then turning up like he did? It's been a difficult thing, for sure." After clearing his throat, he said, "The store's empty. You want to speak with Walker in here? I need to go in the back and put this hen in a better cage."

"It's up to you, Walker. Is it okay to talk right here?"

After glancing at his boss for the space of a breath, Walker shook his head. "Can we just go sit in your car or something?"

"Sure. We can do that. We can go sit wherever you want," Luke said easily.

But as he led the way outside, a familiar buzzing sounded in his ears.

He knew what that buzzing was—after ten years on the force, he'd gotten real good at sensing when someone was putting their guard up.

And that was definitely the case with this kid. Something was going on with him. And maybe with the man, too. Their expressions were too shuttered, their words too forced.

Well, Luke was here to break down those walls and find out exactly what Walker knew.

Chapter 3

"Perry didn't necessarily care to work. But, of course, what boy his age does?"

MR. SCHROCK

Walker thought the policeman looked completely out of place in Crittenden County. With his pressed khakis, starched white dress shirt, and polished loafers, he looked like he would be more at ease just about anywhere but the middle of rural Kentucky.

Actually, the man looked more like an insurance salesman or a banker than a cop. Well, except for the cane he was using and the brace fastened on top of his left leg.

Then there was the way the man's eyes seemed to notice every detail in his path. He was definitely more than a little scary to be around.

"So, you want to go sit in my Explorer?"

It was pretty evident that the guy was in no hurry to sit with his leg all bent up. "We don't have to sit there; I just didn't want to talk in front of Mr. Schrock."

"Fair enough. Let's walk a bit." Knocking his knuckles against the brace, he almost smiled. "It will do my leg some good. You tell me when you want to stop."

The man's manner was too easy, his words were too agreeable. Felt fake. It made Walker nervous. "Sir, how old are you?"

"Twenty-nine. Why do you ask?"

Yeah, why had he? "I don't know." Feeling dumber by the second, he added, "I guess I just wanted to know a little bit more about you. You said you and Sheriff Kramer were friends . . ."

"Yep. We don't seem much alike, huh?"

"No, sir."

"Funny thing, friendship. It can spring up between the most unlikely people," he said cryptically. "Do you want to know anything more about me?"

Walker wanted to know a whole lot more, beginning with why the man was bothering him, why he was here in Marion, if he was carrying a gun, and if he'd ever shot somebody. But if he asked all his questions, the man would probably answer them all— and then Walker would feel obligated to talk a lot, too.

And he didn't want to do that. "Nope. I'm good."

"I wanted to talk to you about Perry Borntrager." He paused. "You knew him?"

Warily, Walker looked around them. The parking lot was empty. So was the wide front porch that ran the length of the store. His friendship with Perry had never been a secret, but now even mentioning the guy's name felt like he was doing something he shouldn't. "I knew Perry. Sure."

"He worked here awhile, right?"

He'd worked at Schrock's for years. "Right."

"Were you friends?"

"Kind of." When the detective stopped and stared at him, Walker felt even more uneasy. "We worked together, me, Jacob, and Perry."

"Jacob . . ."

"Jacob Schrock. He's out of town."

"Really? Kind of poor timing, don't you think?"

"Jacob's at a horse auction in Lexington." At least that what he was telling everyone.

The detective pointed to a bench under a tree that protected them from the rain that was starting to fall. "Here okay to sit? Leg's starting to cramp."

"Sure."

As Walker plopped down on the bench, far more slowly, the other man sat, gingerly placing his palms on the seat of the bench before easing down next to him. Then he pulled out a notebook and pen and wrote a couple of things down. "So you boys worked together. And now Jacob is out of town . . ." He paused, then looked at Walker directly. "And what do you think happened to Perry?"

The man was making him really nervous. The way his gaze zeroed in on him made Walker feel like he could practically read his mind. "I think someone tossed him down a well." Though his answer was unoriginal, Walker couldn't help but grin. After all, that was all anyone really knew about what had happened to Perry.

The detective didn't look amused.

"Let's try this again. What do you think happened to Perry, before he was dumped in an abandoned well and left to rot for months?"

Walker felt himself flush. As his mind raced to imagine what Perry had looked like, broken and decaying, he started feeling woozy. "I don't know, sir."

Before Walker could take another breath, the detective continued. "I'm wondering who would have any reason to hurt him."

"I don't know."

As the man stretched his leg and sighed, Walker wished that he was anywhere but here.

"Before I came here, I spoke with Lydia Plank. She knew Perry pretty well. You know her, right?"

"I've met her," Walker corrected. "I don't know her well. She's Amish."

"Perry was Amish and you knew him."

"That was different. I worked with Perry."

After pausing, and staring at him too long, the detective nodded. "Ah. Well, Lydia told me Perry had picked up some bad habits."

"Not really," Walker said quickly, then wondered why in the world he'd even come to Perry's defense. The guy had lied and hurt more people than Walker could count. Months ago, he'd sworn to himself that he'd never do anything for that guy again. "I mean, everything wasn't bad."

"So when was he good?"

The question caught him off guard. Was it really that simple? That someone was good, then bad? Switching personalities like a light switch? "I don't know . . ."

"You must have an idea," the detective prodded. "I mean, you seem like a pretty together guy. Mr. All-American. I'm sure you weren't hanging around a loser."

Walker squirmed and wished again that he was sitting anywhere other than where he was. "Perry was a decent guy when I first met him, which was about four years ago. He wasn't my favorite person, but he was good enough to hang out with."

"Even though he was Amish?"

With effort, Walker kept his expression neutral. People who didn't live in their community just didn't understand what it was like, living with the Amish. They seemed to think the two groups lived side by side and never intermingled.

Or they thought all the good people drove buggies and all the bad ones drove cars. "Just because a person is Amish doesn't mean he's all that different," he said slowly. "All it means is his religion is different."

"Ah." It was obvious the detective was struggling to understand what Walker meant, but Walker wasn't in any hurry to give some outsider a tutorial on living with the Amish.

"Anyway," Walker said. "Perry used to be okay, but then, things happened . . ."

"Like what?"

"I don't know for sure," Walker replied, glad that at least this was true. "Perry got mixed up with some bad people and started doing some things I didn't want to be around."

"Bad, like how?"

Walker turned to Luke in surprise. He'd thought Perry's activities were well known. "Bad, like drugs. Bad, like drug dealers." He paused and backpedaled fast. "I mean, that's what people said."

"What kind of drugs?"

"I don't know." He shifted. No way was he going into any more detail. Why had he even said anything?

"Did you meet these drug dealers?"

"No."

The man's eyes narrowed. "Sure?"

Walker hated the guy's voice, like he was being super sarcastic. "I never met his drug dealers, okay?"

"I'm still trying to figure out how Perry, who was Amish, would ever meet up with someone who sold drugs." He paused. "Are you sure it wasn't the other way around? That you were the one who introduced Perry to the 'bad' people?"

Walker was stunned. The sheriff had never asked stuff like this. "I didn't."

"I'm not here to get you in trouble, son . . ."

The "son" comment grated on him like nothing else. "Just because Perry was Amish doesn't mean he was innocent," he snapped. Giving into his temper. "You outsiders think you know everything. You don't. And just because I'm the *Englischer* doesn't mean I'm going around smoking pot."

"Ah, so that's what he was selling?"

"I don't know," he said quickly. "I just was using that as an example." If only Perry had just been selling pot. But he knew the drugs were a whole lot worse than that.

The detective nodded. "I'm sorry, you're right. Every once in a while I find myself slipping into the hope that the Amish are immune to the outside pressures of the world." He lowered his voice. "I've seen so much, I guess I hope that there are some people in this world who didn't screw up their lives so much."

"I'm not Amish, but my grandfather is. He might not have all the pressures of the outside world, but it doesn't mean he doesn't have pressure in his life. We all do. And we all react differently."

"That's a good point." He drummed his fingers on one of the metal braces surrounding his leg, then twisted two fingers and cracked his knuckles. The popping jarred against the sleepy sound of the pattering rain.

Then the detective turned to Walker, his expression completely void of emotion. "So far you've told me nothing I didn't already know. Tell me something new."

Pure relief filtered through Walker's bones. For a minute there he'd thought he'd let something slip. "I don't have anything else to tell you," Walker said quickly, doing his best to sound as detached as he wished he was. "I once was friends with the guy. Then I wasn't. I'm sorry he's dead, but I didn't have anything to do with it."

"Okay, well, what can you tell me about these drug dealers. Where did they come from? Were they local?" He paused. "You're in college, right? Maybe they came from your college?"

"I don't know where they came from," he retorted. "I never knew their names." Feeling Luke's skepticism bearing down hard on his shoulders, he added, "I didn't want to know." Looking out across the parking lot, at the thicket of trees, he ached to get away. To hide. To be anywhere but here being questioned.

"Were the guys Amish?"

Walker shook his head before he thought the better of it.

And that made the detective smile.

But still Luke didn't look like he believed a word of it. "Come on, Walker. Give me something I can use. Don't you want to know what happened to your friend? What were they? English? Amish? Old? Young?"

Walker felt his world about to change. The last thing he wanted was to get further sucked down into Perry's pit. "Both," he finally said.

Luke narrowed his eyes. "The drug dealers were both English and Amish?"

"No. They were all English. They were both old and young."

"And their ages?"

"Late teens, early twenties," Walker said, feeling as helpless as a bug in a spider's web. "Maybe someone even older, closer to thirty."

"From around here?"

"I don't know."

"Come on, Walker. Talk to me."

"All I know is they didn't go to high school with me. But the county is big, and a lot of kids don't go to the public school. They were homeschooled or they drop out."

"What do you know about Perry and Lydia?"

The change in questioning made his head spin. Clenching his jaw so his voice wouldn't shake he said, "They dated for a while. Then they broke up a few months ago. "

"And you said you don't know her well?"

"I know her well enough to say hi on the street, that's about it."

"She never confided in you?"

"Back when they were dating, they were Amish, I was not. It's not like Lydia would have had any reason to confide in me. We weren't friends."

"What were Perry and Lydia like together?"

Walker felt his mouth go dry. The detective was pushing all kinds of memories forward that he would have been perfectly happy to forget. "When they were still together, before Perry got mixed up in . . . they were good. Perry . . . he used to say that he'd do just about anything to make her smile."

The detective raised his eyebrow. "Why? Was she not normally happy?"

"I think she was normally quiet. Perry could be outrageous," he clarified. Remembering a time when Perry had made Lydia laugh so hard she started crying.

"Outrageous, how?"

Just remembering made Walker smile. "One time Perry got a hold of a unicycle."

"A unicycle?" the detective prodded.

"Yeah, like the circus clowns use? Anyway, somehow,

he'd taught himself to ride it. One day, Lydia came to the store and he rode that thing down the center aisle. Just as he got close, he lost control and knocked over a display of baked goods." Before he could stop himself, Walker found himself grinning. "Mr. Schrock was fit to be tied, but Lydia had laughed and laughed. Perry later said hearing her so happy was worth his punishment." Looking at the detective, Walker took a breath and spoke from his heart. "That's how Perry used to be, Detective. He was my friend. But once he changed . . . Either way, he didn't deserve to be murdered."

Luke stared at him for a long moment, then shifted and pulled out a card from his wallet. "Well, I'll be here awhile looking into Perry's death. Take this and give me a call if you remember something new. Call anytime, day or night. Okay?"

"Okay. Sure." He stood up and started walking before the detective got to his feet. But once he rounded the corner of the building, his footsteps slowed. And suddenly, it was impossible to not think about better days, easier times.

Back when he and Perry had been partners in crime . . . but just the kind of crime that meant harmless shenanigans and lots of laughs.

"Hey, Walker," Perry called out as he flew through the front door. Late again. "Don't tell Schrock, okay?"

Walker crossed his arms over his chest and tried to sound irritated. "Where were you?"

"With Lydia."

"Again. And what were the two of you doing that made you lose track of time?" he'd asked. Just to give Perry grief.

But in a flash, Perry's whole demeanor changed. "Nothing like that, English. Lydia's a nice girl. She's special."

He held up his hands. "Sorry! I was just kidding. You know that, right?"

But Perry walked right by, snubbing him. Walker knew that the damage was done. Perry was going to hold a grudge for the rest of the day. . . .

The detective's car door slamming brought him back to the present. Shaking his head at the memory, he strode into the store.

But the moment she saw him, Mrs. Schrock clicked her tongue in dismay. "Walker, you're soaked to the skin! Go in the back and dry off before you catch your death."

"Yes, ma'am," he murmured, glad for a little more time to collect his thoughts.

And to throw out the detective's card. The detective might want more information, but Walker knew one thing for certain—if he never talked to the man again . . . why, it would still be too soon.

Chapter 4

"Sure, I'd thought Perry had jumped the fence. Where else would I have thought he'd gone?"

JACOB SCHROCK

One of the best things about her parents, Lydia decided, was that they always gave her time to relax after work. When she walked into the house after spending most of the day on her feet in a warm greenhouse, her mother would greet her. And here she was now, with a plate of chocolate chip cookies, a tall glass of lemonade, and her book.

"Go rest for a while, dear. I heard you had a busy day at the greenhouse."

"I sure did," she said around her first bite of cookie. Looking at the kitchen, with the smooth wood plank floors and the butcher-block table that had once been her grandmother's, Lydia tried to concentrate on happier things instead of the detective's visit. "Everyone was coming in for seedlings. Daed and I must have sold forty perennials before noon."

Her mother picked up a bowl of sugar snap peas and started shelling them. "That's *gut* news, *jah*? We worked hard to get those seeds to do their jobs. I'm thankful to them."

Lydia couldn't resist smiling at her mother's soft look of pleasure. "Oh, Mamm. You always do talk about the plants as if they have feelings."

"Oh, I know they don't have feelings," her mother retorted quickly as she shelled another peapod. "But I know they are workin' hard for us. I want to give them their due. It's only right, *jah*?"

"Of course. I just wish I'd inherited your gift for coaxing the best out of plants. I'm afraid my talents only revolve around selling them."

Her mother stilled, a funny look on her face. "What 'gift' are you talking about, Lydia?"

Lydia down the half-eaten cookie. "You know what I mean. Everyone is supposed to inherit traits from their parents. For some reason, your green thumb skipped me and jumped right to the other kids." When her mother looked at her strangely, Lydia began to grow uncomfortable. "I'm just teasing ya, Mamm."

"My talking to plants is just a silly habit. It's certainly nothing to wish for."

She didn't understand why her mother was so touchy about the subject. "Oh, I know," she said airily. "It was just an observation."

"You'd do better to observe other things, child," she said as she carried the bowl to the sink. "I think you must be *shlayfadich*. Go outside and rest."

Lydia wasn't the least bit sleepy, but she didn't argue. "All right. I'm on my way." Pausing at the door, she added, "I'll promise to do my best to listen to the plants while I'm sitting out here. Maybe even report back to you what I hear."

"Oh, you. You are a terrible daughter," her mother said,

her cheeks turning rosy, the hint of a smile on her face. "I should know better than to talk to you about the plants."

Lydia was still chuckling as she left her mother at the stove, then walked out of the kitchen.

"Enjoy yourself, *maidle*," her mother said as Lydia opened the screen door and walked outside.

Because the ground was so wet and muddy, she carefully took the steppingstones toward the back garden. They were spaced a little far apart for her stride, so she stepped slowly. The slower pace let her breathe deep and find peace in the glory that surrounded her.

Why, in another month, the garden would smell like heaven and be full of vivid colors. At the moment, however, it was merely a sunny spot with the barest rosebuds on the bushes.

Lydia sat down on the damp bench and sipped her lemonade. Little by little, she pushed aside the conversation with her mother and let a true sense of peace filter through her. As much as she liked to tease her mother about talking to the plants, Lydia knew she felt the same way about nature. Nothing made Lydia happier than to sit outside and smell the fresh, clean air and feel the warm sun caress her skin.

Cookies and drink forgotten, she rested her neck against the back of the bench and closed her eyes.

But instead of finding relief, memories of Perry filtered through.

Perry walking by her side. Sipping lemonade with her in the kitchen.

Then later, Perry laughing at her.

Just weeks before they'd broken up, he'd teased her about all sorts of things. Including her somewhat restrained and quiet ways. Though it used to be something he'd liked about her, all of a sudden it was yet another part of her that he'd found fault with.

"Lydia, why do you have to be so serious all the time? I tell you what, sometimes being with you is like being with my maiden aunt," he'd said one evening at the end of a singing. "You need to learn to cut loose and have a good time."

"Like you?" she'd snapped. His cynical looks, and the way he'd find the one thing she wasn't good at and point it out—it made her feel on edge and exposed.

"Of course like me," he'd answered, his whole posture becoming more argumentative. Aggressive. "Come on, Lydia," he'd goaded as they'd walked farther and farther into the cornstalks and away from everyone else's curious stares. "You need to loosen up or you're going lose me to somebody else."

She'd opened her mouth and drew in a breath. She'd fully intended to tell him exactly what she'd thought about his attitude toward her. But before she could get a word out, he'd leaned close and kissed her. Hard.

She'd lifted her hands to his shoulders to steady herself before pushing him away. But instead of feeling her push, he'd taken it as an invitation to pull her closer.

And though she'd never intended to kiss him. Or to embrace him. Though she'd intended to chide him for being so forward . . . she'd kissed him back.

And then had felt so ashamed of her behavior that she couldn't break things off. She tried to convince herself that she still loved him. After all, only a wanton woman would behave in that manner with a man she had begun to distrust.

And surely that couldn't be her. That was not how her mother had raised her to be.

Perry, being Perry, had recognized her weakness and had laughed. "I told you you were gonna have to change. And now you are! You learn quickly," he said with a grin. "Why, the Lydia I used to know would have never done something like that."

Because his words were true, she'd kept silent. But was she really changing, or was Perry bringing out a dark side of her that had always been hidden inside . . . waiting and lurking for the right time to come to surface?

Had she become the type of woman to kiss men out in the open? Had she become the type of person who took more risks than she should?

"Lydia? Hey, Lydia, are you asleep?"

With a jerk, she popped her head up and opened her eyes. Stared at the English boy standing in front of her. "Walker?"

It was hard to see his eyes under the brim of his baseball cap, but the lift of his lips relayed that she'd made the correct guess. "Yeah. It's kind of a surprise I'm here, huh?"

Lydia blinked hard, trying to come to terms that Walker was standing in her rose garden, looking for all the world like he was nervous to be speaking with her. "I'm surprised. I mean, it's been a while since we've seen each other," she finally said. "Not since I saw you at Schrock's in December . . ." Her voice drifted off before she allowed herself to finish the thought. No way did she want to think about that evening again.

Filling the silence, he said, "I'm back at work there."

"I heard. Why?" she blurted. She would have thought Walker would get a job someplace else. Someplace without all the memories.

Looking uncomfortable, he shrugged. "Once Perry was gone, it didn't seem like such a bad place. Plus, they were hiring. I just had to promise Mr. Schrock that I wouldn't take off again before giving notice."

"Ah."

It was awkward, looking up at him. When she started to stand up, he stepped forward. "Hey, I just wanted to talk to you for a few minutes. Your sister Becky said you were out here and that you could probably talk. That is, if you have time." He paused, then cleared his throat. "Do you have time?"

"I have time, sure." It wasn't like she could say she didn't. After all, only a lazy girl with time on her hands would pass the afternoon dozing in a garden.

"Thanks."

His voice was deep and a little hoarse sounding. She wondered if the tone was new, or if he was feeling just as awkward as she.

"Perhaps you'd like to sit? I think there's room for two on this bench. It would seem kind of odd for us to talk this way, with me down here and you up there." She attempted to smile, though her stomach was turning into knots.

He would have stopped by for one reason, only: to talk about Perry.

But still he hesitated.

She didn't blame him. There wasn't much room for two, not really. But even if their legs brushed against each other, it would be less disturbing than if he remained standing in front of her, looming over her like an overgrown bush.

"Come sit down, *Englischer*," she said, putting in the *Englischer* title to make him grin.

It worked. "*Englischer*, huh?" he asked, his eyes lighting up with amusement. "And here I thought you were the type of girl who treated everyone so politely."

"I am being polite. Mighty polite. After all, an *Englischer* is what you are."

"And here I thought I was so much more than that," he murmured.

As soon as she scooted over, he sat down next to her. His presence sent little bursts of tension through her spine. Up close, Walker was even more handsome. He was wearing faded jeans, scuffed cowboy boots, and a snug-fitting T-shirt. She remembered someone saying that he'd been the star pitcher for the high school baseball team.

And now that the hint of tension was gone, she wanted to avoid the reason for his visit for as long as possible. Struggling to remember much about him, she tilted her head to one side. "It's been a while since we saw each other. Are you still taking college courses?"

"Yeah. Well, I mean, I'm at the community college over in Paducah. I thought I'd go a couple of years there before transferring to somewhere bigger. It's easier to pay for." He shifted the cap. Now he stared at her directly. His eyes, so brown, the color of melted chocolate, met her gaze, making her blush.

"Ah." Of course, his plans were foreign to her. No Amish boy she knew had plans to go to college.

"And you? What are you doing now?"

With dismay, Lydia realized that in a lot of ways nothing had changed. "Nothing new. I'm still working at our family's greenhouse. I just sat down after working all day."

"And here you are, still outside? Around roses, no less."

His voice didn't sound condescending. No, it sounded a little amused. Maybe more than a little amused. "I guess I can't stay away from plants," she quipped. As soon as she heard her words, she ached to yank them back. It probably wasn't possible to speak more childishly!

But instead of making a face, Walker merely nodded. "It's good you like plants. I remember Perry talking about your family owning this big greenhouse. It's a popular one, isn't it?"

Before she could answer, he continued. "One day, maybe you could show me around. I mean, it looks like a real nice place."

"I'm surprised Perry told you anything about the greenhouse. He didn't care for it."

"Well, of course he didn't. I mean, it was Perry, right? He didn't like much."

That was so true. While they'd been courting, he'd become harder and harder to read . . . and harder and harder to please. She'd thought he'd only been that way with her.

Perhaps not.

And just like that, her anxiety rose. She really didn't want to have to talk about Perry with anyone else. He was dead. What could she do?

Dead. Not passed away. Not lifted into heaven. Dead.

It sounded so harsh. Disrespectful.

Though her blood felt like it was turning cold, she shrugged. No way did she want Walker to guess how affected she was by Perry's death. His murder was shocking. Never had anyone been killed in their community. The violence stained them all, changing what they knew into something dirty and foreign.

But so were her feelings about him. She should be only mourning his loss, not thinking about how he'd made her feel the last time she saw him. She shook her head, refusing to allow herself to go there.

Walker cleared his throat. "I came over here, thinking we should talk about Perry. You know, see what each other remembers about him."

"I don't see why we need to share stories."

"You know, the sheriff asked some city detective to help him investigate. I think maybe they're thinking someone who knew Perry killed him. Someone like . . . us."

She'd gotten that feeling as well. The detective had raised all sorts of suspicions in her head and made her feel uneasy. "I know about Mr. Reynolds. He came over and asked me questions. When I told him I knew nothing, he left. So now I doubt he will contact me again."

"Oh, no, Lydia. He didn't leave. He's still here, and he's still asking a lot of questions. After he talked to you, he went to the store and asked me about a hundred questions about Perry. I didn't think he would ever leave . . ."

"And did you have much to tell him?"

For the first time, he looked disturbed. "I don't know. I answered him as best I could. I didn't really have a choice. He's with the police, you know?" After glancing toward the kitchen door, he lowered his voice. "The detective wanted to know about the people Perry started hanging around. He kept asking me about what I knew about Perry's private life. About the things Perry didn't want anyone to know."

"What did you tell him?" she asked, flushing as they both realized she hadn't asked what he knew.

What he'd told and what he knew were two very different things.

"I said I didn't know much," he said after a moment. "And that's true. I don't know much."

"Did he believe you?"

"Honestly? I doubt it." His eyes darted away, as if he was reluctant to meet her gaze. When he faced her again, he asked the inevitable. "You know, Detective Reynolds asked about you, too, Lydia. I think he's starting to get the idea that there was a whole lot more to Perry than most people realized. And a heck of a lot more than we want to admit."

Lydia knew that to be true. But even if it was, it didn't

mean she had to get involved. "I bet the detective will go away soon. He's from Ohio, right?"

"Yeah, but I don't think he's going back there until he solves this," Walker said slowly. "Actually . . . I think he might come back here and talk to you some more."

"He shouldn't. I told him I didn't know anything."

With a grunt, Walker stood up. "Listen, I don't know how much you knew about Perry's secrets. But if you knew even half as much as I do, you need to listen to me. If we don't keep our stories straight, we're going to get burned."

Even though she knew what he meant, she played dumb, if only to gain a few precious seconds to process everything. "Burned?"

His voice turned kind. Almost patient. "You know . . . caught. We're going to become real suspects."

Perhaps they should keep their stories straight, especially about that evening in December. But if they did, it might mean that Walker had something to hide. And what if what he was hiding was dangerous? What if he had something to do with Perry's death and he was lying?

She really didn't know all that much about him.

Shaking her head, she got to her feet. "Well, thank you for the warning."

His jaw looked set as he reached into the pocket of his jeans and pulled out a ballpoint pen. "Give me your hand."

She did as he asked. Cradling her hand in his right, he wrote a series of numbers on her palm with his left hand. When he was finished, he curved her fingers over, making a fist.

Hiding the numbers from view.

"That's my cell phone number. When you're ready to talk to me about what you really know . . . or about what we saw in December . . . don't come to the store or call my house. Call this number."

She didn't need to ask why he wanted any conversation between them to be kept secret. She felt the same way. Their town was too small to be able to count on privacy. It didn't matter if he was English and she was Amish.

Someone in their circles would notice them talking together and comment on it. "And then?"

"And then, we'll figure out a way to talk. Without the detective finding out."

She couldn't help but touch his arm with her unmarked hand. "I think if we do talk it should be out in the open," she said, changing her mind about meeting. "Otherwise, we'll raise suspicions."

"Fine, we'll meet in the open."

His voice was so clipped, yet another wave of unease filtered through her. "Walker, do you think, really think, we need to be so worried?"

Instead of moving away from her hand, he stepped closer, making her full palm curve around his bicep. "Lydia, I think if the detective realizes that all of us knew Perry better than we're saying, things are going to get really complicated. More complicated than either of us can imagine. And that makes me really worried."

Walker turned and walked away before Lydia could think of any retort that made sense.

Instead, she sat back down on the bench and tried to calm her shaking nerves. She had known things were going to get discovered sooner than later. She'd known it as certainly as she had known Perry wasn't the right man for her.

She'd just hoped the truth would come out at a far later date.

"Lydia, is everything all right?" her mother called out from behind the screen door.

"It's fine." Thinking quickly, she said, "That was just my friend Walker. He stopped by to say hello, that's all."

Her mother leaned closer to the screen door—so close that her nose was pressed up against it. "I didn't know you were friends with any *Englischer* boys."

"I'm not. I mean I'm not friends with very many. But Walker is nice."

"Is he now? And how old might he be?"

"I don't know, Mamm." And because it was yet another thing that she didn't know about in her life, her voice turned sharper. "Truly, *muddah*. He only came by to see how I was doing. See, he knew Perry, too. And the detective has spoken to him also."

"Well, unlike that *Englischer*, you had nothing to do with Perry's disappearance."

So that was how they were going to refer to Perry's death. "Walker did not, either."

"But you can't be sure, can you?"

"I can be sure that I trust him as much as anyone else. He's a nice man, Mamm." And she could also be sure that he was hiding information. Just like she was.

"Perhaps," her mother said before turning away in an uncharacteristically quiet fashion.

Ten minutes later, after she heard her mother leave the kitchen, Lydia hurried to her room. She carefully wrote down the phone number on the back of an old Christmas card, then locked herself in the bathroom and scrubbed her hand until it was raw.

At least the numbers were gone.

If only the memories could be erased as easily.

When they'd first started courting, Perry had been sweet and had brought her daisies and had blushed when he talked to her. He'd had a faint Kentucky drawl that had mixed with his Amish accent, creating a soothing, lilting cadence. She'd liked to just listen to him talk.

Back then, she'd been sure that Perry was the man for her. She'd gone to sleep dreaming about weddings and days spent walking by his side.

And then, practically overnight, Perry wasn't so sweet at all.

He'd yell at her. And show up late. And his accented voice developed a hard edge to it that hurt her feelings.

She began to avoid him.

And then they had fought about his new dreams and her old-fashioned values. Just remembering how he'd teased her about not wanting to do more than kiss him good night caused her to tremble. The way he'd grabbed her upper arms and trapped her next to his body. The way his kisses had turned painful and his heated gaze had turned cool when she'd pushed him away. Closing her eyes, she breathed deep, preferring to inhale the residual tang of Pine-Sol and bleach on her hands than to recall the sharp scent of rain-soaked leaves that surrounded their feet in the woods.

When she had prayed that she'd never see Perry again.

But that prayer hadn't come true.

Chapter 5

"Perry could ride a unicycle, juggle three oranges at a time, and run faster than you could ever imagine. He always thought it a shame that none of that mattered in the real world."

ABRAHAM BORNTRAGER

Walker had no idea if his visit with Lydia had been a mistake or not. Saying she was reserved was putting it mildly. The girl had seemed to keep every single emotion she was feeling to herself. As he drove his old Chevy truck off of the Planks' property and hit the state highway, he played their conversation over and over in his head.

"I don't see why we need to share stories. The detective will leave soon."

The words had fallen from Lydia's lips like they'd been recorded messages—tinny and canned sounding. Could she have sounded any more guarded or wary?

Had she been afraid of him? Or was this her normal way of conversing? And if it was, what had Perry even seen in her?

Probably that she was, well . . . beautiful.

The opinion caught him off guard. Back when Perry had dated her and their paths had crossed, Walker didn't remember her being that way. But now that he thought about it—maybe he'd never taken a good look at her. The first time he'd met Lydia had been when Perry had been standing by her side. As soon as Walker had heard the word "courting" he'd taken an emotional step backward.

After all, there was an unspoken rule between him and most of his friends—guys didn't even think about other guys' girlfriends. But he wouldn't have looked at an Amish girl closely, anyway.

Back when he'd been in high school, he'd been all about being part of the in-crowd. He'd been a four-year letterman for baseball, and he'd worn his letter jacket around like it was a big deal. Just about any cute girl he'd wanted to date had acted flattered and excited just to be noticed by him.

Walker knew his head had gotten so full, it had been a wonder it still remained on his head! After a while, he'd started to only worry about his appearance and his reputation.

Then he'd gone off to community college and had found out real quick that he hadn't been as special as he thought he was. A late-night conversation with his dad let him know the truth—that his parents had been patiently waiting for him to get over himself, knowing that he'd been simply going through a phase.

Being out of his small bubble made him realize that the world wasn't just about him. And, that it wasn't a nice place, either. That feeling hit home more than ever when the detective showed up, rattling his cage.

As he pulled into his driveway, he spied Abby sitting on the front steps of their house, waiting for him. Unfortunately, his sister was sitting as she usually did. Looking a little bit lost and a lot in need of a friend. He wasn't sure why she'd never fit in at school like he had. Maybe it was her awkwardness in social situations? Or maybe it was her way of always analyzing things to the nth degree.

But whatever the reason, he always felt a rush of protectiveness toward her. She needed him like few other people in the world did.

He parked his truck off to the side of the driveway, and waved his hand as she watched him approach.

"What's up?" he asked, keeping his voice steady and easy as he threw an arm around her shoulders. "How was school?"

"Fine."

"Hey, 'fine' is better than usual." Walker tried to tease a smile from his sister.

Now that everyone knew she'd found Perry's body, her reputation at school had gone from being just another awkward girl to the weird one. It was painful to know that she was the new constant source of gossip and ridicule.

"'Fine' means no one went out of their way to talk about Perry with me today." She bit her lip. "And 'fine' means that Jessica didn't make fun of me in chemistry."

"Hey, that's a start, huh?"

"I don't know. I think she was just too busy with her new boyfriend to pay me much attention."

"Maybe she's finally realizing that there's more to you than she thought." Jeez, he sounded like some kind of Dr. Phil wannabe, but he couldn't stand her being so depressed. "I mean, you've been standing up to her and the other girls in her clique more and more, right?"

She shrugged. "I don't want to talk about it anymore."

"You should. Hiding won't help."

Brushing a hand through her blond hair, so curly in the humidity, she looked him in the eye. "I've actually been waiting for you for another reason."

"Which is?"

"Are you, um, busy right now?"

"It's five. We're going to eat dinner in an hour."

"But after? Are you busy after dinner?"

He was worn out from talking with the detective and Lydia. More than a little ready to just sit and watch TV. Plus he had a couple of chapters to read for Biology. But there was such sadness mixed with hope in Abby's voice that he couldn't bear to put her off without giving her a chance. "I'm just going to watch TV and study. Why?"

"I wondered if maybe we could go visit Grandma Francis and Grandpa James."

He hadn't seen that one coming. "Tonight?"

"Well, yeah."

"Why do you want to go see them tonight?"

"I don't know." She looked down. Fussed with a hole in her faded jeans. "You don't have to stay there if you don't want. You could just drop me off," she added quickly.

Walker didn't want to go, but at the moment he was more interested in why she was going than the logistics of it all. "If I left, how would you get home?"

"I could probably stay with them overnight, and then Mom or Dad could pick me up sometime tomorrow."

"But you have school . . ." Dismay filled Walker as he began to realize that this was probably yet another one of Abby's schemes to get out of being at school. "You can't miss again."

"I won't be missing anything. Tomorrow's a school holiday—teacher workday or something."

Walker nodded, hoping to give himself some time to try to figure out what to say. Though they all loved his father's parents, it wasn't a usual thing for him or Abby to want to visit them on the spur of the moment. Usually, visits to their

Amish grandparents were accompanied by complaints about the heat, or the chores, or the quiet stillness that surrounded their home.

"So, what brought this on?"

"Oh, nothing."

Yeah, right. Abby's voice was airy and she wasn't looking him in the eye. "Come on. I know you pretty well, right? Suddenly, you've just decided that you want to go spend the night with our grandparents? Do they even know you're coming over?"

"No."

"So you just want us to show up? Without an invitation?"

"They've always said we could stop by anytime. That means we don't need to wait for them to ask, right?"

He supposed she was right, but it still felt like it would be rude to just drop by unannounced. "I don't know, Ab."

"Come on. It's not like they're strangers." She kicked her feet out in front of her, then crossed them. Then shifted again. Just being restless. Just being Abby. "They're our grandparents, you know."

"They're also very polite and kind. Probably too polite to turn you away."

"I already talked to Mom about it. She said I could go if you didn't mind taking me."

She might not have minded, but Walker had a feeling she probably wasn't too happy about it. "But what about Dad? They're *his* parents."

"She said Dad would never stop me from seeing them."

"Would never stop is a long way from being happy about this visit."

"Walker, if you won't take me, just say so. Okay? I don't need all your opinions right now."

Her words, and that sad look of acceptance, took the wind out of his sails. "Sorry."

"It's okay. I mean, I know this isn't what you want to be doing . . ."

His sister looked so heartbroken, he didn't have the heart to tell her no. Seeing his grandparents was complicated for him, too. Though it was never spoken of, he'd often felt the tension that rose between their father and his parents. Sometimes it seemed as if their dad was embarrassed by what he now thought of as important—his job, his car, the life he'd built for himself. It also seemed that there were a lot of unspoken conflicts that were never solved.

However, none of it was his business. He had enough problems without worrying about Abby's. "How soon do you want to go?"

"You'll take me? Really?"

"I'll take you right after dinner. But you get to tell Dad yourself."

"I will."

Now that the burden wasn't on his shoulders, he added, "Be sure to pack an overnight bag, too. But keep it in the truck. If you get the feeling that they'll let you spend the night, then you can get it out. Okay?"

Her smile told him everything he needed to know, and pushed away the rest of his doubts.

Chapter 6

"I fished next to Perry once for three hours. When he caught the biggest bass of the day, he grinned, admired that fish, then threw it back. And forbid any of us to tell his parents. Don't know why."

JACOB SCHROCK

Grandma Francis smelled like sugar cookies. Abby was pretty sure she always had. She couldn't remember a time when her grandmother hadn't been surrounded by the scent of wholesome goodness. Even as a child, Abby recalled toddling into her grandmother's kitchen, looking for both a cookie and a warm hug.

Yep, she had always equated her grandmother with everything good and trustworthy on the earth.

"Abby! Walker!" Grandma Francis exclaimed the moment they opened up the truck doors. "How *gut* it is to see you!" Smiling happily, she trotted down the narrow dirt driveway toward them like she was greeting long lost relatives. "What brings you two here this evening?"

When Walker merely raised an eyebrow and glanced her way, Abby felt nerves overtake her. Obviously her brother was going to let her do all the talking. That was the right thing to do; after all, the reason for the visit had been hers. However, it felt strange to be taking charge. Usually she was more than content to let him do the talking. And he was usually happy to do it.

As the seconds passed, Grandma Francis's smile of pleasure was eclipsed by a frown of worry. "Oh, no. Is someone sick? Did something happen to your *daed?*"

"Oh, no, *Mommi,*" she said, using the Pennsylvania Dutch word for Grandma. "Everyone's fine."

"Then why are you standing there like a lost sheep and acting twice as quiet?"

As their grandmother continued to look at her patiently, Abby cleared her throat. "I wanted to see you and Grandpa. Walker didn't mind driving me. Is that okay? I mean, I know you didn't ask me over."

"Of course, child. If you want to visit, you are always welcome." Crossing arms over her comfortable girth, she winked her brother's way. "You too, Walker. Though you are standing there looking like a tree taking roots, you're always welcome here."

He laughed. "*Danke.* Sorry for the tree impersonation. Guess I'm just tired."

"You don't need to be anything but how you are, Walker," Grandma Francis said sweetly, starting to usher them inside, her gray dress brushing against her ankles..

Though Walker looked at ease, Abby knew she had more to ask. "Um, *Mommi,* I was also hoping that maybe I could spend the night, too? Would you mind terribly if I slept over and then Mom or someone could take me home tomorrow?"

"I wouldn't mind." Her voice slowed as she looked over Abby with a steady gaze. "Is anything wrong?"

"No. I, um, just wanted to get away for a little while."

After a pause, Grandma Francis nodded. "If you are seeking to get away, I think you picked a perfect place to get to. Now, where is your bag?"

"In the back of Walker's truck. I could go get it."

"I'll help Walker get the bag, Abby," Grandpa James said as he stepped out of the shadows. "I'm not so old that I can't do that. But you have to give me a hug first."

She stepped into his embrace. While her grandma always smelled like cookies, the scent of leather and horses always clung to her grandfather's skin. She inhaled deeper and felt the muscles in her shoulders relax. "I didn't see you there."

"I know," he said simply. "But we're together now, *jah*?"

"*Jah*." She nodded when they parted.

He turned to her brother. "Now, Walker, how about you show me where your *shveshtah*'s suitcase is?"

"Sure, *Dawdi*," Walker replied and walked with his grandfather to his truck.

Grandma Francis led Abby toward the house and curved a soft hand around her arm. "Now, how about I show you where you can sleep?"

"All right." As they walked, Abby noticed that Walker and her grandfather's voices had lowered. Their tones sounded hushed and private-like, speaking about things they didn't want her to hear.

Three cement steps brought them up to the front door. When her Grandma opened it, Abby walked into the dim entryway, smelling the familiar scents of vanilla and lemon oil and embers. Immediately, a sense of calm engulfed her. "Your house always smells the same, Mommi."

"Well, I should hope so. My James and I have lived here for years."

Abby chuckled. "No, I mean it always smells like you've just been baking something and just tamped down a fire in the fireplace."

"Most likely that is because that is what has usually happened! It is a rare day that I don't bake something new, and with this damp March weather, I find my bones yearning for the heat of a fireplace."

Abby bent down and pulled off her flats, preferring to feel the wood floor under her bare feet. "Maybe I could bake something with you tomorrow? It's been a long time since I've made cookies with you."

Grandma Francis paused. "You're not going to be anxious to head home?"

"I was hoping to stay here until Friday afternoon. Or Saturday. If you don't mind?"

Resting a hand on her shoulder, her grandmother shook her head. "I don't mind . . . but I sure would like to know what provoked this impromptu visit."

"I just wanted to see you both."

"And I just happen to like peaches in the summer, but it don't mean I go gallivanting around orchards in March. What's going on?" Her brown eyes narrowed through her glasses. "Are you still having nightmares about finding Perry?"

She was, but she hated to talk about them. She far preferred to ignore the dreams that visited her every night. They seemed to be as inevitable as being talked about at school.

"The dreams aren't too bad," she lied as they walked upstairs.

"Something is, though, yes?"

Abby felt her cheeks heat with embarrassment.

Her grandmother paused in front of the first closed door on the left. "Abby, you are my granddaughter and are welcome to stay here for as long as you like. I am also happy to bake with you, too. But I would rather have your honesty. Please tell me what's on your mind. And I want to hear everything, too. Not just the parts you think are good for my *ohr*," she said, pointing to her ear.

Feeling caught, Abby hedged. "It's complicated."

"That's all right. I've lived long enough to understand complicated stories."

Abby stared at her sharply. Was Grandma Francis teasing her?

Her grandmother didn't budge from her post in front of the paneled oak door. It seemed as if she wasn't going to move until Abby explained everything.

But she had gone to her grandparents' house to escape from everything, not to make sense of her feelings. "I'm not sure you'd understand."

"Believe it or not, I've had thorny things happen to me," she said gently. "I wasn't always old, you know."

"You're not old."

"I'm far older than you! Now are you ready to talk?"

"I don't want to talk about finding Perry." She was so tired of talking about that day. So tired of revisiting the memories.

"If you're not upset about that, suppose you tell me what has gotten you so spun in circles."

Across from the landing was a window looking out onto the driveway. Directly below, she could see her brother leaning up against his truck, arms folded across his chest like he always did, laughing. He looked tanned and healthy, happy and handsome—he looked confident and sure of himself.

And completely the opposite of Abby. As she watched her brother talk, Abby felt tears prick her eyes. They were only three years apart in age, but had always been so far in attitude and demeanor. "I'm not anything like Walker," she blurted.

"I would hope not. One Walker is enough for this family."

Instead of smiling at the joke, she felt even worse. "No, Mommi. He was popular at school. *Really* popular." She sputtered, suddenly wondering if such things even mattered if you were Amish. "Do you know what that means?"

"Popular? Oh, yes. I've heard that term a time or two over the years."

Abby flushed as she realized she was sounding condescending. "Did you ever care about things like popularity?"

"Did I ever?" she murmured with a faint smile. "Me? Not so much. For others though, I think it mattered more." She opened the door to the bedroom and waved Abby forward. "This is your room. Come sit down on the bed with me and we'll talk more, *jah?*"

Abby sat down on the beautiful white quilt. It was covered with tiny white stitches in the shape of flowers.

Taking care to keep her feet off the quilt, she perched on the edge. "Why didn't it matter to you?"

"I think because I was happy with myself. I was lucky, I think, Abby. I was one of those few people born knowing what I wanted in life. I grew up next to your grandfather, so I knew I wanted to always be with him one day. And I always wanted to be like my mother, fussing with a houseful of *kinner.*"

"I don't know what I want to do when I grow up. Sometimes I don't even know who I want to be."

"Well, of course you don't! You're too young to know such things."

"I'm eighteen."

"Eighteen ain't all that old, Abby. I promise that, though you love to analyze things, there is no hurry. Give yourself some time to simply enjoy each day."

"That's not easy to do."

"It's not easy because you've had a difficult time of it lately. But, I promise, there's a reason for everything. I suspect that the Lord probably wants you to rest for a spell."

"If that's what He wants, I'm not so sure I want to follow the Lord's advice." She felt so haunted by the memory of discovering a dead body and so alienated by everyone knowing, all she wanted was a chance to start over. The idea of having to wait longer made her stomach clench in knots.

She had to do something soon. Thinking of her father, and the way he talked about wanting to be different than the way his parents wanted him to be, she asked, "Mommi, did it bother you when Dad didn't want to be Amish?"

"Yes."

"Were you mad at him?"

Slowly, she shook her head. "*Nee*. I wasn't mad, I don't think. I felt more sad than anything, to be sure. I knew if Tim wasn't Amish that we wouldn't see as much of each other."

"Did Grandpa James feel the same way?"

"He did, to be sure." With a soft smile, she added, "It's hard to let your children grow up. But that's why we have the Lord, I think. We need to trust in Him to help us make decisions, and for Him to help our children, too. When your father told us he was going to be English, we prayed and prayed. Then your father admitted that he'd been praying about it, too."

"I didn't know that."

"Perhaps he would tell you about it now, if you asked?"

Abby shrugged, not sure how to approach her father with those kinds of questions.

Her grandmother smiled softly. "After a bit, your grandfather and I decided we couldn't change his heart. And if he had been praying, and if he truly felt like the Lord understood his reasons, well, that had to be enough for us."

Her grandmother's words were so simple and heartfelt, and made so much sense, too. "You really do want me to take time and pray about what I want, don't you?"

"For me, prayer is the only way to make decisions. The Lord is just waiting to guide us—but if He is missing in your life, it makes all those big decisions harder." Clasping her hands in front of her, she smiled. "Of course, everything with your father happened a long time ago. Care to tell me why you are thinking about it now?"

"I guess I was just wishing I was closer to you and Grandpa James," she hedged.

"Abby, you are my *kinskind*, my grandchild. No matter if I'm Amish and you are not, *my* world is yours, too, *jah*? We can be as close to each other as we want to be."

"I guess you're right."

"Ach! I know it."

Abby laughed. Her grandmother made it sound so easy, but it wasn't. Finding a place to be comfortable and happy was hard. Harder than she'd ever imagined.

"Now tell me where you want to be more popular."

"At school," she blurted. "I don't fit in."

"Fitting in isn't everything, child. In God's eyes we are all perfect. Besides, one day, before you know it, you'll wonder how you ever thought you didn't fit in."

Abby doubted that. "Mommi, in my high school, I stick out like a sore thumb. And now everyone talks about Perry Borntrager, and how I'm the one who found him."

"Finding a body like that would shake anyone up."

"I was with some girls and we were smoking." She looked at Grandma Francis. "Did you hear about that from Mom and Dad?"

"I did."

Abby waited to hear the lecture about smoking, but none came. Instead, her grandmother just continued to sit on the bed and waited with a kind, patient expression.

Which was all the encouragement she needed. She took a breath and blurted the rest of her story as quickly as possible. "Now those girls don't want to talk to me, and the other kids think I'm weird because I found a body but don't want to talk about it." She took a breath. "And Mom and Dad keep asking me why I was smoking with them in the first place."

"And you said?"

"I said, I don't know." She paused. "That's not really much of an answer. Is it?"

"I think it sounds like a fine answer. Everyone sometimes does things for no special reason."

"You think?"

"I know. We're all human, *jah*? Now, I suppose we'd best get back down with the men before they come up here wondering what we are doing with ourselves."

As her grandmother stood up with a sigh, she added, "Don't forget about how God works with us, Abby. He has the answers. We, on the other hand, merely try to figure things out. Remember the saying? . . . *I know not what the future holds, but I know Who holds the future.*"

Abby hadn't heard that saying, but she thought it made sense. "If that's how God wants things, he must be real happy with me right now. I don't know have any idea what's going to happen with my future."

Her grandmother laughed as they headed downstairs. "Abby, you are going to have to come here more often. You make me smile like no other."

And to her surprise, Abby felt herself smiling too as they took the steps together.

Chapter 7

"The problem with me and Perry was that he had too many secrets and I had too few."

LYDIA PLANK

"Lydia, we need to speak with you for a moment, if we may," her father said.

Looking up from the bowl of frosting she was mixing, Lydia gazed at her father with concern. It wasn't his way to ask her to talk. Usually, he just approached and said what was on his mind. "Right now?"

"I think that might be best. Unless you can't stop your baking?"

"I'm only making frosting, Daed," she said as she turned to the sink and quickly washed her hands. "Where do you want to talk to me?"

"Come to the porch, Lydia," her mother said. "We can sit on the rocking chairs for a spell. It's so peaceful out there."

Both her parents were waiting on her? And her usual bossy mother was standing to the side, waiting for Daed to talk? Something must have happened. "I'll be right there," she said quickly.

As soon as she dried her hands, Lydia went out to join her parents. Hanging from the front-porch railing were a series of baskets filled with marigolds. Usually the flowers and the fresh air gave her a feeling of peace, but all she felt at the moment was a sense of foreboding. It washed over her in waves as she saw their serious expressions.

"Is something wrong?"

"*Nee.* I mean, not really." Her mother flashed a smile that disappeared almost as quickly as it had come. "Come sit down, child."

Her bare feet felt chilled as she walked across the thick planks of decking. When she sat down in one of the white-washed rocking chairs, she noticed that her parents' hands were clenched together tightly.

"You two are starting to scare me. Is this about the police detective's visit?" That was the only thing she could think of that would cause her parents to wear such stricken looks.

"It's not about the detective's visit. It has nothing to do with Perry," her father replied. "Well, not really." Her parents exchanged looks.

"What's happened?"

"Well, when those English girls first discovered Perry on the Miller farm, it caught us by surprise."

"I think it caught everyone by surprise."

"The Lord does watch over us all," her mother said, "but He also does things for a reason, I believe."

After looking at her mother for a long moment, her father cleared his throat. "Lydia, when we heard that Perry's body was found, it got us to thinking."

"What about?"

This time her mother answered. "Well, that there had to be a reason he was murdered and then hidden in the well.

He must have had secrets. No one could have imagined that such a thing would happen in Crittenden County. And especially not in our community."

Lydia nodded. Perry's death had been a shock, for sure. But she still had no idea why her parents wanted to talk to her about his death now.

Her parents exchanged looks, then her *daed* spoke. "It made your mother and I realize that keeping secrets wasn't such a good thing."

Lydia blinked. Her father's Amish accent was slowly becoming stronger with every sentence he spoke. That was a sure sign that something was really bothering him.

Or that he was nervous.

What was going on? Why were they talking about secrets? Did her parents not trust her? "I haven't been keeping secrets from you. Or from the detective," she added quickly.

Then, as she realized that she'd kept many things about Perry close to her chest instead of telling the policeman, and that that was almost the same as lying, she amended her words. "I promise, I hadn't been courting Perry for weeks. I hadn't even seen him since December." She ached to add that they hadn't even been all that serious, that the two of them had liked the idea of their union more than actually spending time together.

"We believe you," Mamm said. When she hesitated, awkwardly looking toward her husband, her father spoke again.

"What we're talkin' about, it's not about Perry."

"Then, what?"

Her parents exchanged uneasy-looking glances again.

"You two are really startin' to worry me. Is someone sick?"

"No one is sick." Her father braced his hands on his knees, then took a deep breath. "The Lord works in mysterious ways, daughter. When we were first married, we hoped for a *boppli* right away. But after two years, we realized that *Gott* had other plans."

All her life she'd been taught to listen to the Lord's guidance instead of her own will. "Yes?"

"Patience, Lydia," her mother warned. "What we are saying is of great consequence."

Tucking her head, Lydia kept silent.

Her mother continued. "Daughter, I don't know how to fully describe how I was feeling. See, I wanted a *boppli* badly. All I ever wanted was to raise a family. Soon, it became all I could think about. That, and how it didn't look like I was going to get my wish."

Lydia felt sorry for her mother, but still didn't understand why they'd decided this information was of great importance—or that it had to be shared right that minute. "God listened, right? I mean there are four of us. You did get the family you always desired."

"*Gott* did listen, indeed." Her mother flashed a smile. "But my wish didn't come true in the way I had imagined. You see, we began to get desperate, and so we started asking people about adoption."

Lydia's mouth went dry as the words sank in. "I didn't know that," she said slowly, still wondering what they were trying to tell her.

"Lydia, we went to an adoption agency. Quite unexpectedly, we heard there was a baby girl who'd just been born . . ." her mother's voice drifted off. "For reasons we never learned, the baby's mother had decided to put the baby up for adoption. The administrator said the woman had been looking for a warm, loving family." Glancing her father's way, her mother finished her story. "She was lookin' for a couple just like us."

Still confused, Lydia leaned forward. Waited for the second half of the story. "And?"

"And we adopted that baby," her father said with a shrug.

Lydia still didn't understand. They were speaking of the past, but all this was new. "So," she said hesitantly, "you are going to raise another child?"

Her mother smiled slightly though that happiness didn't reach her eyes. "That child was you, dear," she said softly. "We adopted you."

Adopted? A cold chill raced through her, as sharp and jarring as a pitcher of ice water. "What? I'm not yours?"

"Of course you're ours, daughter," her father said emphatically. "Don't you understand? We adopted you."

Looking almost helpless, her mother spoke quickly. "You are my daughter. The daughter of my heart, Lydia."

She was a daughter of her mother's heart? What in the world was that supposed to mean? "Mamm?" But as soon as she said the word, she felt tears prick her eyes. Was her mother even her mother?

"I know this news must surely be a surprise to you, Lydia," her father said matter-of-factly. As if they were discussing her grades in school. Or the vegetable garden. "However, you should know that almost as soon as we agreed to raise you, your mother became pregnant with your brother."

Beaming, her mother nodded. "It was a wonderful-*gut* blessing, for sure!"

A sick, terrible ache formed in her middle and held on tight. Why were her parents beaming? "So no one but me is adopted?"

"*Nee.*"

"None of them? Not Reuben or Petey or Becky?" Only after she asked the question did she dare to feel guilty. How could she want her siblings to be adopted, too? Shame filled her as it waged war with resentment. Struggling to contain the mixed emotions was causing her head to pound.

"You are the only one. We never told you because we didn't want you to feel different than the others."

When her *daed* paused, Lydia quickly spoke, filling in the gaps. "No different from the others who are really your children."

"You are my daughter," her *mamm* soothed. "You are just like the others."

The words sounded forced and faked. "I am not. I am someone else's daughter. Some . . . some other woman's," she sputtered. "But for some reason she didn't want me." Confusion spun with feelings of sadness. She was twenty years old! How could her parents have kept this a secret for so long?

Her father frowned. "Lydia, it wasn't like that."

"You were always a blessing to us," Her mother said. "That is what we are trying to tell you."

"I hear what you are saying," Lydia allowed, but now she didn't even know if that was the truth anymore. Her mind reeled. What did it mean when everything she had thought was true was now lying on its side? "I don't know what to think."

"You shouldn't think anything is different. We are still your parents, and you are still our daughter." Her father said with such a determined expression that she supposed he thought she was eight years old again. That all he had to do was say that something was the way he wanted it, and she would accept his word.

But it was now obvious that his word couldn't be trusted anymore. After all, he'd lied to her about who she was her whole life.

"Why are you telling me all this now? Does my real mother want to meet me?" She ignored the flinch her mother gave. "Has she ever contacted you? Have you been contacting her all this time?"

But instead of seeking to give her more answers, her father retreated behind a mask of propriety. Reaching out, he clasped her mother's hand and threaded his fingers through hers. Making a solid connection. A bond. "This is your real mother, child."

"You know what I mean." Forcing herself to be strong, to ignore the tears that were threatening to fall, Lydia held herself stiffly. "Did she ever say she wanted to know about me?"

Her parents exchanged looks. "*Nee,*" her mother finally said. "The woman who gave birth to you never wanted to know you, and she never wanted you to know about her. That was part of the agreement," she added, looking torn and guilty.

The small ray of hope that had been threatening to rise vanished completely. There was no happy news here. Her real mother had given her away like an unwanted kitten and had moved on with her life. Her real mother had never wanted to hear about her. She never wanted to get to know her.

Though it didn't make all that much sense, given that she'd just found out about it all, the harsh rejection stung. Hurt more than Lydia could ever imagine.

"Why tell me now?"

Her father leaned toward her. "With everything that happened with Perry, we started realizing that the Lord gives each of us only a small number of days on this earth," he said quietly after glancing toward her mother again, "We began talking about the time of your birth, and how you are twenty now. An adult. One day soon you'll find a man and get married. We realized that time is precious. It is probably best not to count on many more tomorrows. Instead, it is best to do things right away."

"I didn't want to wait any longer, even though I knew this news would upset you, Lydia," Mamm said. "We thought it was something you would want to know before you married and had *kinner* of your own."

"What was she like? What was my mother like? Was she young? Old? Married? Unmarried?"

After exchanging glances, her father answered. "We never asked."

"We didn't want to know, Lydia. You were all that mattered to us. And you were *wunderbaar.*"

"Were they Amish? Or were they *Englischers*?"

"I don't know," her mother said. "It wasn't important."

Lydia had never heard of an Amish couple giving up a baby. Therefore, it was highly likely that her birth parents were English. Which meant . . . what? "If my parents were English, am I even Amish?"

"You were raised by Amish parents. You were brought up Amish. Of course you are Amish."

"But I have not yet professed my faith," she pointed out.

"That is only a matter of time, though, *jah*? In no time, when you are courting again, I'm sure you will be ready to be baptized."

Now Lydia wasn't so sure of that. "Maybe. Maybe not."

"But this is your heritage."

"*Nee*, I thought I knew my heritage by birth," she corrected. "Things are different now." Her voice drifted off as she realized now there were so many holes and blanks in her past, it was as if half of her life had gone missing.

Before her eyes, her parents' attitudes hardened. With a

glare, her father said, "You are making this more complicated than it is."

"You've kept a secret about my part in this family for twenty years. It's pretty complicated to me."

Her father crossed his arms over his chest. "But nothing has changed, Lydia." After a pause he added, "And there's no reason for you to talk to your brothers and sister about it, either."

"You want me to keep the secret now?" She felt completely betrayed. Here they'd tossed this information in her lap and now didn't want her to mention it again.

Her mother's chin lifted. "It is for the best. Your siblings might not understand, you know."

Oh, she knew. Feeling like her whole world was spinning, she stumbled to her feet. "I think I'm going to go for a walk now."

"Now? You can't. You have work today."

"I am not going into the greenhouse. Reuben can work for me instead. Or you two can."

Her mother leapt to her feet. "That's it? That is all you have to say?"

What could she say? For some reason, her parents expected her to take their news, smile, and then go walk to the nursery and work by their side until dark. It was far better to get some space between them before she said something she would regret. "*Jah.* I'm going to go for a walk. I might be a few hours."

"If you are not going to go to work, you need to do your chores. You have obligations to our home."

It had been that way all her life. Her mother talked about God and how He guided their lives. She talked about how each person in the family had a special place where he or she belonged, and how they all needed to do their part to keep the house and business running.

But at the moment, she didn't feel as if she belonged anywhere. Lydia straightened up and with a determined voice answered. "I don't think I'll be doing my chores today."

"Lydia, you must! You are still a member of the family."

Unable to hold her tongue any longer, she spoke. "Am I? Am I really? As far as I'm concerned, I'm the girl you've lied to for years. Years!"

And with that, she ran inside and grabbed her purse from the top of the kitchen table. Her parents followed on her heels, but then stopped when she pulled open the front door.

"Lydia? Please come back and talk to us about this!" her mother called out.

Refusing to answer, Lydia pulled the screen door shut and let it slam behind her. As she heard her parents voices rise, she kept walking. Within seconds, she reached the end of their property. Taking a left, she passed the Yoders' herd of cows, and heard the faint roar of the waters running in Crooked Creek.

In the weak morning light, the dark woods around the creek beckoned her. There, she could get lost on one of the many trails and paths that ran along the water. Picking up her pace, she rushed forward. And, to her surprise, didn't have the desire to look back at all. In fact, at that moment, she wished she could keep walking forever.

To get far, far away. As far away as possible. Then she would figure out what to do next.

Chapter 8

"The thing about Perry was that he never seemed Amish to me. 'Course, in a lot of ways he didn't seem like anything at all. He was just Perry, for better or worse."

WALKER ANDERSON

"Yeah?" Walker said into his cell phone after hastily grabbing it from amid the clutter atop his dresser.

He heard a faint rustling in the background, then a throat clearing.

"Walker? Is that you?"

A curious buzz rang through him as he recognized the voice. Low and sweet and faintly accented. "Yeah, it's me," he said, unable to keep the smile out of his voice. "This is Lydia, right?"

"Yes." Pure relief filled her tone. "I was afraid I'd read the number wrong. Is this a bad time to talk?"

"Not at all. You called at the perfect time."

"Ah. *Gut.* I mean, good." Her voice was rushed but still thready-sounding. Far less sure than when they'd spoken face-to-face.

"Walker, when you said that you were willing to meet me to talk about things, did you mean it?"

"Sure I did." Of course, while he had meant it, he wouldn't have bet a nickel that she'd take him up on it.

"Then could we meet? Soon?"

"Yeah. Sure." Running a finger along the only empty area on his messy desk, he cleared his throat. Realizing that she was most likely outside at one of the Amish phone booths that some families shared, he said, "Did something new happen? Did Detective Reynolds make you scared or something?"

"Something did happen, but it wasn't with the police detective. This is more personal."

"Is it about Perry?"

"No," she said after a moment's pause. "It's just that, well . . . something came up that has surprised me very much. My mind is so muddled, I've realized that I need to talk it through. To, ah, someone who isn't Amish."

Walker was as confused by her statements as he was by the way she was choosing him to confide in. They hardly knew each other. "And I'm the only non-Amish person you know?"

"Of course not."

"Then why me and not somebody else?" He could almost feel her apprehension through the air. But he wasn't going to give her an easy way out. No way did he want to agree to meet her alone, just to get blindsided. He'd had enough of that with Abby—she was a champion at finding any excuse to corner him in order to talk about her problems.

"Because of everything with Perry, and the way you know how much I'm struggling with his secrets, you might be the only person who could understand."

She sounded so upset, he quit questioning her. "How about we meet tomorrow afternoon?"

"I could do that . . . if you wouldn't mind picking me up at my family's nursery?"

Picking her up sounded like a date. And though that wasn't what she meant, warning bells went off in his head. Picking her up would give anyone who saw them together a reason to ask questions.

She seemed to realize that. "I could also meet you in town at the Pizza Hut around five. Would that work better for you?"

"Yeah. That works better for me." The Pizza Hut was on North Main, one of the closest streets to Highway 60 and the Amish community. From her house to the Pizza Hut, it was only five or seven minutes by car. But by buggy or bike, it could take almost an hour. Maybe even longer if she was walking. "Lydia, are you sure you can get there?"

"It won't be a problem."

Used to worrying about Abby, he almost asked Lydia how she was going to get to town. But then he stopped himself. How she got to Marion wasn't his business. In addition, now that plans were set, he was a little uncomfortable with the idea that an Amish girl was going to meet him there.

"Lydia . . . listen, I don't know what I was thinking. I can pick you up at the nursery. Do you want me there at five or earlier? I can come as early as two."

After another moment, she blurted, "If you could pick me up at three, I would be grateful. *Danke*, Walker. I mean, thank you."

After they discussed directions, they hung up, and he found himself staring at the phone. There had been a lot of background noise. He wondered where she'd called from.

What could have happened in her life that would change her whole demeanor so much?

Only one thing came to mind—Perry. Even though she

said her reason for meeting didn't have anything to do with him, Walker figured it had to, at least indirectly.

After all, what did they have in common besides Perry?

Or maybe it was that he felt like his mind was never all that far from Perry. Not even after all this time.

Perry had always been happy-go-lucky, but there was a point when he just started pushing boundaries . . .

Back when they'd been working behind the front counter together, during a lull, Perry had casually opened the cash drawer, pulled out a twenty, and stuffed it into his front pocket.

"Perry, what the heck are you doing?" he'd asked. "You can't do that."

"Sure I can," Perry said simply. "I just did."

"But you can't steal from Mr. Schrock."

"He ain't never going to miss it."

"Yeah, he is." Walker knew he would when he counted the cash drawer at the end of the night.

"What are you going to do about it? Get the twenty back? Fight me for it? Go tell Jacob?" He'd grinned with open amusement. Daring Walker to fight him. To tell.

"I don't want to do anything—"

"Gut. Then don't." More softly, Perry said, "It's just a twenty, Walker. I've taken a couple before and old Schrock's never said a word."

"I can't believe you're stealing."

"Oh, Walker, who would've believed that out of the two of us, you'd be the one who was so honest. So sweet and good?" His voice had turned syrupy.

Walker had been very sure that Mr. Schrock would have never believed him over Perry.

So, to his shame, he didn't do anything. He'd been too afraid that Mr. Schrock wouldn't believe him. That Perry would find a way to get back at him.

He'd even been worried about his reputation. No one wanted to be known as the kid who tattled on his friends.

So he'd held his tongue and hadn't said a word. And as each day passed, Walker had stood by and watched things get worse. And it had. More money went missing.

Yeah, that day with the cash box had been the first of many bizarre things that happened between them.

And that had forced Walker to put as much space between him and Perry as possible.

In the end, he'd quit.

Because by then, he'd felt like spending time with Perry meant lying to just about everyone he knew.

Luke Reynolds was lonely. His leg hurt, it never seemed to stop raining, and while the folks in the county were friendly enough, most kept their distance. So much that he was starting think that he had a sign on his back that told everyone to stay far away from him, like he was a leper or something.

As he took the front left booth at the Marion Café, he pretended to find interest in the menu. It was difficult to do, though. There was little on the laminated cardboard he hadn't already tried.

"I'm waiting for the day you ignore the menu completely," his server said around a saucy smile. "If I was a betting woman, I'd say we've got about two more visits before you take the plunge."

"Only two more visits, huh?" He looked at the fortyish woman with the salt-and-pepper hair with some amusement. "What do you think I'll do then?"

"What everyone else does, of course. Tell me you want the usual." She grinned, displaying a full set of crooked teeth stained by years of tobacco. "Then it will be up to me to do the remembering."

Glancing at her name tag, he said, " Nancy, that's my problem. I don't know what my usual even is."

To his surprise, she sat down across from him, her snug uniform pulling at the buttons running down her chest. "That's because you're too easy to please, detective. Most folks want what they want. You seem to be just fine thinking about things awhile."

"I'll have the roast beef sandwich."

"With fries or soup today? Soup's vegetable."

"Any good?"

She shrugged. "Good enough."

"I'll take the soup."

She slid out of the booth. "It'll come right up." After two steps, she paused, her white-soled shoes squeaking slightly. "And detective? . . ."

"Yes?"

"Don't you be takin' it personally, now."

"Take what personally?"

"The way everyone's keepin' their distance and such."

Luke was vaguely embarrassed that his outcast status was so visible. "So the rudeness is intentional?"

"Yep. More or less." When he raised a brow, she prattled on. "No one's aiming to be rude, honey. Just standoffish, that's all. Nobody wants a fella like you peeking into their private life. Some things are better left undisturbed, you know?"

He supposed that made sense—to someone who liked to keep his head buried in the ground. "I can't ignore a murder."

"The boy was Amish, though."

Luke was familiar enough with the workings of the community to know that meant next to nothing. Most people knew everyone else. "He worked at Schrock's Variety, which is close to town. Anyone could have had something to do with it. Or they could know something."

"Maybe. Maybe not."

"People can't cover up a crime, Nancy."

"No one else wants to cover anything bad up, neither," she said in a rush. "But, you know, there's a big difference between wanting justice and digging up old hurts. Don'tcha think?"

The way she phrased the words caught him off guard. There was something in her tone—something almost eager, almost pleading—that he couldn't leave alone. "You think finding Perry's killer is going to dig up someone's old hurts around here? Why is that?"

"Perry had been a good boy, but over the years, he changed," she said baldly. "I've heard round that some folks want to pretend otherwise, but that's the honest truth. He wasn't good, and he wasn't planning on getting better anytime soon. And because of that, folks started giving him wide berth."

"How wide a berth? Nancy, did you think Perry dangerous?"

Before he could ask more, another customer called her and she turned away. Leaving him with more questions than he'd had before.

When he looked around him again, he noticed that more than a handful of people had come into the diner, and not a one of them seemed eager to look his way.

With a sigh, Luke flattened out the menu and stared at it again, trying to pretend he hadn't just done that moments before.

He needed to help out Mose as quickly as he could, then get on out of Crittenden County. He was too comfortable in the city to ever get used to acres of rolling hills and miles of fields and woods. The Amish community just north of Marion felt particularly confining. The roads were narrow and winding, the streets and shops barely marked well enough for a stranger to see. Interspersed with the Amish homes were a wild array of brand new oak and stone farmhouses and abandoned trailers.

And the people, while pleasant enough, didn't seem to have much use for a city detective from Cincinnati. More often than not, level stares met his questions, making what should have been a rather routine investigation something far more challenging.

As Mose had tried to tell him.

Luke realized now that he should have listened.

Chapter 9

"Perry's eyes were deep hazel. Never green, never brown. It was as if God had chosen that particular shade just for him."

LYDIA PLANK

Lydia hadn't meant to thank him for picking her up and taking her to Pizza Hut. Actually, she hadn't meant to thank him for agreeing to meet her. After all, she'd already thanked him on the phone. More than once. Being so grateful for a kind gesture seemed too eager, too weak.

But when Walker looked at her the way he did—his gaze solid and slow, his expression carefully guarded but search-ing, her mouth started running off in spite of herself. "I hope all this wasn't too much trouble for you. Picking me up and going to get pizza I mean," she blurted.

When he glanced her way, she rambled on. "Pizza Hut is kind of out of the way."

"Not if you have a car."

"Oh. *Jah.* For sure. I mean . . . I suppose not."

As if he sensed his manner was making her jumpy, he winced. "Hey—I'm sorry. I guess I've been sounding kind of rude." He cleared his throat, illustrating that for him, too, this conversation was turning completely awkward.

After shaking his head, he smiled slightly. "What I'm trying to say is that it was no trouble at all. I told you it wouldn't be."

"I'm glad of that."

They spent the rest of the drive in silence. When they passed a pair of Amish girls that Lydia knew from school, Lydia made sure she kept her face averted.

Walker seemed to be just fine with her keeping quiet. She kept waiting for him to play with the knobs on his dashboard, to turn on the radio or something. But he didn't. Instead, he simply drove with one hand on the wheel and the other propped on top of the open window.

The cool air fanned her cheeks and made her feel more at ease.

After he parked his truck, he opened the restaurant door for her and guided her in. A couple of people who were sitting in booths looked at them strangely, but no one said a word.

When the hostess guided them to a booth in a back corner, Lydia felt her spine relax. The last thing she wanted was to sit at one of the square tables in the middle of the restaurant. There, they'd be on display, for better or worse.

After they sat down and were handed menus, Walker looked at her in that direct way of his. "Sorry, I was a little late picking you up. Did that cause problems?"

"*Nee.* I mean, no." Now she was the one stumbling over her words. "I didn't have to wait long at all." Actually, she'd been ready a full thirty minutes early, feeling like it would be terribly rude to make him wait for her.

Instead, he'd come ten minutes late, causing her to wait on the bench at the front of the nursery. Just like she had nothing better to do. Reuben had berated her for sitting around but she'd told him to mind his own business. Her parents, on the other hand, hadn't said a word. She could tell they were disappointed by her choices. But there was no need for him to know that.

Walker seemed satisfied with her answer, flipping open the menu and scanning it. "So, what pizza do you like?"

"Oh, I don't know."

His head popped up. "Which one do you usually get?"

"I haven't eaten here before."

She waited, half prepared to answer his questions about why she chose a place to meet that she'd never been to before.

But instead of launching into a barrage of questions, he grinned. "Oh, boy. Well then, get ready for the best pizza you've ever had in your life."

She laughed. When she looked at him, finding the strength to meet his eyes and act, well, normal, she saw his own soften. Suddenly, she began to have hope that this idea to meet hadn't been the worst idea ever. Perhaps if they could laugh about pizza, there was enough of a connection between the two of them to inspire trust.

And she so needed to trust someone.

"I'll look forward to trying it."

"Want to get pepperoni? It's my favorite."

"If it's your favorite, I'm sure I'll like it *verra* much." She was just about to ask about the salad bar when their waitress approached. She was wearing a pair of snug dark denim jeans and a fitted T-shirt.

And a smile that seemed just for Walker.

"Hey, Walker," she drawled with what Lydia was sure was a flirty smile. "I couldn't believe my eyes when I looked over and saw you sitting here. I haven't seen you in a while."

"Not since high school," he replied.

"Forever."

"So, uh, Kim, how've you been?"

"Good. I'm good." Her smile widened as she cracked her gum. "Time goes by so fast, don't it? It seems like just yesterday we were in chemistry class together." She shook her head wryly. "I can't believe it sometimes."

"Yeah." He looked her way. "Lydia? Is pepperoni okay?"

"I'm sorry?"

The server cracked her gum again. "Walker just asked if a pepperoni pizza is okay with you. Is it? Do you even know what that is?"

"It is fine." She didn't look back at the server, afraid the other woman would see the irritation in her eyes. Of course she'd had pepperoni pizza before.

Walker glanced her way again, then after another pause, he held up two fingers. "We'll take two Cokes, too, Kim. Thanks."

"All right. Sure, then." With a swish of her hips, she turned away, leaving them alone.

"What just happened, Lydia? Everything okay?"

What could she even say? "Nothing. I'm sorry. My head went wandering. That's all."

"You sure?"

"Oh, yes. I'm sorry."

"Don't apologize. It's not like you don't have things to think about." His mouth tightened. "There's a lot going on. So what did you want to talk about? I mean . . . you said it was nothing to do with Perry, right?"

"No. I mean, not really." As much as she'd been dying to talk to someone about all her feelings about Perry 's death, now none of it seemed as important as her current situation.

But it was still hard to get the words out.

Walker shifted, signaling that he was losing patience.

It was time. "A couple of days ago, my parents, they . . ." She paused. Forced herself to continue. "They said they needed to talk to me." Warily, she glanced at him. He looked at her and nodded, encouraging her to continue. "What they told me was a shock. I'm adopted."

His eyes widened and his mouth went slack. Completely mirroring the way she was feeling, the way that she had been feeling since her parents had oh-so-calmly told her the news.

"You had no idea?"

"None. Until they gave me the news, it never crossed my mind that I was different from them at all."

"Really? You never thought you looked different? Or acted different?"

"Every once in a while it crossed my mind, but my mother was always sure to brush off my questions." She shrugged. "When my *mamm* told me not to question why God gave me blue eyes and the rest of my family brown, I listened to her."

She shook her head, realizing that surely there were a hundred little things that she should have wondered about, from her slim build when her mother was far curvier, to the way she was impatient, to the way she didn't like sweets when everyone else in her family had a sweet tooth. "I'm the only one, too."

"Only one what?"

"Of the kids in my family to be adopted."

"No way."

Lydia nodded, feeling vaguely like she was gossiping about strangers. Truly, her story felt like it belonged to someone else. "*Jah*. There're four of us kids, but I'm the only one who's not a biological member of the family."

"What are you going to do?"

She was glad that he wasn't correcting her, trying to make

her feel like she shouldn't be so rattled. "I'm not sure, but I want to do something." And even as she said the words, she realized that was the truth. She wasn't sure what to do next, or even if she should want to do something. To be sure, there was no set of rules explaining how to deal with situations like her own. All she did know was that keeping everything inside was clawing at her sense of worth.

Was there even anything to do?

Kim arrived with their pizza and drinks. Lydia was thankful for the interruption. As Walker reached for one of the white plastic plates and picked out a slice, she sipped her soda. The cold, sweet tang to the beverage was at once familiar and foreign. Usually, she didn't crave anything more than water or coffee, but at the moment, the sugar seemed to revitalize her senses and bring clarity to a foggy situation.

The slice of pizza did the same thing to her emotions. The cheese and sauce were hot and spicy, and the thin crust delicious.

Walker said nothing as he ate across from her, but the amusement that played across his features revealed that he'd noticed her enthusiasm for the pizza and Coke.

Moments later, Kim returned with a pitcher and refilled their glasses. "Need anything else, Walker?"

He looked her way. "Lydia, want anything?"

"*Nee.* I do not need anything more."

His lips twitched. "We're good, Kim," he said at last.

She shifted, popping a hip out. "Sure about that?"

"Positive." He picked up his pizza while Kim still stood at his side, obviously hoping he'd have more to say to her. If Walker was aware of the other woman's interest, he gave no sign of it.

As Lydia observed the whole exchange, she found herself

wondering more about him. He was so different than most of the Amish men she'd spent time with, far more outgoing, less reserved. Walker seemed to project an easy confidence with just about everything he did. What would that be like? she wondered. What would it be like to know yourself so well that nothing could rattle you?

And how come she was feeling the exact opposite?

"What?" Walker blurted.

She blinked. "What do you mean?"

"You keep staring." He brushed his pale blue T-shirt for nonexistent crumbs.

"I'm sorry. I don't mean to be rude —"

"No, is something wrong? I mean, beyond your news?"

"Not at all. I was just thinking that you seemed so relaxed here. And so relaxed with Kim."

"Oh. I should be. I mean, I've known her forever."

"Yes, of course." Mentally, she rolled her eyes. Why had she even mentioned it?

"Are you upset? Kim's kind of rude, but don't take it personally. She's like that to just about everybody."

"It's not Kim." Lydia paused as she tried to explain herself better. "I'm not uncomfortable being here. I guess I'm just uneasy about life right now."

He eyed the rest of the pizza pie on the table, obviously debating whether to eat more or leave it. Then he met her gaze. "So, what are you going to do about your parents' news?"

"I'm not sure. My parents don't want me to do anything."

"Seriously? They just expected to drop that bombshell on you and move on?"

She wasn't exactly sure what he meant, but she got the gist of it. "Yes. They'd like me to keep it a secret, too." Of course, she hadn't.

"That's hardly fair."

"I feel the same way. I don't want this secret."

"You're an adult. You need to do whatever you need to do. I mean, that's what I think."

She smiled. "Thank you. I needed to hear an outsider's opinion. Someone who wasn't Amish."

He slowly grinned. "Like me."

"Yes. Like you."

"So, did they tell you who your real parents are?"

Here was her chance. It was either time to bring her concerns to the forefront of her mind or to push them away.

"No . . . But I think I need to find out who they are. Good or bad, I need the truth."

"That sounds logical."

"Even if I never get to know them, I should at least know who they are, I think."

"You're completely in the dark? Your parents didn't give you any information?"

"Walker, they couldn't even tell me if my birth parents were Amish or English." She sighed, and asked the question that had been lingering in the corner of her mind since her parents told her the news. "Walker, if my birth parents are English . . . do you think that's what I am meant to be? If they were English, do I need to be English, too?"

"I have no idea."

The simple words, combined with the steady, serious expression on his face, confirmed her fears. There was no blueprint to this situation. No one knew exactly what she was supposed to do now. And no one could provide her with an easy answer. This was something she was going to have to figure out on her own, by herself.

Chapter 10

"I remember when Perry and Lydia broke up. He told me it was her fault, but I never really believed that."

WALKER ANDERSON

Walker wished he was anywhere but where he was.

"Do I need to be English, too?"

Lydia Plank was gazing at him like he was some kind of hero, when the truth was he'd never be anyone's hero. Not with all the things he'd done in his life.

He grabbed the last piece of pizza and bit off a big bite, needing the time to figure out what to say. "I don't know the answer to that." When Lydia flinched, he closed his eyes. He was sorry he'd frightened her, but still feeling completely out of his element. "Lydia, look . . . I'm just a guy from a small town in Kentucky. I'm not Amish; I'm not even close to being sophisticated. My big life event was playing in the state championships in high school. Why would you think I would know what you should do?"

Her cheeks turned rosy. "Since you know a lot of English girls, I thought maybe you could tell if I had something in common with English girls our age. And that maybe then I would have an idea of what I should do."

"Well, I don't. I'm not some expert on Amish and English, or even American teenagers. I only agreed to meet because I thought you wanted to talk about Perry."

As her face clouded with uneasiness, he blurted, "There's no news, is there? The last thing the detective told me was that they were questioning Perry's friends."

She leaned back in her chair. "Was that what I was? For a time, I thought I was his sweetheart."

"Then you broke up?"

"*Jah*. I hadn't talked to him for some time."

"I hadn't, either," Walker said wistfully. "But I told the detective I didn't know what Perry had been doing before he went missing."

"But you knew. Right?"

There was more to her question than he was prepared to answer. And so he pushed the questions back to her. "Why? Where did you think he'd disappeared to after New Year's?"

She blinked. "I thought he went to Lexington. Maybe even St. Louis."

"I did, too. He was sick of being here. Once I heard him talk about meeting some guys from out of town."

"I saw him with some of those men." She shivered. "They looked so different from us. They had on fancy clothes and sunglasses." Leaning forward, she whispered, "I don't know if those were the people who were selling him drugs."

"Yeah," he shook his head, not sure what to say.

"Did you ever tell anyone?"

He'd told the detective, but he wasn't going to tell her that. "No way. It wasn't like I knew anything for sure."

"I never said anything, either," she admitted. "It felt wrong to say things like that about a boy I had loved. Plus, I wasn't even sure anyone would believe me. I didn't have proof."

He swallowed. It made him uncomfortable to realize that they had something in common. It was easier thinking about how pretty she was when she was practically a stranger. It was easier imagining what it would be like to have her look at him in a soft way, when he knew they were worlds apart.

After looking around, fearful for a moment that everyone had stopped minding their own business and was listening to their conversation, he leaned forward. "Once, he said he'd smoked something to have more energy." Remembering the conversation, he said, "He acted like it was the best thing in the world. He offered to give me some to try."

Her eyes turned to saucers. "And what did you say?"

"I said I wasn't interested." He was afraid it was meth—there had been no way he'd get near that. "I'm not into drugs. I don't even drink." She looked so worried, he had a sudden thought. "Hey, did he ever offer you anything?"

She shook her head. "Never. But he started drifting away from me. From us. From everything we believe in." She paused, her eyes widening. "I mean everything Amish."

"Did you ever talk to anyone about Perry?"

Her expression turned troubled. "When I was seeing Perry, I pulled away from my girlfriends. They didn't like him, you see."

"But you did?"

She shrugged. "I thought I did. I wanted to; I'd known him forever. And my parents had encouraged us. They thought he was still the same, you see."

Now he understood. She felt like she was completely alone. The guy she'd once trusted was gone. Her parents had encouraged her to date a guy who'd been lying to just about everyone. And then it turned out that they'd been lying to her, too. Now her siblings weren't even her real siblings.

That was why she'd forced herself to see him. Because he was one of the few people who had been honest with her. "You know, my grandfather says it's not who you are that makes a person, it's what you believe."

"Walker, I'm not even sure what I believe anymore. I don't know who I am, and I don't even know who to trust."

It was on the tip of his tongue to tell her that she could trust him. But he held the words back. After all, they hardly knew each other.

After sipping her drink again, she opened her purse and pulled out a ten-dollar bill. "Thank you for meeting me here, Walker."

"You can pay next time. Put the money away. I've got this."

She turned to him in surprise. "Next time?"

Walker knew he should feel relief. She didn't want another thing from him. She didn't want to meet him again.

He should feel happy. Really glad. They'd lived this long in Crittenden County without crossing paths all that much. There was no need to see her again or to deepen their friendship.

But as he looked at her, and as he thought about Abby and how lost she always seemed to be, he knew he had to do something. For whatever reason, their lives were now intertwined because they'd once known Perry. And if he knew anything, it was that God didn't do anything without a reason.

"Look, we never got our stories straight about that night at Schrock's. Meet me tomorrow at Stanton Park."

She shook her head. "Walker, there are a lot of people there. Already, I'm sure everybody's wondering what the two of us would have to talk about."

"The park will be crowded. No one would notice us." It was

true. Stanton Park wasn't known to be a hangout for Amish or for college students. No, it was a place where people down on their luck hung out.

She bit her lip. "I don't know . . ."

"Look, it's the only place for us. It's close. No one will see us. No one will know. It will be our secret."

Apprehension flashed in her eyes before she slowly nodded. "All right. I'll see you tomorrow at the park at four o'clock. I think I had better go now."

"Wait a minute. Aren't you going to let me drive you home?"

"There's no need."

"But with my truck, it's no problem to take you home. It's not out of my way at all."

"I've already taken up enough of your time."

"Driving won't take me long at all."

She smiled softly. "I imagine it wouldn't. But I'd rather walk."

After setting her napkin on the table, she slid out of the booth and walked out, her back straight in her royal blue dress. Her head held high with a perfectly creased white *kapp* covering her light brown hair.

Never looking back.

By now, Luke had interviewed over twenty people about Perry. From what he could discern, Perry Borntrager had been both a pillar of the community and the worst sort of bully. He'd been kind to animals and small children, but had taunted them as well.

He'd been always amenable and patient. He'd also been mean and irresponsible and difficult.

For all these reasons, no one liked him.

But everyone was really sad he was dead.

Luke was growing more frustrated by the day, and more certain that his time was being wasted. "Mose, I think I might be going soon," he said as they left Mose's office, one half of a trailer behind the bank building. It was raining again. He'd put on his ball cap from the police academy but had refrained from putting on his slicker.

The light rain pattered against his flannel plaid shirt and cotton twill slacks. Mose had on a ball cap that read "Ice Road Truckers" and was dressed in loose jeans, a tan sheriff's uniform shirt, and a red down vest. Luke figured that this was the first time in a while that they looked alike. Their strides matched, both easy and measured; instead of looking like a Kentucky Mennonite and a city guy from Cincinnati, he and Mose looked like a pair of friends.

Much like they'd looked when back at the academy.

"Wish you wouldn't," Mose muttered.

"Staying here would only be a disservice to you. Fact is, I'm not making much headway." Thinking about the hours of useless conversation he'd had, where the Amish men and women had talked in circles, practically daring him to delve into their personal world just so they could shoot him down. "Actually, I'm afraid I might be making things worse."

Mose glanced his way. "How so?"

"People are clamming up the moment I get near them," he said grudgingly. Feeling like the worst sort of rookie. "Or, even worse, they're telling all kinds of stories about Perry that don't add up. One minute it seems like the kid was a saint. Other times, that he was the worst sort of sinner."

"That sounds like most of us, don'tcha think?" Mose chuckled.

Luke was not amused. He was frustrated and sitting here

admitting his faults. "Mose, I'm trying to say that I think you would do better without me."

"I disagree. Yes, you're a stranger here, but I know you'll see some connections that I've been missing. Here in Crittenden County, our whole lives are intertwined; it's hard to sometimes tell the good from the bad. Things might be making more sense than you realize."

"The information I'm getting and recording is only going to confuse your investigation."

As they walked along the sidewalk, Mose nodded to the few people they passed. Tipping the bill of his cap at a pair of elderly ladies; smiling at a pair of shy Amish girls—who didn't look Luke's way for even a second.

"Maybe not. Maybe you're helping more than you'll ever know."

"I doubt that." Even as he said the words, Luke wanted to cringe. He wasn't the type of man to whine like this. Or to give up easily.

But he was the type of man who dealt with realities. And the reality was that he was destined to remain a fish out of water. The majority of his experience was on the city streets and alleys of Cincinnati. He was used to informers and snitches and a whole team of forensic specialists to appear at a moment's notice. Driving around the hills and valleys and woods in the county, talking with *Englischers* who rarely talked to their Amish neighbors or to the Amish who were so entrenched in their farms, families, and community that they weren't aware of other's gossip was difficult at best.

And while he didn't mind a difficult investigation, he did mind failing.

"I appreciate your honesty. I do for sure," Mose replied, sounding much like the Amish man he'd grown up as. "But

I promise you this, I wouldn't have asked you here if I didn't think it would help, Luke." Mose didn't wait for an answer as they increased their pace, crossing the street and heading toward the veterans memorial. When they stopped in front of a trio of crosses, he spoke again. "I still believe that it will."

"You sure you want to bet on that? I'm costing you time."

"Don't sell yourself short. Besides, if you don't help me, what else are you going to do while you recuperate? Sit in front of the TV and watch Sports Center?"

Luke had no doubt that his friend had used the TV reference on purpose. Back at the academy when they were roommates, they'd watched endless hours of Sports Center when their bodies were too tired to take another step and their minds were too tired to study another law, citation, or procedure.

Mose had only been two years out of his Amish community, and still had an almost whimsical appreciation for all things ESPN. He'd grown as attached to Sports Center as any preschooler with *Dora the Explorer.* In a way, the two of them had bonded while watching it.

Luke was just about to tell Mose that not even that reminder could soften his stance when nearby a pair of teenagers opened a truck's back cab, and stealthily pulled out a couple of six-packs of beer and not very discretely stuffed them under their hoodies. The high school's name was proudly printed on those sweatshirts, practically beckoning any and all law-enforcement officers to crack down on underage drinking.

Seeing the kids act so foolishly—and knowing he could do something about it—almost gave Luke a rush of pleasure. "Guess we could go take care of some business, huh?"

A slow smile lit Mose's face while they watched yet another

two kids scurry out of the truck, one with what looked to be a full bottle of Kentucky bourbon nestled in his arms like a baby. "Your leg up for it? This could get squirrely."

He patted his brace. "I'm up for it, no problem."

"Then I'd be obliged." Raising his voice, Mose called out, "Boys, you want to tell me what in the Sam Hill you're doing?"

Luke groaned as the kids started running. "Somehow, I figured they'd do that. I got the one on the right."

"You're only taking one?"

"I'm good, but I'm injured."

"Oh, fine." As they all took off, Mose called out, "Jeremy? Is that you?"

A pause, then a hoarse, squeaky reply floated through the air. "Yes, sir."

Some things never changed, Luke thought to himself as he picked up his pace and grabbed the boy on the right. "Don't even think about tackling me, son," he said as clearly as possible. "If you make me be on crutches again, you'll be arrested for assault on a police officer."

Only later, after the boys had been taken to the police station, parents had been summoned, and more than a little fear had been put into a pair of fifteen-year-olds, did Mose bring up Perry again.

"I know he was dealing, Luke," Mose said, his voice heavy with certainty. "I know he was dealing, and he was making a whole lot of people in this community miserable while he was selling that poison to them. I want to know what he was doing, and I want to know who thought they were justified in killing him. Someone was really angry. Someone was angry enough to kill the kid and stuff him in a well. I want to know who did it, Luke. I want to know it enough to risk everything."

He paused, then looked at Luke directly. "I want to know these answers so badly that I'm willing to tell you I can't do it alone. Please, don't go."

It was the "please" that did it. Mose had been raised Amish, and therefore came across as naturally self-effacing. But he was also a talented professional. He wasn't the kind of man to show weakness, especially not in his career.

His friend needed him, and he believed in him. For the moment, that was enough. "I'll go visit with his parents tomorrow. Again."

"That sounds like a fine idea," Mose murmured. "That sounds like a real good idea. I'm obliged, Luke."

"Don't be grateful yet; I haven't done anything."

"But you will. I'm certain of it."

Luke replied the only way he could. He punched the guy lightly in the shoulder.

Chapter 11

"Perry was a dear boy. When he was eight, there was none better."

BETH ANNE BORNTRAGER

"Lydia, can you help those customers near the annuals?"

"Sure, Mamm," Lydia replied. After waving her brother Reuben over to help with the register, she hurried to the back of the property. In a corner, right next to a pond with a waterfall that hadn't been easy for her father and Reuben to build, was their flowering plants and low-level shrub area.

In between each row of plants were neat gravel-lined paths. They connected to each other in a mishmash way, reminding Lydia of a crossword puzzle. The area was one of their busiest areas in the spring, both with customers wanting to purchase plants and for visitors. Many in the county claimed their nursery and garden was one of the prettiest in the area.

As she approached, Lydia noticed that there were several groups of *Englischers* standing around in clumps. Lydia looked at each, wondering which ones were waiting for her to come help them. As she approached, though, none were looking in her direction with an expectant look.

Feeling slightly confused by the summons, she wandered down another aisle, her gaze darting left and right. Then she stopped and a lump formed in her throat as she saw a tall man with wheat-colored hair, a pair of worn, faded jeans and heavy tan boots. "Walker?" she blurted before she could catch herself.

Walker looked just as taken aback as she. "Lydia." After meeting her gaze for an instant, he turned away. "Hey, we, I mean my mom . . . she . . . needs some flowers."

"Way to make me feel good, Walker," a petite redheaded lady said by his side. "You couldn't sound any less interested." Her teasing tone deflected her snippy words.

And made Lydia grin. "I don't know many men who care all that much for flowers," she said. "So I guess maybe Walker ain't alone in that."

The woman's smile broadened. "Walker, do you know this smart girl?"

"Yeah. I mean, yes." Somewhat clumsily, he performed the introductions. "Mom, this is Lydia Plank. Lydia, this is my Mom, Chrissy Anderson."

"It's nice to meet you," Lydia said. Now that the introductions were out of the way, she jumped to business. "If you are here looking for plants, I'd say you came to the right place. I'd be pleased to help you."

"I'm looking for some spring flowers that will do well in the sun. A couple of flats."

"Geraniums and vincas will do nicely." Guiding them forward, she showed them some of the fresh red and bright pink blooms. "These are all easy to take care of as well."

"Perfect. We'll take four flats of each."

Walker groaned. "Mom, I'm going to be planting flowers all weekend."

"Abby will help you." With a wink at Lydia, Mrs. Anderson grinned slyly. "Maybe."

Lydia was intrigued by Mrs. Anderson's humor. She liked how playful she was with Walker. Especially since his mother's banter seemed to transform him from a confident boy to one far less assured. "I'll fill out a slip for your order," she said easily, "then help you carry the flowers to your car."

"I can carry them out, Lydia," Walker said. "Don't trouble yourself. You're in a dress."

"I'm always in a dress," she said with a laugh. "Besides, it's no trouble. It's my job, *jah*?"

Though Walker looked embarrassed, his mother appeared charmed. "Well, now. Aren't you a sweet thing? Yes dear, please go help Walker while I look at the apple trees you have in the back." And with that, she darted away, leaving the two of them alone.

After his mother was out of sight, Walker cleared his throat but still didn't look all that relaxed. "Here we are, together again."

"Jah. I'll go help you with the flats, then. Follow me, if you please."

He followed her toward the back. After she put four flats of vincas on a cart, he set the same amount of geraniums next to them. "Should we take them to the register now?"

"No. I'll remember what your mother ordered. There's no need to carry them up there." Feeling that he was standing too close, she waved a hand. "You lead the way and I'll follow with the cart to your car."

He stepped forward, then turned and looked at her, his expression sheepish. "I feel a little weird, letting you do this."

"You shouldn't. It's my job. I do it all the time."

But for some reason, it didn't look like her comment made him any happier. "Let's go, Walker," she prodded. "I've got much to do today."

"All right." He led the way to the parking lot. On the first row was a tan-colored vehicle. After unlocking the back hatch, he helped her set the plants in the trunk. When the sleeve of her dress brushed against his arm, they both acted like they didn't notice. When he reached around her to pull the hatch down, she pretended she didn't feel a sudden burst of awareness or smell the tangy scent of his cologne.

Then they returned to the inside of the greenhouse. "Do you still want to meet me this afternoon?" he asked.

"Jah. I mean, yes."

His eyes warmed, making her realize that she had spoken quickly. Really quickly. "I mean, I scheduled time off work," she added.

"Do you work a lot?"

"Almost every day." When his brows rose, she explained. "It's my family's shop, you know. We all must work together to keep it running. It's a big place."

"Do you ever wish you didn't have to work so much? I mean now?"

"Now that I know I'm not really a Plank?" The question hit her hard, though it came from her own worst fears.

He held up his hands. "You said that, not me. I was thinking that it would be hard, with you mourning Perry and all."

"Sorry." Shaking her head, she said, "I guess I can't help but jump to conclusions sometimes. . . ." She paused.

He prodded. "And?"

"And? And now that we're talking about things, I have to say that I'm glad I'm still working some. It keeps me from thinking about things too much. And well, now I can kind of see the humor in it all. Everything that's happened is surely beyond my greatest imaginings."

"If you can laugh, maybe it means you're feeling better."

"Perhaps." She shrugged. "I don't know. All I do know is that I've always liked working outside, even if I sometimes wish for more free time. Or if my dress gets dirty," she couldn't resist adding.

He laughed. "I deserved that." He shifted, stuffing his hands in his back pockets. "I guess I'm trying to tell you that I'm glad you're okay."

What could she say? Sometimes she did wish she was doing anything but waiting on customers, up to her elbows in dirt. Of course, sometimes she wished that she had gone to high school . . . or perhaps chosen a different path in life instead of living the way her mother had. Especially now. But all that the doubts had gotten her were sleepless nights.

She'd learned years ago to stop wishing for things that could never happen.

Yet another legacy of Perry, she supposed. When he'd begun to change, it had felt like his memory had gone missing, too. He pretended that they'd never talked about a future together.

He'd forgotten her likes and dislikes.

Or more to the point, he hadn't cared. Truly, Perry had taught her that promises sometimes meant nothing. He taught her that sometimes people did things on purpose, just to hurt.

Yes, he'd done that very well.

"Walker, are you ever going to join me over here?" his mother called out. "We've got other things to do today."

"Sure, Mom. I'll see you later, Lydia. At the park."

"I'll be there." She met his gaze with a smile before turning away and joining her brother at the cash register.

After the Andersons left, her mother walked up. "That is the same boy who came over."

"Yes. I told you we were friends."

"How do you know him?"

"Walker?" Lydia considered a few replies, then settled for the truth. "Like I told you, he was a friend of Perry's, too."

"You should stay away from him, then."

"Why?"

"Perry, he was a bad influence." Her voice turning sharper, she added, "And he had to have learned his bad things from someone. Perhaps it was from Walker."

"Oh, Mamm. Walker had nothing to do with all that."

"But still, he is an outsider, Lydia."

Rarely had her mother sounded so judgmental of an *Englischer*. "Walker used to work with him at the Schrocks'. You know how picky Mr. Schrock is. If he didn't think Walker was a good person, he never would have hired him."

"Even if Mr. Schrock does trust him, Walker is not Amish, Lydia. That is reason enough to stay away from him. You two have nothing in common."

Lydia felt herself nodding before what she was agreeing to sank in. "Mamm, all *Englischers* aren't bad. You know that."

"True, but their modern influences can be a difficult thing."

"I'm not about to start telling you I want a cell phone."

"There's other things to worry about besides telephones. I'm sure that boy is far too worldly for you to keep company with. He would surely take advantage of you. You need to be careful around men. Why even Perry made bad choices."

Even Perry?

Suddenly, it was all too much. Her being adopted, her mixed-up feelings about Perry and his death, the investigation.

And now Walker was in her life, making her feel things she had carefully tamped down after Perry had pushed her . . .

In a flash, she remembered the feel of Perry's mouth on her neck. His fingers on the collar of her dress, the weight of him when he'd leaned over her on the floor . . .

And just like that, she wasn't okay at all.

"Mamm, I thought I was okay, but maybe I need some more time off from the nursery." Before her mother could start questioning her, she said, " There's so much going on. I need a break from all the stress."

"Plants aren't stressful."

Oh, she was deliberately misunderstanding. Deliberately ignoring the truth. "You know what I mean, *muddah*. I want some time off. I need some time to think about everything. To process it all. I don't know who I am anymore."

"You are Lydia Plank. You are Amish. That it all you need to know."

That was the problem, she was starting to realize. For most of her life, she'd never thought twice about who she was or what she wanted. She had assumed that she'd join the church one day, marry, and follow in her mother's footsteps. Now, however, she wasn't so sure that was the path God meant for her to follow.

And if that wasn't the path meant for her . . . ? She couldn't even begin to imagine what He had in mind.

Chapter 12

"There's a place down by Crooked Creek that is the perfect hiding spot. Perry told me he once stood there for hours and not a single person saw him."

WALKER ANDERSON

Walker looked up when Lydia approached. "You came," he said.

Why was he surprised? Did he not trust her? "I told you I would."

"Still, things come up." He shrugged.

"Things do." She smiled. "All morning, it felt like everything that could have gone wrong did."

"Murphy's Law."

"I'm not sure what law that is, but I feared I wasn't going to be able to get here."

"But you did."

"I did." She lifted her chin. Feeling somewhat proud of herself. She looked around at the windy trail, at the children's playground equipment. At the soccer field. "Where would you like to go?"

"How about we just go to the swings for now?"

She walked by his side, walking with him, but still staying

just enough apart that if an observer saw them together, he would think they just happened to be going in the same direction.

Taking hold of the swing's chains, she sat down on the rubber seat with a sigh, leaned back, then pushed herself off with her feet.

Suddenly, the air whooshed around her, sweeping across her skin, cooling her cheeks. Beside her, Walker did the same. "I haven't swung in ages."

"Me neither." He flashed a smile. "When was the last time you were on a swing set?"

"Years ago." She tried to recall a single event, but all the memories floated together and meshed in her brain. "One time me and Reuben came here when we were dodging chores."

"You, Lydia? I would have never guessed."

"Why is that?"

"You always seem so contained. So perfect."

Remembering all the things she'd done over the years, she shook her head. "I promise, I've never been perfect."

"Me neither." He pumped his legs a bit and sailed higher and higher. "The last time I was here was when I was dating Jessica."

Unexpectedly, she felt a sickening in her stomach at the thought of him bringing another girl to that same spot. With effort, she did her best to keep her features even and schooled. "I suppose this would be a good place to take a sweetheart."

"Oh, she wasn't a sweetheart."

Lydia blinked, then realized they were having a communication problem. Every once in a while, the differences between being Amish and English were very pronounced. "Calling someone a sweetheart just means you're courting.

Not that you are in love and about to get married or any-thing," she explained.

"Ah. Well, we weren't really courting, either. We just went out a few times."

"Jessica is a pretty name."

"Yeah, it is." His lips pursed and he gazed out into the distance, looking like he had a hundred things on his mind.

Or at least that he was thinking about something far away. He pumped his legs again, leaning back so that his elbows locked.

"Are you still seeing her?"

"Jessica? No."

"Are you seeing anyone?" She was curious about him. Though she hated to admit it, her mother's words were still spinning in her head. Had Walker been part of the reason for Perry's fall from grace?

His head snapped her way. "Why do you care?"

She wasn't sure. "I wouldn't want one of your English girls to get the wrong impression."

He grinned. "Yeah, I bet they'd be really worried if they saw me out here swinging with other girls."

Now she felt embarrassed. Yes, she supposed to a college man like him, sitting alone with an Amish girl was about as meaningful as walking to class. But in her world, you didn't spend one-on-one time with a member of the opposite sex unless you were courting.

Confused about her rambling thoughts, she kept her voice prim. "You don't need to sound so full of yourself, English. Just because I don't know your usual habits doesn't mean I'm not aware of how men and women date." She let her legs still and relax. And with that, her swing slowly fell, until it was barely swaying at all.

"Sorry. You're fun to tease." By her side, his swing fell as well. "You know, I've been thinking about what we talked about at Pizza Hut. About your parents' news. Have you decided whether you're going to do anything about it?"

That "anything" felt like a challenge. She'd been struggling with the idea of both forgetting about their revelation and investigating it further. "I don't know," she said finally.

"Are you mad at them?"

Was she? "I don't know." Now with her feet solidly on the ground, she attempted to explain what was happening. "My parents seem hurt that I haven't taken their news, smiled, and kept on living as if nothing changed."

"Really? They thought you'd be unfazed?"

"I think so." Or did they? She was close to her parents, but no matter how close they were, conversations like this weren't something they did much. "I'm not altogether sure how they thought I would react." She thought about it some more. "I guess they knew I would be upset. Otherwise they would have told me earlier, right?"

Walker nodded.

Still half talking to herself, Lydia added, "My parents wanted me to put the conversation behind me and go on like nothing was different. I couldn't do that." She turned to him. "I guess I am mad."

Hopping off the swing, he held out a hand to her. "I would be."

She took his hand and stood up. His hand felt calloused and warm against her own skin. For a moment, his grip tightened, then his hand dropped.

"I'm mad," she said again. "And yet, at the same time, I feel almost grateful to them, too."

"Why?"

"All my life, I've wondered about myself. I've felt like part of the family and all, but a little different, too. Sometimes, things would happen and everyone else would just nod and go along with it, but it wouldn't feel the same for me. It felt like something was missing."

"Maybe God was biding His time? Waiting for the right time to let you know?"

"Maybe." She frowned. "But I don't understand why He thinks now is the right time."

His expression was shadowed as he pointed to the sidewalk that circled the perimeter of the park. "Hey, want to walk for a while?"

"Sure." Happy to leave the conversation behind, she fell into step beside him. Together, they walked silently along the cracked path. Weeds had grown along the edges, and the narrowing path forced them to either walk single file or closer together. They moved closer together.

As the breeze rustled her black bonnet covering her *kapp*, she sighed. "It's pretty out."

He glanced her way, seemed to look at her closely for the first time. "It is pretty here," he said, sounding a bit surprised.

Her cheeks heated, though surely the way she'd felt his gaze hadn't meant anything? Glancing his way again, she noticed that he was staring straight in front of him. However, his stride had shortened to match hers. She was shorter than he, the top of her head only reached his chin. But walking like they were, staying side by side, it felt like they were a pair.

They continued walking, dodged a pair of branches that needed trimming. All the while, Lydia found herself appreciating the silence. Somehow being quiet by his side was better than being alone with her thoughts.

Perhaps this was what she needed to do more often? Just walk and let things happen? Just be happy with her situation? After all, did it really matter who her birth mother was? All she really needed was her faith and the family who raised her, right?

"One of the reasons I wanted to talk with you is that I've been going through some of the same things," Walker said.

"Things like what?"

He shrugged. "Did you know my grandparents are Amish?" She shook her head. "Who are they?"

"Francis and James Anderson. Do you know them?"

"*Nee*, though the name sounds a little familiar."

"They don't live real close to here. About forty minutes away."

"That would explain it. If they're in a different church district, our paths wouldn't cross all that much."

"Maybe so. Anyway, my sister, Abby, really likes being with them." He glanced at her quickly. "She's never said anything, but sometimes I get the feeling that she'd rather live with them than with us. Maybe she wants to be Amish? I don't know."

"Really? I've never heard of someone wanting to be Amish."

"But it happens sometimes, right?"

Lydia nodded. "I suppose it does. I guess I was wrong using the word 'never.' Sometimes people do join our community. It just doesn't happen often. It's a different life, *jah*?"

"It is." They rounded a bend and stopped. An ancient ash tree had fallen across the path, blocking their way. Walker pressed a boot on the trunk but it didn't budge. "Looks like this is as far as we can go."

She walked to his side. "I guess you're right." Taking a breath, she said, "Walker, that night in December . . . when we were all outside the Schrocks' . . . did you have a feeling that something bad was going to happen to Perry?"

He shook his head. "Nope. I was trying to stay away from him, if you want to know the truth. I was sick of him."

"I wanted to avoid him, too," she murmured. In December, she'd still been so rattled by the things he'd done. By the way he'd tried to force himself on her. Clearing her throat, she said, "That night, he stopped to talk to us."

"I remember."

"We were cruel."

"All anyone did was ignore him."

"Not Jacob," she reminded him.

"What Jacob did isn't any of our business."

Lydia supposed Walker had a point. But she still didn't feel like she could let that episode go. "But, Walker, maybe if we had tried harder to keep Perry on the right path . . . if we'd been better friends, maybe Perry would never have left. Maybe he'd still be here."

His lips thinned into a hard line. "Don't go there. No sense feeling guilty about something we can't do anything about."

"I never told the detective about that night. Did you?"

"Of course not."

"Maybe we should tell the detective that we saw him—"

"If we do that, he'll never leave us alone. He'll want to know everyone's name who was there." Staring hard at her, he said, "You know the others won't appreciate us for talking, Lydia." Turning away, he started walking back toward his car. "We should say nothing."

She rushed to keep up, her black tennis shoes slipping a bit on the slick spots. "You know, the detective's going to keep askin' us questions about Perry and what we knew until he gets more answers."

"I suppose it's his job to do that," Walker said. "But I don't want to worry about those questions until we have to."

"You don't think we're just hiding our heads in the sand?"

"No . . . Besides, I don't know who killed him."

"I don't know either," she said quickly.

Pain flashed in his eyes. "You're going to think I'm horrible, but sometimes I wish Sheriff Kramer would give up. You know—say that there's no way anyone is ever going to find out what happened. Then we could all forget about it."

Lydia didn't bother telling Walker that she felt the same way. Her feelings weren't something to be proud of, and they weren't something to be shared. If she wanted the police to forget about murder, then it would mean that she wanted to forget about Perry . . .

Although that had been what she'd been trying to do.

Embarrassed by her train of thought, uncomfortable about their decision to keep their secrets hidden, she blurted, "When is your next day off work, Walker?"

"In three days. Want to meet me here at the same time? Can you do that?"

"Yes. I'll be here."

He opened his car door. "You want a ride back to your place?"

"*Nee, Danke.* I'd rather walk. Goodbye, Walker."

"Hold on a sec—"

But she kept walking. Talking to him had brought up too many emotions. She was embarrassed that she was more worried about getting questioned than helping the detective discover the murderer. Embarrassed about the feelings she was starting to have for Walker . . . and as confused as ever about her relationship with her parents.

So even though it was rude of her, she kept walking.

Sometimes a person had to follow her instincts . . . even if those instincts weren't anything to be proud of.

"Abby, you ever going to tell us why you are spending so much time here?"

Abby looked up from the scrapbook of postcards her grandparents had collected from their latest trip. She'd gotten a ride over before Walker got busy. She was happy to come and help her grandmother make yeast rolls, and to hear about their recent bus trip to Washington, D.C. "I'm here because I like being with you and Grandpa."

"We like being with you, too. But I don't think that's why you're spending your days here. A young girl like you should be with your friends, don'tcha think?"

Abby bit her lip. Gathering her courage, she followed Grandma Francis into the kitchen. "I don't have a lot of friends right now."

"And why is that?"

Abby wanted to lay the blame on finding Perry's body, but it was so obvious that that discovery had been the least of her problems. "I'm different."

Her grandmother eyed her carefully before nodding and turning to a pitcher of lemonade. "Care for some lemonade, Abby? Perhaps we could sip on it while we go outside. It was getting a bit stuffy in the living room, I think."

"All right." After her grandmother poured two glasses, she followed her out the back door.

To Abby's surprise, instead of stopping at the wooden swing hanging on the front porch, her grandmother kept walking. And walking.

They passed the large barn, and the smaller barn that held the chickens and extra grain and hay. They walked along the carefully manicured walkway with blooming roses and freshly planted begonias and geraniums, entered a fenced-in area, and finally stopped at the front of her grandmother's vegetable garden.

It was large; no doubt three or four yards wide and at least double the amount in length. Row upon row of freshly tilled soil greeted her. Only a few sprigs of green were visible.

"Grandma, I don't think I've ever been out here before."

"No, I didn't think you had. It's a *gut* garden, don'tcha think?"

"It looks bigger up close than from your porch."

"Most things do look bigger up close, I imagine." Still sipping on her lemonade, she scanned the area. "This garden gives me great comfort, Abby."

"I bet."

"It didn't used to. Used to be, when my *mamm* would send me out to weed, I'd wish I was anywhere but here." She frowned slightly. "I promise, no one could think of as many other *important* things to do instead of weeding than I could."

Abby grinned. "I'm trying to imagine you shirking chores. I can't."

Bending down, Grandma scooped up a small handful of dirt and cupped it in her hand. "One day when I was working so hard to do anything but what I was supposed to . . . something occurred to me." Her hand splayed out and the dark rich soil fell through her fingers back to the earth.

After watching it land with a satisfied smile, she glanced Abby's way. "I realized that weeding the unwanted debris makes the plants we're nurturing have more room to grow. When I made that decision, I didn't mind being out in the garden near as much. Abby, maybe you, too, should stop fighting what is in front of you. Perhaps you should put aside some of your worries and concentrate on what is really bothering you."

"I'm not fighting anything—and I already know what is really bothering me. I need a new start, Grandma."

"Maybe what you need is to stop and give thanks for what you have to be grateful for—your family, your friends . . . even your independence. Perhaps it is time to look at it all in a new way." Poking the dirt with one finger, she grinned. "Ah, look at that, wouldja? Another dandelion weed." With a fierce tug, she pulled it from the soil. "Ah, now I am sure this tomato plant will have room to grow." Turning to her, she said, "Abby, it's time. . . . It's time to let the past stay in the past and spend some time with some people your age."

Her grandmother was speaking in riddles. "But I like being with you and Grandpa."

"We like you being here, but for you to only be here . . . it's not right."

She flushed. "Grandma, I haven't been spending so much time here because I'm avoiding my life."

Grandma Francis raised her brows but said nothing.

Which made Abby realize it was time to blurt the truth. "I've been coming over because I think I want to be like you two. I want to be Amish." Abby held her breath, half-prepared for her grandmother to start tearing up. Or get all emotional and hug her close.

Telling her how happy she was.

But instead, her grandmother leaned back on her heels and looked anything but happy. "Oh, Abigail. Truly?"

The lump that had been forming in her throat almost choked her as Abby struggled to express herself. "I've thought about it a lot, Grandma. A whole lot."

"Hmm."

She rushed on. "Because I've been thinking about this so much, I'm sure becoming Amish is the right thing for me. I don't like makeup and I do like to help you can vegetables."

"I see." Her tone sounded skeptical. "No makeup and liking vegetables . . . these things mean you should change your whole life?"

"Of course not. But you know what I mean." Feeling slightly foolish, Abby pressed her case. "Plus, if I become Amish, I can stay here with you and help you. All day long."

"And you think I need all that help?"

Gesturing toward the fields where Grandpa James was out walking, she said, "This is a big farm, Grandma. Plus, if I'm here, helping you, I won't have to go to school anymore. Or go to college."

"Ach."

Abby flinched at the word. Warily, she glanced at her grandmother.

Her quick glance turned into a full-fledged gaping stare as she realized what was happening. Yep, it was true. Her grandmother was laughing. "Grandma? Are you laughing at me?"

A lined hand clasped her shoulder and pulled her close. Next thing she knew, Abby was being hugged by two thin arms with a force so strong and stalwart that it didn't seem like anything could disturb it. "I'm not laughing at you, child. Well, not too much."

"But I thought you'd be happy with my decision."

"Hmm. You've certainly taken me by surprise."

"I promise, I've thought a lot about this. And I'm serious, Grandma. I think I'd be a great Amish woman."

Her grandmother stepped away and led the way from the garden. She seemed to be deep in thought as they walked back to the house. Abby took that as a sign to be patient.

When they got to the front porch, her grandmother sat on the front stoop and gestured Abby to sit next to her. "You don't have to be Amish for me to love you, Granddaughter."

"I know that. I want to be Amish because I think I'll fit in better."

"You fit in with your grandfather and me just fine."

"I mean I'll fit in better with everyone else."

"And have you mentioned this decision to your family? It seems a mighty big one to make."

"I told Walker."

"What about your parents, Abby?" she asked patiently. "What about your father?"

Abby shrank from the question. Though her dad had always made it clear that he loved his parents dearly, it had also been very clear that he had no regrets about the choices he'd made regarding his religion.

And though she'd never asked him what he might think if she became Amish, she instinctively knew he would be upset. "I haven't told my parents," she finally admitted.

"Your father is going to be upset about this news."

"Probably. But I bet you and Grandpa didn't like the choice he made." Feeling wise beyond her years, Abby said, "Grandma, I think everyone, sometime, has to decide how to live life . . . even if it doesn't make other people happy."

"What you say is true . . . but I still think you should take things more slowly."

"How old was my dad when he told you and Grandpa his decision?"

She blinked, looking completely taken aback by the question. "When he was about your age."

"So I'm not too young to know my own mind."

"You're never too young." Her grandmother hesitated.

"It's just that I don't want you to have regrets. With your father, we knew he wasn't suited for our way of life. He was impatient and dreamy. Always." Looking beyond Abby, she added, "He was a good worker here, but he lit up when he was around the English. He loved learning and mechanical things, and a faster way of life."

"So he knew."

"*Jah.* But I, for one, think it is easier to step out into the world than retreat into our ways. You would be giving up a lot. Coming to visit and canning is not embracing our way of life. You might change your mind."

"Or I might not." Feeling braver, she added, "Grandma, Walker wasn't all that surprised."

"No, I wouldn't think he would be," she mused. "Your brother has always had a way about him that was older and thoughtful."

Abby's pride stung. It sounded to her like her grandmother thought Walker would be a better Amish than she would.

This wasn't how she'd planned for the conversation to go. She'd imagined her grandmother being so excited about her announcement.

Not pushing off her statement like she was an immature kid.

Slowly, she got to her feet. "I'm going to go find my cell phone and ask Walker to come pick me up."

"You want to leave already? I thought you were going to keep me company all day."

Once again, Abby felt as if she was being talked down to. "Grandma, I'm kind of upset right now."

"Abby, dear, look at me."

When Abby met her gaze, she noticed that her grandmother's eyes looked just as contemplative and serious as she felt inside.

"Abby, just because I'm worried about you, it doesn't mean I don't trust your feelings. If you truly want to think about joining the order, I will be more than happy to help you."

"Really?"

She nodded. "But we're going to take things slowly. I'm going to talk about my life and about what I do every day. You're going to listen and think, truly think if this is the life-style for you." Pointing to the pile of weeds, she said, "And you are going to promise me you're going to pull away all the things that don't matter from your mind . . . And then we're going to pray. Okay?"

"Okay."

Grandma lifted a finger. "And then, after you've prayed and thought and been patient, we'll talk to your parents. No way do I want to start doing things without your parents knowing."

"But what if they don't agree?"

"Oh, I don't think they will!" She smiled then, taking the sting out of her words. "But if you are as grown up as you say you are, you won't worry about that so much. And you'll figure out how to honor your parents while honoring your goals, too."

Abby felt dismayed. She'd always thought of her grand-mother as a very kind and reserved woman. Someone who kept to herself and didn't ever risk hurting other people's feelings.

But now she realized she'd been seeing her grandmother from a child's point of view. Now with fresh eyes, she real-ized that her grandmother was actually a very strong woman.

A woman who was willing to step forward—and step on toes—if she thought the situation merited it.

"Abby, what do you say to my plan?"

There was only one answer. Getting to her feet, she said, "It's a fine plan."

"Even if it takes years?"

Abby started. "Years? I had thought we could do this a little more quickly."

"*Nee*. It does not happen like that, Abby. If you are serious about being Amish, you will have to learn to wait for the Lord's timeline."

"Oh."

"All right, then." After she clambered to her feet, she brushed her skirts. "Let's go visit the hens, then."

"What are we going to do?"

"You are going to gather eggs."

"What if one of the hens gets mad?"

"You'll get pecked, I imagine." Her grandmother chuckled at the expression Abby wasn't able to hide. "Come now, Miss Amish In Training. You want to live my life, you'd best get used to making friends with my hens . . . and their beaks. Just be glad I don't ask you to wring one of their necks."

"That's gross, Mommi."

"*Nee*, that's being Amish," Grandma said with a chuckle.

Abby found herself grinning as she followed her grandmother—and as she realized that she was finally feeling hope instead of despair.

Chapter 13

*"Of course I knew Perry. We all did. But that doesn't mean
any of us knew him well."*

FRANNIE EICHER

Luke walked down to the first floor of the bed-and-breakfast
he was currently living in, saw Frannie Eicher, and almost
turned right back around.

But Frannie saw him first. "Mr. Reynolds, hello there. *Gut
matin!* And how are you today?"

The owner of the B&B was a young woman, petite and
slim and possessing pale eyes that seemed a true mix of
gray and light blue. Her skin was fair and her hair was a rich
auburn color. But all that youthful beauty was wasted on a
know-it-all attitude.

The fact was, she nearly drove Luke crazy every time their
paths crossed.

He knew it made no sense. Frannie was nothing if not
polite. She cooked well, and ran the inn diligently.

But her close tabs on his coming and going made him feel
like he was living in a prison instead of a well-run inn.

At the moment, he ached for the cool anonymity of a

Motel 6. "I'm just, ah, going to the dining room to get some coffee."

She paused, a line of worry appearing between her brows. "Mr. Reynolds, I'm afraid I've put away my coffeepot."

"At nine A.M.?"

"It is nine thirty, actually."

She loved to do that. Loved to correct him. "Okay. You've already put away the coffee at nine thirty?"

Instead of looking embarrassed, she met his gaze directly. "I'm terribly sorry for your inconvenience. I've been up for hours you see, and my other two guests ate at seven. I thought, perhaps, you had decided to sleep in."

Her simple explanation made him feel like squirming. She seemed to have the same effect on him as Mrs. Creighton, his second grade teacher. "Coming downstairs at nine thirty in the morning is hardly sleeping in. I would have thought you would have been used to guests relaxing. I mean, isn't that what people are supposed to do here?"

His words obviously hit their mark because she flinched, then blushed. "Perhaps you are right. Well, I can go make you a fresh pot of coffee now. If that is what you would like."

Her tone sounded like she was about to actually pick the beans, roast, and grind them. "That's okay. Don't put yourself out on my account. I'll get coffee at a restaurant or something."

"Mr. Reynolds, you paid for breakfast."

"But you didn't save me any." She looked so affronted, he said, "And listen, like I've said before, please call me Luke. The only Mr. Reynolds I know is my father."

"Well, you are the only Mr. Reynolds I know."

There she went again, challenging him about nothing. "Just call me Luke, would you?" he asked again, his voice turning sharper. "Why in the world do you make everything so difficult?" He hurried to the door, anxious to get out of there.

But her melodic voice stopped him in his tracks. "Luke, I don't mean to pry, but are you all right?"

There was new concern in her voice. He turned around. "Why would you ask that?"

"Well, I know I put away the breakfast things, but that really was because I didn't think you wanted any. Every other morning, you were downstairs by seven. And now you're going out for coffee this late. That's not like you."

This was what made him prickly. In the city, no one butted in on your life, your comings and goings. Now that he had slept in, he felt like he was about to get a talking-to. "I overslept," he finally admitted. "I was up late working on notes."

He waited for the comment. Because, he was learning, Frannie never let an opportunity to share her opinion slide. One second passed. Two.

"Ah," she said.

That was it? Feeling curiously let down, he folded his arms over his chest and glared her way. "I'm waiting."

Her brows rose in confusion. "For what?"

"For you to say something about me not sleeping when the sun went down. About how I probably won't be able to do my job if I'm wasting the morning. Come on, I know you're dying to tell me what you think."

"I most certainly am not. What you do in your room is hardly any of my business," she said in a rush. "We both know that."

He might have believed her if her cheeks hadn't turned so pink.

Because what they both also knew was that she'd practically

made it her goal in life to get into his business. Some days, it seemed like it was all she did, noticing when he was coming and going. "It may not be any of your business, but that doesn't usually stop you."

Her pale eyes flashed hurt. "Mr. Reynolds, I don't know why you are so upset with me. I already told you I'd be happy to make you coffee. And I most certainly have not gone out of my way to comment on your life."

"Come on, don't disappoint me now. Ever since I've gotten here, you've commented on my days, on what I eat. I'm surprised you haven't started chiding me about taking vitamins or something."

A multitude of emotions flickered across her face. Before she looked at him directly. "Are you taking Vitamin C?"

"See—" he began. Then stopped when he spied the mirth in her eyes.

She was making fun of him. Teasing.

Running a hand through his hair, he felt as cool and collected as a jar of captured bees. "Sorry. I guess I couldn't have been more rude, huh?"

"You could have . . . if you'd asked me my age and weight."

He blinked, then felt his face flush like a teen. Because, well, even though she drove him as crazy as a loon, he'd never once had found fault with her appearance. She really was one of the prettiest women he'd ever met.

Not that she needed to know that.

"This investigation has been challenging," he finally said. "Plus, all the rain has been making my leg ache like a . . ." He paused, trying to think of a suitable analogy for Frannie's ears. "Like a burn."

Her eyebrows rose. "Ache like a *burn?*"

Now he just felt foolish. And he needed caffeine fast.

"Listen, I'm going to get out of here. I'm afraid I used up all my good manners about two days ago. Now I'm just wandering around the county asking questions that no one will answer."

"I'm sorry—"

"Stop. Hey, I know I'm being difficult. I'll do my best to make sure our paths don't cross anytime soon."

He waited, ready for her to come up with some kind of snippy retort, one that would put him in his place. But instead, she stepped forward and clasped her hands primly behind her back.

"Are you hungry?"

Her simple question spurred a simple response. "Yes."

"I can make you some breakfast while your coffee brews. Would you care for some bacon and eggs?"

Already his mouth was watering. "That sounds great."

She nodded. "All right ,then. If you come to the kitchen in ten minutes or so, I shall have it ready for you."

"Thank you, Frannie."

"You are very welcome . . . Luke."

When she turned away, Luke pretended he wasn't thinking about how tiny her waist was. How he could probably span it with his two hands. Or that he kind of liked how she stood up to him—most women didn't.

And how very different she was from Renee.

As Frannie disappeared from sight, Luke took a seat on the bench by the front door and straightened his leg.

And thought about the woman he'd been sure he was going to marry one day.

When things settled down. As soon as they both had gotten tired of dating and clubs. When their careers were on track. When they both had some vacation time coming and could fit it into their schedules.

Renee was driven and forthright and successful. A lawyer. She enjoyed the idea of dating a cop.

He enjoyed how she'd never asked too much of him. How she gave him a little bit of class on his arm, and how she always called before showing up at his apartment.

Now he couldn't believe how foolish he'd been. Had he really thought that love and marriage could be fit into his life like a lunch break?

Which just went to show—he'd probably been in Crittenden County too long. The last thing in the world he needed was to start feeling something for one of the women who lived here.

Too bad his conscience wasn't relaying that message to the rest of his body. Because all it seemed to be thinking about was a hot breakfast and a surprisingly tender smile.

And all his heart was thinking was that it was nice to be around a woman so different than Renee. So different from just about anyone else he'd ever met.

"Lydia, when are you coming back to work?" her sister Becky asked in that melodramatic way of hers.

Without looking up from the fabric she was carefully cutting out, she answered. "I don't know."

"Don't you think you've been sitting around long enough? Reuben says you have."

Surprised, Lydia turned to her. The line that always formed between her seven-year-old sister's brows when she was disturbed about something was there, alive and well. "I've hardly been sitting around at all, not that it's any of Reuben's business. After all, I'm working on a quilt now. Right?"

Becky stepped forward and fingered the one square Lydia

had pieced together. The flower box quilt pattern was a favorite of theirs, and Lydia knew that the contrasting shades of yellows and white were going to fetch a terrific price at the local craft store.

That is, if she could bear to put it up for sale.

"It's real pretty," Becky pronounced. "But it ain't work."

"I don't need to work all the time," she snapped. Really, hadn't she done enough in her twenty years? Didn't anyone ever think she did enough? "Becky, I don't even know why we're discussing my days. What I do—or don't do—isn't any of your business."

"I think it is."

"And why is that?"

"Because when you don't do something, the rest of us have to do it."

"You're only seven. I promise, you're not expected to do too much."

"But Reuben says that because you are sittin' around, working on a quilt, he's running around at the nursery like a chicken with its head cut off."

Lydia couldn't believe her brother had said such things to their little sister. Determined to put an end to it, she said, "I've worked plenty, Becky. Don't act like I haven't."

Pure irritation flared in her sister's eyes before she turned and walked toward the door.

But just as Lydia picked up another swatch of fabric, her sister turned back around. "I saw you with that *Englischer*."

It took every ounce of patience Lydia possessed to not clench her hands and wrinkle the fabric she was holding. "What are you talking about?"

"I saw you with that boy. The one who came to the nursery with his mother."

It wasn't easy, but she played dumb. "I have no idea who you're talking about. Lots of folks come with their parents to the nursery."

"I think his name is Walker. I heard he knew Perry, too. And, I know that you're playing dumb with me now."

Embarrassed to get put on the spot by a seven-year-old, Lydia lashed out. "If you have all the answers, I don't know why you're questioning me."

Becky froze.

Her heart going about a thousand beats per second, Lydia waited for her sister to turn and walk away. But to her surprise, her little sister stepped forward instead, tears in her eyes. "Lydia, what has made you start acting so different?"

"Nothing. And I'm not acting different."

"Is it because of Perry dying?"

"I told you, I'm not—"

"Is it 'cause Mamm and Daed said you were adopted?"

Now her heart felt like it stopped. "You know?" Her voice fell to a whisper.

Slowly, Becky nodded. "Reuben was going to help me get a snack when we overheard you and Mamm and Daed talking in the kitchen." Just as Lydia was going to berate her, her sister added, "We didn't mean to eavesdrop, it just happened."

"Did you two already tell Petey?"

Becky shook her head. "Reuben said we'd better not, 'cause even though Pete is eight, he can't hold a secret for nothing."

"That's something, I suppose. Petey would go tattle."

Looking deep in thought, Becky pursed her lips for a moment. Then she blurted, "I truly am sorry for you."

Her sister's kindness caught her off guard and was a good reminder about the right way to act. She was doing no one any favors by holding her anger close to her heart. "It's okay. I'm not happy about the news, but my being adopted isn't your fault. I don't want you to worry about it."

"How can I not worry? You're upset. And you're my older sister, no matter who your *mamm* was."

Lydia studied her for another minute, trying to determine if there was more to Becky's words than she was letting on. How would she not see Lydia differently now?

"Things will get better. I just need some time. Mamm and Daed understand that." After a moment she added, "If you could, I'd appreciate it if you could give me time, too."

"Do you want to be English now?"

Lydia realized that her sister was no longer being catty . . . she was seeking to understand her. And so she did her best to respond in kind. "I don't know."

Her sister's temper surfaced once again. "I think you're just biding your time until you jump the fence and leave us all behind."

She wanted to promise her sister that she'd never to do that. She wanted to promise Becky that she wasn't thinking about leaving their community.

But she couldn't. Not yet.

Chapter 14

"That Perry, I could always count on him to talk to the customers about special sales. Chaos didn't bother him none."

AARON SCHROCK

"Walker, you just going to stand there like a bump on a log, or are ya going to help me with these guinea pigs?"

Inwardly, Walker groaned. When he'd first seen the man enter the store with a wire container full of furry animals, he'd been tempted to quit. His boss surely had to be the craziest store owner in the whole county. "Sorry. I'll carry that for you."

After he carried the crate the rest of the way into the store and set it on the main counter, he bent and peered into the cage.

Seven tiny, furry orange and white bodies with beady eyes started right back at him.

They were cute, if you liked those kind of animals. He did not. "Mr. Schrock, who in the world decided that we were going to start selling guinea pigs?"

"Mrs. Schrock and myself, of course."

Walker had known them long enough to recognize a tall

tale. Mrs. Schrock was a very organized and competent woman—selling small rodents didn't seem like something she would do. "Are you sure about that?"

Looking a little embarrassed, Mr. Schrock bit his lip. "Well, maybe Mrs. Schrock didn't have too much to do with the decision. But the pigs are going to be good business, Walker. Mark my words," he said with a little shake of his finger. "People like pets."

People liked dogs and cats. Maybe hamsters. Horses, even. But cinnamon-colored guinea pigs? Walker wasn't so sure. Besides, having to take care of these little creatures until they found owners was going to take a lot of time. And it wasn't hard to figure who was going to be in charge of cleaning up after this new stock. "Mr. Schrock, maybe we should rethink this."

"Nothing to rethink. The animals are for sale. Ten dollars each, Walker. And look here, this is going to be their new home."

Walker glanced over to where Mr. Schrock was gesturing and frowned. It was an open square surrounded by chicken wire. "Are you sure that's going to keep them contained? It looks a little flimsy to me."

"They're going to be happy enough. Now start taking them over to their new home. Take two at a time and be quick about it, wouldja? The store's about to open. I'm not paying ya to hear your opinions."

"Yes, sir," Walker said with a grin. Mr. Schrock was truly one of the nicest men he'd ever met. He was kind of eccentric, but he was full of good humor and always had a plan for some new sales idea.

He was just carrying two creatures over to the bigger pen his boss had made when the front door opened and two little girls scampered in with a lady in a raincoat and matching boots.

"Hi, Mr. Schrock," the lady said with a sunny smile. "Do you think it will ever stop raining?"

"Not in my lifetime," he replied. "What can we be helping you with, Mrs. Krienze?" As he spoke, he pulled out two more guinea pigs from the carrier—just as the little girls caught sight of them.

The girls squealed, scampered closer, and reached out with eager hands. The pigs didn't care for that idea and squirmed.

Mr. Schrock lost hold of the animals, and they fell to the floor with a batch of frenzied squeals. The poor little guinea pigs, who by some miracle had survived the fall without any lingering effects, squeaked and ran in two separate directions.

"Walker, do something!" Mr. Schrock ordered.

"Yes, sir." But just as Walker was about to set the wriggling pigs in his hands in the pen, the little girls, seemingly delighted about more fluffy animals to pet, rushed forward.

Actually, they pretty much lunged at Walker. Startling him. And the little creatures. And then, just like that, they squirmed out of his hands and were gone.

Four were now on the run. No doubt pooping and chewing their way through the store. Which he was going to have to clean up, of course.

Walker felt a headache coming on. What a mess.

"Walker, look what happened!" Mr. Schrock exclaimed. "The pigs, they've run off!"

"I noticed," he said dryly.

The woman grabbed the hands of the two little girls. "Mr. Schrock, I'm so, so sorry. I feel like this is our fault. What can we do to help?"

"There's not a thing you can do, Mrs. Krienze. These things happen, jah? Don't worry none. We'll find the pigs." With a glare Walker's way, he added, "That is, my employee here will."

Mrs. Krienze sent a sympathetic look his way. "Good luck, Walker."

"Thanks," he said. What he didn't say was he had no idea how he was supposed to round up four baby guinea pigs that had a whole shop to run around in.

After Mrs. Krienze rounded up her girls and sheepishly guided them out of the market, Mr. Schrock clapped his hands. "Get busy now, Walker. We need to find these animals. Fast."

"I'll do my best."

"Get down on your hands and knees, son. You won't be able to spy the creatures from your height."

"You make it seem like a bad thing that I'm six feet."

"It is today." Mr. Schrock pointed to a line of shelves. "I think I heard a bit of squeaking over there. Get down and look, wouldja?"

Obediently, Walker got down on his hands and knees and looked under a line of shelves. Feeling the fool, he crawled to the next section, and almost yelped when a pair of beady eyes met him head-on. "Come here, you," he murmured. Like guinea pigs even listened to directions.

Reaching out under the shelves, he had almost grabbed the little rascal when—

"Walker?"

He groaned as he recognized Lydia's voice, his humiliation complete. Yep, just when he was sure things couldn't get worse, they did. "Oh. Hey, Lydia."

After a moment, she crouched down beside him, the hem

of the violet dress she was wearing brushing the ground. "Whatever are you doing?"

"Looking for pigs. Watch where you step, okay?"

Obviously looking like she was fighting a smile, Lydia lifted one palm off the floor. "Or perhaps I should watch where I crawl?"

Her humor in the situation made his mood lighten. Getting to his feet, he reached out a hand and helped her up. "I don't think either of us should be crawling around here on the floor."

Her lips curved into a full-fledged smile. "Should I even mention that I thought pigs belonged outside?"

"These are tiny furry pigs. Guinea pigs."

Those blue eyes he couldn't ever seem to ignore lit up with laughter. Now it looked like it was taking everything she had to contain herself. "I'll say it again. Shouldn't those pigs be outside?"

"I just work here. I'm not supposed to have an opinion about them."

"Come now, Walker," she said with a laugh. "I know you well enough to know you have an opinion about most everything. So tell me, what are you going to do about—"

Lightly pressing a finger to her lips, he said, "Shh! Mr. Schrock has moved on to chatting with that couple over by the bulk food barrels. If he hears you, I'm going to be back on my hands and knees."

"If it would solve your pig problem, I might consent to help."

Walker relaxed, realizing that now he, too, was grinning broadly. The reason was obvious. He was happy to see her. Happy to have someone to share the circus that was the

Schrock Variety Store. Happy to have someone in his life whom he could laugh with.

But against his fingers, Lydia stilled.

He dropped his hand. "Oh. Hey. I'm sorry. I was just fooling around." Yeah. And he didn't notice that her lips were really soft. Not at all.

"Oh, I know you were just playing." Cheeks blooming, she stepped backward, putting more distance between them.

Walker did the same, no longer caring if the little varmints ate the entire store. Now there were two choices. He could apologize again for touching her so personally.

Or he could pretend nothing had happened. "So, can I help you with something?"

Lydia knew she was being a foolish girl, but at the moment, she could hardly remember her own name. That was how much Walker's innocent touch had affected her.

"Lydia?"

Candles. She'd come in for candles. And white thread. "I just need a few household goods."

"Want some help?"

Help from Walker meant walking by his side and having to pretend a little longer that she hadn't been completely taken by his gesture. "*Nee.* I only came here for candles. I don't need any help."

"Oh." He stepped back. "All right. Well, let me know if you change your mind."

"Walker, go help check these customers out, wouldja?" Mr. Schrock hollered from the front of the store.

"Yes, sir," he said, before turning to the pair of women waiting at the counter. "Did you ladies find everything you were looking for?"

"All that and more," one of them said.

As he began to ring up the women, Lydia darted down an empty aisle. And, when she was sure it was all clear, leaned back against one of the posts, and closed her eyes.

For a moment, all she had been able to think about was kissing Walker. Right there, in the middle of the Schrocks' store.

Thank goodness they'd both come to their senses. After all, the last thing either of them needed was a relationship. She needed a friend she could confide in, not a romance.

And especially not with an English boy. If she went about falling in love, it needed to be with someone Amish. Someone who believed in the same things that she did.

Those words of advice had been told to her over and over for most of her life. She didn't doubt that her mother meant every word.

But of course, her mother had also lied to her for most of her life as well.

Just like that, her true origins rushed right back. She hadn't been born Amish. She'd been adopted into the life.

She'd blindly accepted everything her parents had told her, because she liked fitting in with her family.

But now, well, they weren't really her family, anyway.

All her thoughts disturbed her greatly. She wasn't some young teenager. She was twenty. She had a job and a great many responsibilities. The time for *rumspringa* was passed. But how could she ever move forward in this life if she didn't even know where she came from?

And now, she found herself standing in the middle of a store wishing for Walker's hand against her skin again. Wishing for his kiss.

"The candles are down the next aisle."

"What?" Seeing Walker's knowing gaze, she managed to become even more flustered. "Oh, I was just looking at the . . ." What was she standing in front of . . . ?

"Pills for upset stomachs?"

With a sinking feeling, she looked up and stared at the row of products she'd been gazing at. Pills for diarrhea and constipation.

He folded his arms over his chest and almost smirked. "Are you feeling poorly, Lydia?"

"No! I mean, I wasn't reading those labels."

"Are you sure? Because it's okay if you need some medicine . . ."

"I do not." She was just about to turn and dart down the aisle, when a brown furry blob raced across her path. "Ack!" she screamed, scooting backward.

Right into Walker's arms. "It's okay," he murmured from behind her, not really sounding like he minded her backing into his chest at all. "It's just a guinea pig. They're on the loose, you know."

"I heard." She shook her head, just as Mr. Schrock showed up.

He stopped abruptly, stared at Walker's hands still clasped on her shoulders, and then frowned. "Walker, now you are manhandling the customers? What am I going to do with you today?"

"I'll try to do better, Mr. Schrock," he said as he slowly slid his hands down her arms and stepped to the side so they were facing each other again.

Lydia felt like digging a hole in the floor as Mr. Schrock glared at Walker again, and then stared at the shelf both she and Walker had been discussing. "Lydia, are you sick, child?"

Oh. This was horrible. "Nothing is wrong. Listen, I think I'm just going to go."

All traces of amusement left Walker's face. "But didn't you come in for candles?"

"I'll get them another day. I'm running late," she blurted over her shoulder as she strode toward the door, keeping a careful eye on the ground for darting guinea pigs as she went.

Walker was right behind her. "Hey, Lydia?"

"What?"

"See you at the park? Tomorrow, right?"

There was only one right answer. Even though she was worried about her future, and confused about her past, she was desperately sure that there was only one way she wanted to go with Walker, and that was forward.

"Of course," she said as she darted out the door.

Chapter 15

"Perry loved coconut cream pie. Summer, winter, Christmas?
It didn't matter the occasion. If he came in to the restaurant,
why, he'd order it."

MARY KING YODER

"Have you had much of an occasion to visit Mary King's?"
Mose asked after Luke had shaken his hand and they'd exchanged greetings.

"Nope." Luke looked around at the modest restaurant,
housed in a double-wide trailer situated at the edge of town.
In Cincinnati, he wouldn't have gone inside the place unless
he'd been told to do so by his sergeant.

But he was learning not to be quite so particular about
appearances here. In Crittenden County, appearances were
proving to be deceiving. Some of the plainest of places were
turning out to be pretty terrific.

Like the current restaurant where they were eating. "Frannie Eicher told me this place was pretty good. I'm looking
forward to getting a chicken fried steak."

Instead of agreeing and opening his plastic menu, Mose
tilted his head to the side. "Frannie told you that?"

"Uh-huh. Do you know Frannie? She runs the Yellow Bird Inn."

Mose chuckled. "I'm sorry. I keep forgetting Frannie is in charge of that place. She didn't used to be."

"She is pretty young. How did she come to own it?"

"I'm not rightly sure, if you want to know the truth. Rumor has it that she was good friends with the Gowans." Mose drummed his fingers on the laminate table. "They were the original owners. Now that I think about it, maybe she lived with them for a time and worked there, too? Or, maybe Mrs. Gowan was her great aunt? You'll have to ask her for the full story."

Yeah, that would be the day. He could just see himself asking Frannie all about her childhood, just days after he'd been frank about how his schedule wasn't her business.

"Mose, what'll you have?" the server asked, suddenly appearing at their side.

"Chicken fried steak, of course."

"Mashed potatoes?"

"Uh-hum."

"Beans or corn?"

"Both."

"To drink?"

"Iced tea."

"Sweet?"

"Always."

Luke bit his lip, having enjoyed watching the conversation lob between them like the final set in a tennis match.

"Sir?" the gal asked.

"I'll take the exact same thing, except make my tea unsweetened."

"You got it." When she turned around, menus in hand, Luke couldn't help but do some teasing. "So, I guess you come here a lot. You and that waitress have your order down pat."

Mose grinned. "I come here often enough. And Martha and I do know each other well. A man needs a decent meal every once in a while, you know?"

"I know."

As he thought about his buddy, and how well-entrenched he was in the county, he couldn't help but wonder why he hadn't put down more roots. "Mose, why haven't you married yet? There's got to be some woman around here who would have you."

Luke waited for his buddy to say the same right back at him. But to his surprise, Mose looked uncomfortable about his situation.

"It's not so easy finding the right woman, Luke. Especially, you know, given my situation."

"I thought everyone came to terms with you leaving the order and becoming a sheriff a long time ago."

"Oh, they're perfectly happy with my decision . . . as long as I don't bring their daughters into the mix." He shrugged. "Even though I made my choice years ago, sometimes I still feel like I'm straddling the fence."

Luke knew what he meant. It was hard to fit in one place when your heart hadn't completely left the past. "Maybe you should look into applying to some other sheriff departments. Go someplace bigger. Meet some new people."

"What, suddenly move to the big city, all so I can find some city girl?" Mose's expression would've been laughable if Luke didn't completely understand his point. No matter where you were, it wasn't easy finding a woman who you wanted to date, let alone someone who was interested in dating a cop.

"No . . . though, maybe you might have more of a chance—"

"That isn't going to happen. Crittenden County is my home. And though everyone here doesn't always think of me as family, I think of them that way."

"I understand."

After the waitress brought them their drinks, Luke used the time to sip his drink and consider his friend.

Fact was, Mose was handsome. Years spent in the fields around his house had built up his body in a way nothing else could. It was obvious that he still took the time to stay in shape, and he walked with the steady cadence of a man completely at ease with himself.

Added to his physique were a pair of dark brown eyes and the kind of quiet manner that women seemed to find endearing.

"Sorry I brought all this up," Luke said, feeling like the lowest of the low. "It's none of my business."

Mose waved off his excuse. "Oh, I don't mind. Ask whatever you want, Luke. I've made peace with my situation, for sure. I made the choice long ago to go this route, and come back here and live with the consequences. God set my path, and He knows what is best for me. I just have to keep reminding myself to not forget that."

Luke believed in God, but he wasn't used to being around people who talked about faith so openly. "Your faith is admirable."

Mose shrugged off the comment. "Nah. My faith is part of who I am." Obviously embarrassed by their personal conversation, Mose cleared his throat. "Now, as much as I'm sure you'd love to talk more about your love life—"

"Not," Luke said quickly.

"You got it. So start telling me about what you've learned, Detective, and don't forget to tell me everything, neither."

As Martha placed their plates in front of them, Luke got to work. He told Mose about his conversations with Walker Anderson, Lydia Plank, and Perry's parents. "I tell you what's frustrating—I know they all know more than they're telling me. But no matter how hard I push, I can't seem to get them to trust me."

"You've learned more than I did. It will come."

"It will," Luke agreed. But of course what neither of them said was that time was not their friend. It wasn't like he could stay in the county for an unlimited time. He had a life to get back to, one that he made a living from.

But what was more important than his schedule was the fact that with each day, Perry's trail and final hours were growing fainter and fainter.

"I did get a lead on what Perry was selling," Luke said.

"Wasn't pot, was it?"

"Nope. Looks like meth. Maybe some pills, too."

"I was afraid of that." Mose shook his head. "More and more people in these rural areas are setting up their own labs. We've even gotten some help from the DEA to help track it down." He paused. "But if Perry was selling pills, that's harder to trace. Lot of that is coming from St. Louis."

Thinking about what Walker had said about Perry having some new friends, Luke nodded. "I'll keep looking into things. As for the meth, the dealers might be hard to locate in the middle of rural farmland, but it's not impossible. Dealers don't talk but addicts do. I have a couple of leads, and I'll follow them. I'm going to get to the truth, Mose. I promise you that."

"I'm not the only one who has faith in you, Luke." Mose raised his chin and glanced upward. "Don't you forget that you're not alone. Not ever."

Luke stewed on those words long after they'd ordered peanut butter pie from Martha and ate it while discussing the latest basketball scores.

He stewed on Mose's words as he limped back to his truck and drove along the near-empty streets of the town. And as he sat in bed that night, pretending to read but really thinking about his life back in Cincinnati.

Who did he have there who he truly cared about?

And how come he couldn't come up with a single name?

Arms full of laundry fresh from the line outside, Lydia stood outside the kitchen, listening to her mother chat with little Petey about his homework. Every thirty seconds he interrupted and whined.

Petey had the patience of a gnat.

"Peter, you settle and listen to me," her mother said. Again.

Lydia had to smile. Many of the things her mother was saying were words Lydia had heard more than a time or two.

"Mamm, I am trying. It ain't my fault," he said.

"Ach, but I think it might your fault, son. I think you're playing and daydreaming while in school."

"But my teacher—"

"Your teacher is practically a saint, doing her best to teach you. You need to concentrate more."

"I do concentrate."

"Not as much as you should."

"But that don't mean—"

"I'll hear nothing else about this," she said sternly. "You need to do your best, Peter. Our Lord expects nothing less."

"I don't think the Lord is paying attention to me at school, Mamm."

"He always is. Even at school."

Lydia winced. Her mother now had the tone in her voice that said she had just about lost her composure. It was truly time for her little brother to step back and get quiet.

But obviously, he still had a lot to learn.

"But—"

"Peter . . ."

Lydia couldn't take being a fly on the wall any longer. "Petey," she interrupted as she entered the room. Setting the towels on the table, she added, "Stop talking for once. It's time for you to listen, *jah?*"

"Of course you're going to say that. You do everything right," he retorted with a glare.

"We both know that's not true. Right, Mamm?"

"None of us is perfect, Lydia. That is what I know to be true."

"Well, you're a lot closer to being perfect than I am," Peter grumbled.

"Over the years, I heard plenty of the same things Mamm is telling you now. If you want some advice, it would be to listen and follow directions."

But, as she'd predicted, her brother just glared, then grabbed his bowl of half-eaten soup and noisily placed it in the sink. "I'm done."

"If you're done, go put up the towels," Lydia said.

"That ain't my job. It's yours."

Lydia closed her eyes and hoped she wouldn't have children for years and years. A house full of *kinner* like Peter would surely drive her crazy.

"Child, you are not helping your cause," their mother cautioned.

But Peter just glared, turned away, and gathered up his books. "I'm going to go out and do my chores."

"With your books?"

"I'll put them down first." He grumbled something more under his breath, but thankfully their mother didn't seem to be in any big hurry to decipher it.

Her mother folded her arms over her chest while Lydia stood with her mouth half open. "Mamm, I can't believe him!"

"He's wearing me out, that is true."

"Were Reuben or I that disrespectful when we were eight?"

"Don't you remember?"

She knew her mother was teasing. But what actually surprised Lydia was that she couldn't remember a lot of her behavior during the years of learning to give and take. She remembered her parents' lectures, but not how she reacted to them. "I don't remember as much as I should," she said finally. "That surprises me."

Her mother smiled. "Believe it or not, I was the same way. It's easy to remember the good times, yes? No one wants to remember the bad." After rinsing off Petey's bowl and spoon and setting it to dry, she eyed Lydia up and down. "What are you planning to do the rest of the day?"

It was time to make a choice. She could either be evasive or completely open.

It looked like the Lord had an idea about what she should do, however. After all, here she was, listening to Petey and her mother when she usually did no such thing.

"I'm going to the park, Mamm."

"Oh? To do what?"

It didn't escape Lydia's notice that the question was gently asked. Almost as if she'd been afraid to upset Lydia by being too invasive.

Almost the exact opposite of how she'd been with her brother.

The hesitancy made her move even closer to the full truth. "I'm going to meet Walker Anderson."

"You are still spending time with him?"

"I am."

Everything in her mother's body language signaled a wealth of questions she was so obviously wanting to ask. But still she didn't.

"We are just friends, Mamm."

"Why do you two feel the need for this friendship? That is, if you don't mind me asking?"

"I don't mind you asking. But I will tell you I don't have any set answer. It just seems like we have a lot in common right now."

"Because of Perry?"

Was that it? Was that the main reason? "Because of Perry," she said finally. "But also because of who I am."

"You are my daughter. My special, much loved daughter."

"And you are my mother. I know that. But it's important to me to think about what could have been. If you hadn't adopted me."

"I just want you to know how much we love you, have always loved you."

"I know." Lydia bit her lip in order to not say another word that she might later regret. As the tension between them grew and her mother's eyes watered, Lydia tried harder to explain herself. "Mamm, you asked me where I was going, and I told you the truth. I told you the truth even knowing that it might cause you pain."

What mattered now more than peace and tranquility was honesty.

With Perry, she'd chosen peace. He'd broken her heart and she'd kept to herself, kept her sorrow and confusion to herself. Afraid to make others see her pain, or afraid to inconvenience others.

But all that had gotten her was a series of restless nights and a desperate feeling of being alone.

"I'll be home before dark," she said finally.

Her mother merely nodded—instead of offering her opinion, or cautioning her to be careful.

She appreciated her mother's willingness to allow her some independence. It wasn't her family's way, but given all that had happened in the last few weeks, Lydia needed this space. She hugged her mother tight and whispered "I love you" before she headed out the door and finally let the memories of Perry rush forward like they always did. As she looked at the way the sun was half peeking through the thickening clouds, she recalled another time she'd been standing outside, hoping the rain would hold off, just for a little longer.

When Perry had stopped by to break off their date.

"Lydia, I can't go walking with you, Something came up that I need to take care of."

She'd bit her lip so he wouldn't see how disappointed she was. She'd run around the house like a crazy person, getting her chores done early so she could spend the evening with him. "What?"

"I can't tell you that."

"Why not? What are you going to do?"

"*Nothing you need to worry about.*" *But his eyes had darted away when he'd spoken.*

"*Is it another girl?*"

A slow smile curved his lips. "Nee, Lydia. I won't be with another girl. I wouldn't do that to you." *He'd stopped all conversation then with a kiss. And then another one. And then another one.*

She'd allowed it because she was sure that one day he was going to go back to being how he used to be—kind, patient. . .

Only later had she realized that he'd kissed her like that so she wouldn't ask any more about his plans.

He'd only kissed her to make her be quiet.

Chapter 16

"Sometimes, in the middle of the night when the dream comes back, all I see was how Perry looked, lying at the bottom of the well. And no matter how hard I try, I can't remember what he looked like alive. I don't know why that is."

ABBY ANDERSON

"Can I come along?" Abby asked as Walker grabbed his keys to head out to his truck.

Her request caught him off guard. "Where do you think I'm going?"

"To see the Amish girl."

He stopped in his tracks and glared at her. "How do you know about Lydia? And how do you know I was going to meet her today?"

"I overheard you talking on the phone to one of your friends about how you had plans."

"So you just assumed I was going to see Lydia?"

"Who else would it be? Everyone's talking about your new fascination with Lydia. It's pretty obvious that you like her. I mean, you've never dated an Amish girl before."

"We're not dating."

"Seems like you are . . ." Her voice drifted off suggestively. She was still his little sister and no matter what her age, she would always be into his business and always feel that she had the right to interfere.

"I don't want company, Abby."

"But—"

"That's it. That's all I'm saying." He opened the door, ready to stride through the garage. But the light rain falling stopped him in his tracks.

With anyone else, he would've kept his plans without a second thought. But with Lydia? How did the rain affect her?

Would she still walk to the park in it, or would she opt not to go? Or would she take her buggy instead?

Was she even allowed to use her family's buggy? For some reason, the fact that he had no idea what her situation was at home made him feel even more confused.

"She'll be there, you know. The rain's not going to stop her."

He turned around. Though he was irritated that his sister was still hanging around, he was more interested in what she had to say. "Why do you say that?"

"That's the way the Amish are." Her voice was so strong and sure, she sounded like a mini-authority or something. "They value plans more than problems."

"And you know this because . . ."

"Because of Grandma and Grandpa, of course."

"They're my grandparents, too, Lydia. I didn't know that they felt that way."

"You don't ask."

"And you do?"

A flash of hurt entered her eyes, and because it hadn't been there before, Walker felt his cheeks burn. Hadn't he promised himself to be there for her to be the one person in her life who she could depend on? "Sorry, squirt." He sighed. "Listen, Abby, Lydia won't like you being there. Plus, we've got to talk about some things that are private."

"How about this? I'll only stay for a little while."

"Abby—"

"Just let me ask her a few questions, then I'll leave you two alone. Promise."

"You seem to have all the answers."

"Come on, Walker. Please?"

Suddenly, he had nothing to lose. "Fine. Get in. But if all of this backfires, I'm going to totally blame you."

"Blame me all you want."

Oh, he would. If Lydia did actually show up. Turning on his windshield wipers, he glanced his sister's way. "If things turn out bad, not only am I going to blame you, I'm going to expect you to fix it."

Fifteen minutes later, they were sitting silently in the cab of his truck. Watching fat raindrops splash against the windshield. And waiting.

And then they saw her.

"Well, I guess they do use umbrellas," Abby stated as they watched a solitary figure walk down the main path under a bell-shaped black umbrella. "Do you have one in here?"

"No. Why?"

"Well, where are you going to talk to her? I mean she's probably not going to want to sit in here, right?"

His sister had a point. "There's an overhang by the restrooms. Let's go meet her there."

Abby didn't wait two minutes. She opened up her side and scrambled out, waving and calling to Lydia like they were best friends. Walker felt like sinking into his seat as Lydia stopped abruptly, looked at Abby, then at his truck in confusion.

Then slowly raised a hand and waved back.

There was only one thing to do. He opened up his door and joined them. And pretended that his heart was beating a little faster because he was embarrassed that he'd brought his little sister along.

It had nothing to do with the way he felt around Lydia.

Or that when he'd glanced her way, she'd met his gaze.

And then slowly smiled.

Oh, for heaven's sakes! Walker had brought a friend to their meeting. A girlfriend, obviously, from the way she seemed so at ease around him.

And with that observation, all the warmth and anticipation Lydia had been feeling vanished in an instant. The last time they'd seen each other, she'd been so sure that they had something special between them. Okay, well perhaps that was an exaggeration.

But if it wasn't special, it was good, at the very least.

The problem was that she'd thought he'd felt the same way. Now it was obvious that she'd only been imagining things.

And she'd walked all this way in the rain, too! Looking down at herself, she shook the hem of her dress. The bottom two inches of her dress was soaked through, making her calves cold.

"Lydia, let's go stand under that covered area by the restrooms!" Walker called out. "I've got someone I want you to meet."

Now she had no choice. "Hold your horses," she replied, feeling suddenly like she was sounding silly and immature. "It's raining, ya know?"

"A little bit of rain shouldn't stop your feet from moving."

Crossing over to him, to them, she made a new plan. She'd stand with them for a little while, then turn around and get home. She would be in their company ten minutes, tops.

She'd gone to a lot of effort for such a brief visit, but that couldn't be helped.

"I hope you don't mind that I brought my sister," he said, the look in his eyes fully detailing his apology.

She was brought up short. "Sister?"

The girl stepped forward. Gave a little, half-hearted wave. "Hi," she said shyly. "I'm Abby."

Stunned, Lydia looked from Abby to Walker to Abby again. There, she saw the matching brown eyes. The wheat-colored hair. The same sprinkling of freckles.

And just as importantly, she saw Abby's youth and hesitancy. The girl was nervous around her! But there was something in her eyes, too. A plea for acceptance, to be included.

As Lydia continued to study her, Abby's look of hope dimmed. "Do you not want me here?" She bit her lip. "Walker told me I shouldn't come, but I really wanted to. I'm sorry."

"Nee! I mean, I'm sorry, I didn't mean to stare. When I first saw you two together . . . well, I thought you were a couple, you see."

This time it was Walker who looked struck dumb. "You thought Abby and me were together?"

"You came together. It was an honest mistake." She shook her head from the pesky cobwebs that had threatened to overtake her good sense. "I am sorry for my confusion. Abby, I am Lydia Plank. It is good to meet you."

Around them, the rain and the wind increased, so much so that the water spattered on their clothes even though at least a foot of covering protected them from the rain. Well, Lydia at least was still getting a good drenching.

"Hey, you're getting soaked," Walker said. "Come closer."

Next thing she knew, he was circling her waist with his hand and pulling her toward him.

Rather, toward him and Abby.

The moment she was steady on her feet, he stepped back. "No reason to stand so far apart, right?"

"Right. Of course." His innocent touch had disturbed her as much as the pang of jealously she'd felt when she'd seen them together.

In order to push those unwelcome feelings away, she focused on the girl staring at her wide-eyed. "Why did you want to meet me?"

"Oh. Um. I don't know."

Walker winked. "I told you she was blunt, Abby. Tell her the truth."

"I think I want to become Amish," Abby said.

The words flew out of her mouth before she could stop them. "Now, why on earth would you want to do that?"

Abby looked taken aback. So did Walker.

But Lydia held her ground. "Do you have a reason?"

"I want to be Amish because I think I'd fit in better."

The Amish community was a Christian one. And forgiving of others, for sure. But that didn't mean they didn't have strict rules by which to abide. Lydia couldn't imagine the typical teenager knowingly adopting them. "I'm confused. You don't fit in with . . ."

"She's having a hard time at school," Walker explained, resting one of his hands on Abby's shoulder.

As Lydia watched, his touch seemed to calm his sister. "She doesn't really fit in," he murmured. "And now that everyone only thinks of her as the girl who found the dead guy, it's gotten worse. She's withdrawn . . ." His voice drifted off.

"I don't know if she is thinking about being Amish because she wants to live like her grandparents, or just escape from the situation she's in."

"Ah." Lydia didn't know what to say. After all, she didn't know the girl. And had never walked in her shoes.

"You don't get it, do you?" Abby asked. "You don't get why I would think about changing my life."

"I understand about changing your life. But as for wanting to become Amish? I do not. Being Amish isn't for making new friends, you know."

"That's not what I'm trying to do. I'm trying to find out where I feel best. Have you ever wished for that? To find something that's been missing?"

That's been missing.

"*Jah.* I have wished for that. Lately, I'm been looking for parts of my past, pieces that are missing in my life."

"For things you don't remember?"

"For things that happened to me when I was but a *boppli*—a babe," she corrected. "I don't expect to remember what happened, but I do hope to at least learn some details about what happened to me."

Walker's gaze held steady. "You have every right to want to know the truth," he said softly. Then he turned and looked pointedly at Abby. "And this is definitely none of your business."

"I wasn't going to ask." Abby swallowed hard. "Lydia, can I ask you an Amish question?"

She braced herself. "Of course."

"I've already told her you may not want to answer any of her questions," Walker interjected. "So don't feel obligated to answer."

"Now you have me curious, Abby. Go ahead and ask." As

she waited, Lydia prepared herself to be asked about the pins on her dress. Or her white *kapp*. Or what she ate. Or why she stopped going to school at fourteen.

Abby breathed deep. "Okay. Here goes: Why do you like being Amish?"

The question caught Lydia off guard. "Do you mean what do I like?" she asked, deliberately misunderstanding the question. Just to give herself an added second or so. "Do you mean about our buggies and no electricity?"

This time it was Abby who looked put out. "No," she said, impatience running through her tone. "My grandparents are Amish. I know all about the way they live. But what I don't know is how they feel about it. Do you *like* being Amish, Lydia?"

Well, that was the crux of it, wasn't it? Did she like where she was, who she was—the parts she knew of herself?

With a burst of awareness, she knew that she was just like Abby. Confused about who she was and who she should be.

And confused about why she was confused, which was the most disturbing of all.

"I don't know," she finally replied.

Realizing right then and there that she hadn't given a reply at all.

Chapter 17

"For most of his life, Perry was a good brother to his sister, and a good son to us. That's really all a parent can ask of a child. Ain't it so?"

ABRAHAM BORNTRAGER

"Our boy, he was not perfect, but he was not who you are making him out to be," Mr. Borntrager stated firmly. "I am certain of that."

With effort, Luke held his tongue. He'd been through this scenario countless times. It was never easy telling loved ones about crimes the departed had committed. And it was even harder when it was necessary to try to get more information about the deceased.

No one ever liked to speak ill of the dead—that was one thing that seemed to cross all lines. It didn't matter how old a person was, or what their religion, or even if they were man or woman. Everyone wanted to suddenly pretend that the person they were mourning was better than they remembered.

Luke supposed he'd done the same thing.

For most of his life, he'd reconfigured his father's memory

into something he could be proud of. As the years passed, his father had become kinder and more understanding. Luke sometimes revised his father's work history, too. He hadn't been full of excuses for not finding work. No, he'd just been laid off. For a really long time.

And he'd only yelled at his children because he was stressed, not because he had few parenting skills.

So, yeah, he understood Mr. Borntrager's feelings. But there also came a time when facts had to be acknowledged and justice served.

"I'm sure Perry had his good qualities, sir. I'm not disputing that. But the fact is, there are enough people who witnessed him hanging out with known drug pushers that I'm afraid I have to accept that he was mixed up in some dangerous business."

Before his eyes, Mrs. Borntrager crumbled. "You don't think they are lying?" she asked weakly. "I mean, maybe they were jealous of him for some reason?"

"People aren't jealous of drug dealers, ma'am." When she winced, he felt bad, but still, he continued. "I'd like to search his room again. If you don't mind."

Mr. Borntrager obviously did. "Mose already did that," he retorted, getting clumsily to his feet. "Mr. Reynolds, you've already been in there, too."

"I realize that. However, I'd still like to search it again."

Mr. Borntrager stood rooted to his spot, effectively blocking Luke's way. "I don't have time to stand around and watch you search. Chores haveta get done."

"I understand. Actually, I'd prefer to look around on my own. I want to look in Deborah's room as well."

"But why? Deborah ain't here." Mrs. Borntrager's voice was barely above a whisper.

"She might have known something but didn't tell you." He paused. "Where is she, again?"

"She's in Charm," Mr. Borntrager said. "In Ohio."

Luke pretended he was looking through his notes, though he remembered the detail. "Deborah left soon after Perry's body was found. Isn't that right?"

"My parents live in Charm. The visit had been planned for months," her father replied with a defiant edge in his voice.

"Plus, it has been hard on Deborah," her mother said. "She's lost her brother, you know."

Luke stepped closer to the stairs. "I know this is upsetting, but you need to let me do my job," Luke said.

"Maybe it's God's will that we'll never know the truth," Mrs. Borntrager whispered. "Maybe that's why this investigation has been so difficult. Our son is in the ground. No matter what you discover in his room, it won't bring Perry back. You should listen to the Lord."

"I believe the Lord guides my life, ma'am. And because of that, I believe he gave me the skills to do my job. Now, if you don't mind, I'd like to go on up to his room."

For a moment, both parents stood together, a solid wall against him. Fear was etched in their eyes, as was lingering pain and a flash of irritation. It was becoming obvious that the Borntragers wanted Luke or Mose to produce Perry's murderer out of thin air, then send him to trial and get him convicted. All without involving them or delving into Perry's character.

Of course, that wasn't going to happen. He needed to dig deeper into Perry's life in order to discover exactly who he'd been hanging out with. Doing that meant he was almost sure to uncover some of Perry's activities that his parents didn't know about.

The Borntragers slowly moved apart. Neither met his gaze as he stepped through them and slowly climbed the stairs, his left leg hurting more than ever.

The clamber of his boots echoed on each step as he climbed the staircase.

He remembered the upstairs being very small, and his impression didn't change as he surveyed the narrow hallway branching out into two cubby-sized rooms. Though he knew the left belonged to Perry, he opened the right door. There he saw a room so pristine and sparse, it looked as if a nun had taken up residence. A twin-sized bed rested next to the far wall. Only two other small pieces of furniture kept company with it—a bedside table and a chest of drawers made out of oak. Looking closer, he noticed a figurine with a quote from Matthew written below it. Saw a stack of books.

This had to be Deborah's room. Luke wondered why it was so empty. Had she kept it this way, or had her mother put most of her belongings away?

Or had she taken most of her things to Charm? And if she'd done that, how long was she planning to stay in Ohio?

Thankful that no footsteps had followed him upstairs, he crossed the room and opened the thin drawer of the bedside table, hoping against hope that he'd suddenly find a stash of receipts or a hastily handwritten note addressed to Perry.

Inside, he did find a stack of birthday cards to Deborah. He sorted through them, but didn't find anything of interest besides a pad of paper with hearts and the initials J.S. written on it, then hastily scribbled over.

Quietly, he left the room and crossed the hall. Then opened Perry's door and walked right into another world. Whereas most of the house was Plain, Perry's looked very close to an English boy's room. Clothes hung on pegs—

homemade trousers with suspenders, jeans, and T-shirts. Books of all kinds littered his desk and a wobbly-looking bookshelf. History texts lay between a Bible and a pair of current paperback bestsellers. On his desk were pencils, pens, scribbled sheets of paper, and a few pennies.

Three quilts piled on the bed. A pair of boots stood at attention to the side. A shade was halfway up the window, letting in the bright sunlight, casting shadows on most everything else.

Luke wondered about the differences in the two bedrooms. Wondered about the English clothes that were out in plain sight. And wondered if any of it would help him at all.

Well, there was only one way to find out. He sat back down at the desk and began going through every book and sheet of paper again. He only stopped when he found a letter signed "Frannie."

Abby watched Lydia walk to her front steps and then disappear into her house with a feeling of loss. The whole afternoon hadn't been anything like she'd imagined it would be. She'd thought she'd feel included and eager to be more like Lydia.

Instead, she only had more questions.

"You've been quiet for five whole minutes," Walker said as he shifted into reverse, glanced out the mirror, then backed down the driveway. "I would've thought you'd be talking nonstop."

"I guess I don't have anything to say."

"Why not? Lydia answered all your questions?"

"No." Abby struggled to put her mishmash of emotions into the right words. But her efforts were futile. "I thought she'd be happier or something," she finally muttered.

"Happier about what?"

"Oh, I don't know. I guess since she's older and Amish and everything . . . I was hoping she'd seem more content with her life. But she seems just as confused about her life as me. I didn't expect that." She clasped her hands tightly in her lap, waiting for him to tease her about what she said.

But to her surprise, he looked contemplative. "I think Lydia has a lot on her mind. Just because she's Amish, doesn't mean her life is problem-free."

"I know the Amish have problems, too, Walker." She frowned. "Do you think Lydia is still upset about P-Perry?" Gosh, she still could barely say his name.

"Probably. But that's not what I'm talking about." He stopped at the light and turned on his right blinker. "She found out some things about her family that she didn't know before. Some pretty heavy stuff."

Abby was dying to get details, but she knew if she pushed Walker wouldn't tell her anything. "Well, I thought she'd at least be happy being Amish."

Finally came the bark of laughter she'd been expecting. "Your problem, Abby Anderson, is that you want easy answers to hard questions."

"Not all the time."

"A lot of the time you do. You've always been that way. You've always asked 'why' about a hundred times a day. And you've wanted your answers immediately."

Stung, she said, "Well, one thing that was really obvious was how much you two like each other."

He stiffened. "I've told you we're not dating, Abby."

"Oh, I know that. But you're also not just friends. You're more than that." When he didn't reply, she pushed. "Have you two always been close?"

"What do you mean, 'always'?"

"I mean, even back when she was dating Perry . . . did you like her?"

"I didn't know her."

"Really? I thought sometimes all of you hung out together."

"Not really."

Remembering last December—remembering hearing something about how a group of them had run into each other by chance but had ended up hanging out for hours—she said, "But weren't you all together around New Year's?"

Next to her, his posture became rigid and his expression turned glacial, telling her without a doubt that she'd gone too far. "I'm sorry," she said quickly. "I'm sorry, I know it's none of my business."

Walker said nothing more until he pulled the truck into their driveway. "Abby, maybe your problem isn't that you're not Amish," he said with icy contempt. "Maybe it's your mouth. You say too much and ask too many questions and expect people to give you information that's none of your business."

"I don't—"

"You do," he interrupted. "You do this all the time. Don't ask me to take you to see Lydia again."

"Walker, you know I didn't mean to upset her or get too pushy—" What she wanted to say was that she didn't mean to push him so much.

"But you did," he snapped. "You did, like you always do."

And with that, he unbuckled his seat belt, pulled his keys out of the ignition, and left the truck with her still sitting in it.

Abby sat in the cab for a long time afterward. Watching

it rain. Thinking about the way Lydia and Walker pretended not to stare at each other.

Thinking about her brother's reaction to her simple comment about New Year's.

Right about when Perry Borntrager went missing. Did her brother know more than he was letting on?

Chapter 18

*"I was only afraid of Perry when I thought he would hurt me.
And that happened only one time."*

LYDIA PLANK

Sweat trickled down her spine in rhythm to her motions.
Every time Lydia pulled hard on a dandelion weed, another
drop of perspiration fell. The inevitability of her dress becoming soaked to her skin seemed to mirror the painful
changes that were happening in her life.

No matter how hard she tried, she couldn't escape the fact
that she wasn't who she'd always believed herself to be.

That somewhere out in the world, there was a woman
who'd given birth to her and then gave her away.

Added to the mix of emotions was the strange turn of
events with Walker Anderson. To her shame, Lydia knew she
was attracted to him. The mischievous spark in his eyes and
tempting grin had captured her heart and held on tight. Each
time they spoke, there was a sense of integrity and honesty
that drew her closer to him.

She couldn't have ignored him if she'd tried.

How could so much have changed within a year? Walker

Anderson wasn't the kind of man she'd hoped to marry. Perry had been.

As far as she'd known, Perry was a catch. Perry was handsome and a little mischievous. She'd loved that he hadn't been quiet or too serious. But he had a dark side she'd never imagined. He'd liked to shock her, whether it was his stories about drinking and smoking, or . . . the way he'd tried to force himself on her.

Though it was the hottest morning in memory, she felt her skin chill as she remembered how harsh and bitter he had been when she'd pushed him away.

"Stop, Perry!" she practically screamed, pulling her dress down back below her knees.

After another shove, he rolled her to her side. Breathing heavy, he'd turned his head and watched her in the dim light as she'd fastened her dress better. Straightened her hair and repinned her kapp. "You needn't act so frightened, Lydia," he said. "I wasna going to hurt you."

But he had. Fighting tears, she scrambled to her feet. "I need to go home."

He laughed. "Like that? You better wait a bit, or everyone's gonna ask you when the wedding is. You look like we've been rolling in the grass."

She backed off. "I would never marry you," she'd called over her shoulder before darting through the trees.

The walk home was scary. It was already dark, and the shortcut that was easy during the day was confusing at night. She'd fallen more than once.

But once she'd gotten home, she waited forever, until she was able to sneak in through the back door and run up to her room.

Because Perry had been right. No one would ever believe she hadn't been rolling around in the grass.

Even if it hadn't been by choice.

Pulling another weed, she grimaced. In spite of Perry's warnings, she'd kept what had happened a secret, afraid that Reuben would find out. Or her parents.

Yes, for sure, Perry had turned out to be so different than who they'd all thought he was.

Wiping her brow, she forced herself to think of someone else. Maybe underneath Walker's Englishness . . . he was everything she'd ever hoped a man would be.

She didn't understand why he was in her life at the same time her past was falling apart. She'd rather not be dealing with her attraction to Walker, Perry's murder, and her mysterious adoption all at the same time, but that choice didn't seem to be up to her. As always, it was up to God.

All she could do was trust that the Lord had timed these changes in her life for a reason, and He no doubt expected her to come to terms with them with honesty and forbearance. If possible.

Was it possible? Another drop of sweat rolled down her back, chilling her skin as Lydia sought to untangle her emotions. Back and forth she weighed her choices about what to do next. She could pretend the news about being adopted didn't bother her. She could pretend that she wasn't still mourning the loss of Perry.

She could stop thinking about Walker Anderson.

She grabbed another unwanted weed's stem and yanked hard.

"Lydia?"

With a gasp, she dropped the weed and looked up toward the voice. "Detective Reynolds? Whatever are you doing here?"

"I need to ask you some more questions, Lydia."

"More?" This was what she and Walker had been afraid of . . .

"I know you're tired of them, but there's not much I can do about that. I need your help if you can give it."

She shook her head, hoping to clear the cobwebs. "*Nee*, it's all right. I, um, am fine with the questions. I just was surprised to see you, that's all." She scrambled to her feet.

He gestured to the pile of weeds at her feet. "Looks like you've been busy."

"Always. Weeds are a gardener's worst enemy, I fear." Then, remembering her manners, she cleared her throat. "Would you care for something to drink? Or perhaps you'd like to sit inside?" Sitting inside would open their conversation to other ears, but at that moment, she didn't mind. The detective had such a way of setting her nerves on edge. Maybe if her family was around she'd feel safer.

"If it's all the same to you, I'd rather sit out here. I've been inside a lot today."

"I don't mind at all." She motioned to the nearby benches. "Please sit down."

He limped to a nearby bench and took a seat. "Lydia, I was searching through Perry's room and came across a name I hope you will recognize."

"What is the name?"

"Frannie." He studied her carefully, his gaze never wavering. "Do you know a Frannie?"

"I know of a few, but only one very well. I know a Frannie Eicher." She sat down on the ground, now finding comfort in the earth's heat as she contemplated the name. "She works at the bed and breakfast."

"Owns it now." He looked a little disgruntled. Or perhaps dismayed? "As a matter of fact, I'm staying at her place. At the Yellow Bird Inn."

Lydia grew even more wary. "If you're staying at her inn,

why are you asking me questions? Shouldn't you ask her what you want to know?"

He smiled slightly. "I've found over the years that everyone doesn't always tell me the truth. Because of that, it's better to get an idea of what answers I'm looking for before I ask any questions. Was Frannie ever involved with Perry?"

"I don't know."

"Come now. This is a small community. Everyone pretty much knows everyone else's business."

Funny how even memories of the last time she spent alone with Perry made her pulse race and her mouth go dry. "Detective—"

"Just call me Luke, would you?"

"Luke, I'm not really sure if they were courting or not. After Perry and I decided we, ah, didn't suit, I had kind of a bad patch." Well, she supposed several weeks of depression could be called that.

When he still stared at her, she continued. "I never really talked to him after we parted ways," she lied. "I didn't want to."

"And nobody told you what he was up to? No one gossiped about who he was seeing?"

Luke sounded skeptical. Well, she supposed she didn't blame him.

"If they talked about Perry, I didn't listen." When he continued to stare at her like she was a blight in his vision, her temper flared. "Detective Reynolds, I am not a bad person. I am just a woman who made a bad choice when it comes to love. Perry broke my heart. I thought we would marry. When I found out he was different than the man I thought him to be, I was terribly distraught. I never wanted to see him again. Or hear about him again. Everyone knew that."

"It's a small community. I find it hard to believe you didn't hear any gossip."

Instead of replying, she clenched her hands tightly on her lap.

"And what about now? I've heard rumors that you've been seeing Walker Anderson."

Lydia was sure if someone had covered her face in pink crayon, it wouldn't be more flushed looking. She stood up. "Congratulations, Detective. If you've become entrenched in our rumor mill, you must have finally become accepted in our community. Perhaps even more than I am."

But instead of flinching or looking hurt by her mean comment, the detective merely raised a brow. "Just trying to do my job, Lydia."

"So you've said."

"Well, now. I'm starting to think you are tougher than I thought."

"I think we all are tougher than we thought, Detective. Pain will do that to you."

"Look, Lydia. I still need to find answers, and someone is going to have to trust me enough to talk. What do you know about Frannie and Perry?"

"Very little, Detective. Though we know each other, she and I have been busy with our own lives. She's been busy with the inn, and I've been here. Working. And that is the truth." She turned back around and went back to her weeding.

As she heard the detective shuffle away, she sat back on her heels and sighed.

And realized that she'd become very good at lying.

Luke limped back to his car feeling like ten times the fool, and more than a little bit irritated with a certain Amish woman.

It had been a long time since he'd read somebody so wrong, but he'd definitely misjudged Lydia Plank. Like a young pup, he'd been taken in by a pair of blue eyes, a willowy figure, and an aura of innocence and heartbreak.

Which had led him to stop thinking of her as a suspect and more like a victim—a completely idiotic idea if he ever had one.

Then, while he was neck deep in that paper-thin awe of her, she'd neatly lied to him, he was sure of it. He wasn't sure about what information she was hiding, but he'd been lied to enough to notice the signs. The shifting eyes, the painfully still posture, the constant evading of questions.

He was still stewing as he waited for a pair of ducks to take their time crossing the road—why they weren't flying, he didn't know—when the phone rang.

He only had one guess as to who it was. "Mose, not now."

The feminine laugh that responded nearly caused him to press on the gas and run over a wayward duckling.

"Wow, Luke. Just when I think you can't take me by surprise . . . you do."

"Renee. Hey."

"Well, though you don't call, I guess it's good that you still recognize my voice."

"So, what's going on?"

"I'll take that thread of surprise I hear in your tone as a good sign. I'm happy to talk to you, too."

"Is there are reason you called? I mean, when I left we pretty much agreed that we were through." His fingers drummed the steering wheel as he veered around the last wandering bird and sped off.

"I just happened to see Nancy last night and she mentioned you've got a pile of mail. I thought I'd do a good deed and volunteer to send it to you."

"You talked to Nancy about my mail?"

"Uh-huh. I mean, we do live in the same complex." Her voice had turned cooler, less flirty. "Do you want me to stick it all in a mailer and send it to you . . . or I thought maybe I could come out and deliver it in person."

His stomach clenched. He knew seeing Renee was not what he needed. "That wouldn't be a good idea, Renee. I'm neck deep in a murder investigation and, well, I don't think we would have much to say to each other."

She paused, obviously waiting for an explanation. When he offered none, she spoke. "Oh."

Luke knew he could apologize and tell her that when he got back to Cincinnati they could try to pick up where things had left off. But what was the point? He and Renee were over, and he had no interest in dating her again.

"Renee, if you could put my mail in an envelope and send it out to me, that would be great. I don't have my address on me, but I'll e-mail it to you."

There was a pause on the other side of the line. A lengthy one. "Okay."

"Thanks for sending me my mail, Renee. I appreciate your trouble."

He disconnected before he could reflect further about how distant he felt from Cincinnati. How he hadn't even thought about all his mail. Or what he'd been missing in the city.

And that realization made him admit the bitter truth: He'd become exactly what Lydia had said he was—he'd become entrenched in Crittenden County.

Chapter 19

"I only heard Perry pray once, and that was when his sister Deborah had been rushed to the hospital."

WALKER ANDERSON

"Walker, I can't believe you're helping your sister with this Amish project of hers," his mom chided as he walked into the kitchen late that night. "I'm not really sure what to think."

He'd been studying Western Civilization for the last two hours, and he knew he was going to seriously need some caffeine and food if he was going to get in another two hours of study time.

What he didn't need was to be grilled by his mother about his sister.

"Walker, are you not going to say a thing about this?"

Obviously, he wasn't going to get any reprieve. With his head halfway in the cupboard, he replied. "Since when is helping Abby a bad thing?" No way was he going to touch that "Amish project" jab.

"Since she told me that she visited your grandparents without an invitation and talked to your grandmother about being Plain."

No way was he going to let her twist things like that. "Hold on. I was at the table when she told you she'd roped me into taking her. You know that's what happened. And all I did was drop her off."

"Oh, of course," she snapped, the look in her eyes telling a whole different story. "That's all you did."

After grabbing a couple of granola bars, he walked over to the refrigerator and started looking for the sodas. Hearing his mom on the verge of losing her temper meant it was time to get out of there, fast.

But he still was going to defend himself. After grabbing two cans of pop, he leaned back against the fridge. "Mom, wait a minute—this isn't my fault. Abby had these plans on her own, and would have gone whether or not I was there to take her. Besides, they're our grandparents. It's not like I took Abby out partying or something."

"What about when you took her to see that Amish girl?"

His mouth went dry. After debating whether to pop the tab of the first Coke in front of her, he set it on the counter then spoke. "Abby asked if she could go with me when I saw Lydia."

"So it's 'Lydia' now?"

"That's her name."

"You two must be pretty close if you're already bringing your sister to meet her."

"I took Abby because she asked, Mom. Abby wanted to talk to an Amish girl around her age."

"And?"

"And it wasn't any big deal."

"Because you always do what Abby asks, right?"

Walker flinched at her sarcasm. This conversation was getting uncomfortable. His mother didn't do sarcasm. She was always calm and understanding. "Mom, I don't know why you're so upset. I haven't done anything wrong. And as far as I know, neither has Abby."

She opened her mouth, closed it, then drew a long breath. "You're right. I'm sorry." Slowly, she got to her feet and looked him in the eye. "I really am sorry I sounded like a shrew, dear."

"You didn't sound like a shrew. Besides, Mom, I don't think Moms who wear toe rings get shrewish."

She laughed softly, as he'd hoped. Years ago, she'd tried on a gold toe ring at a fancy jewelry store, then much to her embarrassment, hadn't been able to get it off. Their dad had been so amused, he'd ended up buying it. Ever since, it had served to remind Walker that their mom was, in a lot a ways, just a girl.

Funny how he hadn't thought about that toe ring in months.

Tapping her bare toes on the wood floor, the bright gold glinting whenever the beam from the fluorescent bulbs hit it just right, his mom sighed again. "I'm so completely frustrated with that girl I don't know what to do anymore," she said. "I know discovering Perry's body was beyond hard on her. But Abby didn't want counseling, and she doesn't want to talk to either me or your dad. Now I think things have gotten worse for her at school . . ." She shook her head slowly. "Walker, I just don't know what to do to help her."

"For a start, I think you should talk to her instead of yell at me."

"Maybe." The sides of her lips turned up in a smile, letting him know that she, too, saw the humor in their situation. "I'm more used to yelling at you, though."

Walker grinned because he knew that wasn't the case. Unless he counted a few mishaps when he was in preschool, his childhood had been almost perfect. School and friends and sports had come easy. It had always been Abby who was restless and unhappy.

Which was why, he supposed, he was still trying to come to her rescue. "Grandma and Grandpa really like spending time with Abby, Mom. You know how easy they are to be around. She's comfortable there."

"I'm glad she loves James and Francis. But now she's talking about wanting to become Amish, Walker. That's just odd." She lifted her eyebrows and stared at him. Obviously waiting for him to be appalled.

But he wasn't.

"I know, Mom. I don't know what to say. I don't want to be Amish, but I don't think the way Grandma Francis and Grandpa James do things is bad. I like being with them. I like being over at their house a lot. Abby does, too."

"I know."

Just when he was about to take his drink and granola bars up to his room, she spoke again. "I don't resent her wanting to be with your grandparents. I love them, too. I just wish she'd spend more energy on making more friends at school. If she would have tried out for cheerleading like I asked her to, maybe she'd be happier at school. Like you were . . ."

He did an about-face. "You know Abby's not the cheerleader type, Mom."

"She could've been if she had wanted to be . . ."

"But that isn't who she is. You need to let her be herself." All of a sudden, it felt like God was right there in the room with them, giving him the right words. Helping him help his sister . . . and maybe even himself. "Sometimes we just have to fit where we are meant to, instead of, you know, trying to be something we're not."

"And you think maybe that's what Abby is doing? Trying to find herself?"

"Yes. If Abby is happy, that's really all that matters, right?"

Her lips pursed. "I'm only trying to help her, Walker. Besides, I don't know if she realizes just how different her life would be if she became Plain. I think Abby wants to make her life easier, but becoming Amish isn't the answer."

On impulse, he set back down his drinks, then reached out and gripped his mother's shoulder. "Mom, you know Abby is still having trouble sleeping. She's still upset about discovering Perry's body. You've got to give her some time. She loves you, and she wants you to be happy with her. But I'm getting the feeling that Abby's tired of being unhappy. I think we need to let her try some new things."

Her cool, long fingers covered his for a quick second before she looked up at him with a wry expression. "Is it college that's making you so smart?"

"Western Civ? I don't think so." Grabbing his Cokes again, he started back up the stairs.

"So what is?"

He paused. "Maybe Abby is," he said after a moment's consideration. "She's been through a lot. Never had it as easy as I did. But the whole time, she's kept moving forward, too. Even if it hurts." When he stopped to think about it, his sister was downright brave.

"I never thought about her like that," his mother said quietly.

"I hadn't until lately, and I'm kind of embarrassed about that, too." He started climbing up the stairs. "But I tell you what, after watching how she's handled everything she's been through, I feel like she's made me smarter. Some days I hope I'm just like her."

His mother said nothing more as he marched the rest of the way of the stairs. Not another word about Abby. Not even about the two cans of Coke so late at night.

But even though she was quiet, he knew she was smiling.

Huh. He was, too.

"Watch out, Lydia!" Mr. Schrock called out when she entered the front door of the Schrock Variety Store just thirty minutes after it had opened for the day. "We've got a snake on the loose."

A *snake?* With a gasp, she scrambled backward. "Where is it?"

"If I knew, it wouldn't be on the loose now, would it?"

Looking around the shop, she shared looks of sympathy with the other folks who'd had the misfortune to venture into Schrock's that day. A whole band of customers were standing in a rough semicircle, each wearing a pained look. Like they were trapped in their worst nightmare.

Well, all except Walker. He looked like he was the only sane person in the middle of a roomful of clowns and monkeys. When their eyes met, he winked.

Afraid to move, she lifted her teal dress's hem slightly. "So, do I want to ask why there's a snake running about?"

"That would be *slithering* about, Lydia," Walker corrected from his post by the back door. "Snakes don't run."

"You should know that. You're a smart girl," Mr. Schrock reprimanded.

Lydia knew she was smart enough to realize that she still hadn't gotten a straight answer. Looking around, she scanned the crowd, hoping for a familiar, sympathetic face. She got lucky when she spied Mary King Yoder. "What's going on?"

"Mr. Schrock was fed up with the guinea pigs, you see," Mary King said with a frown.

Looking into the pen, two of the orange rodents stared right back at her. They looked cute and calm and easy enough to handle. "I still don't follow. What's wrong with them?"

"Those are fine," Walker said. "Mr. Schrock is concerned about the ones who got away."

Remembering the last time she'd been in, only to find Walker on his knees looking under a shelf, she shook her head. "You still haven't found the escapees?"

Slowly Mr. Schrock shook his head. "They create a real mess, I tell ya. They've eaten through sacks of flour and popcorn. Poor Walker here's been cleaning up after them nonstop."

Lydia dared to meet Walker's eye again.

He was visibly fighting off a smile.

"Mr. Schrock, I understand your dilemma, but I'd much rather have a pig brush my ankle than a scary snake bite it."

"Oh, child. You should follow that old saying, 'If you can't see the bright side, polish the dull side'!"

Mr. Schrock truly did love his Amish sayings.

He continued, "Besides, Lydia, they're not venomous. The snakes I put out are bull snakes."

It didn't escape, Lydia—or, it seemed, anyone else in the store—that there was now a plural usage of the word *snake*. Almost hesitantly, she said, "Mr. Schrock, if the bull snakes don't eat guinea pigs, then what are they going to do with them?"

"Scare them, of course."

"Scare? If the guinea pigs get scared, what's supposed to happen then?"

As if to illustrate his point, the whole gathering heard a

frantic squeak mere seconds before a flying orange fur ball came shooting out from underneath a shelf.

It paused, looking around a bit. But, just when everyone tried to either catch it or move out of the way, the most gigantic thick black snake slithered out into the open.

The pig froze in terror.

So did Lydia. A sick feeling coursed through her as she realized that it was very likely she was about to witness the circle of life—or whatever it was called when snakes ate guinea pigs—right before her eyes.

Lydia couldn't help it. She screamed.

With the commotion, the snake got scared, too, and quick as a whip, it slithered into hiding again.

And the guinea pig squeaked and ran for safety.

Walker groaned.

"We're all good now, everyone," Mr. Schrock announced with complete false joviality. "Get on to your shopping. Don't let these wayward critters bother you none. The Lord honors all creatures great and small, to be sure."

But the warning came too late. Pretty much everyone was tripping over each other to get out of the store.

"Hold on, Mary King," Mr. Schrock said. "I thought you came for dry goods."

"I'm going to get them somewhere else today," she said.

"But—"

Holding on to the door handle, she glared. "Oh, don't 'but' me, Aaron Schrock. When you rid this place of your creatures, let me know. I'm used to your fool stunts, but this is even worse than the bats you had last year for the flies."

He crossed his arms over his chest. "We didn't have nare a fly in here after those bats arrived."

Her chin lifted. "I got bat dung on my dress. Do you have any idea how awful that was to scrub out?"

His cheeks pinkened. "Actually, I do. My wife wouldn't wash my shirt."

Lydia bit her lip to keep from laughing but laughter was surely inevitable. She dearly enjoyed shopping at Schrock's; there was always something interesting to find on the shelves. But Mary King Yoder was exactly right. Snakes on the loose had to be the last straw.

After a glance Walker's way, she hurried out the door.

And then, to her pleasure, Walker joined her. "Come on," he said with a smile as he reached for her hand. "Mr. Schrock said I could take my break early."

"This early?"

He laughed. "With the way things are going in there, I think he's glad I didn't quit! Come on, let's get out of here. We've got some time."

Only when they walked a few feet did she realize that her hand was still nestled comfortably in his . . . and that more than one person seemed to have noted it.

Chapter 20

"Perry used to walk through our fields in the evening. We didn't care for it much, but he weren't the only one to trespass."

HENRY MILLER

Instead of letting the attention they were getting bother them, Lydia and Walker kept walking. And walking. Little by little, the commotion of the store gave way to the smaller noises of nature. Under their feet, pavement turned into gravel, then finally just a packed dirt trail.

Cars and buggies and noise faded to sights of trees and bushes, and vibrant green vines. The only noise she heard was the sound of footsteps.

"I never get tired of walking around here," Walker said.

"I haven't been on this trail in ages."

"Why not?"

"Too much to do, I guess." But even as she said it, she knew her words were lies. Walking on the trail by herself was scary, and it made her think about how lonely she had been without Perry. It had been hard to break up with him, hard to stay away from him when it meant giving up on all the dreams she'd had. Especially when no one understood why she'd broken up with him in the first place.

"If you're too busy to take a walk, I think you're way too busy," he said with a smile.

They were still holding hands, which was a fairly new experience. Perry hadn't been much of a hand-holder—not that any of the Amish were.

She didn't know any courting couple who would wander around Crittenden County hand in hand.

So why was she doing it?

"Thanks for coming to visit. Did you have any trouble getting out of work?" Walker asked.

His question brought her back to reality. "No. I, um, have been telling my parents that I needed some time to myself."

"Do they know we've spent some time together?"

"They know."

"And?" He glanced her way. "What do they think?"

"Truth?"

"Of course."

"They aren't very pleased. They think I've lost my mind, I'm afraid," she finally admitted. "But I haven't lost it. I mean, at least, not yet."

Walker couldn't help it, he smiled. Everything about her made him smile. "I didn't think you had," he murmured. Then, without his brain being aware of it, he stopped walking and turned so they were facing each other. Once again, he was struck by how pretty she was. The light brown hair framing her face looked shiny and smooth. Her blue eyes seemed to instantly reflect what she was feeling.

He half waited for her to shy away from him. To step back, to fumble with words. To tell him that they should do something else.

Instead, she surprised him.

"Did you bring me out here to kiss me, Walker Anderson?"

"Maybe," he quipped. Though he hadn't. "What if I did? Are you shocked?"

"I have just stood in the midst of a pair of wild guinea pigs and a hungry bull snake and survived! I'm not a woman who is easily shocked."

Her words were teasing, of course. He almost smiled.

Then the rest of his brain told him to stop wasting the opportunity. He dropped her hand. Stepped in closer. "I didn't bring you out here to kiss you, Lydia. But now that you mention it, I think it's a great idea."

Her blue eyes flashed . . . but not in fear, in amusement. "I—I didn't mention it."

"You did. You asked. I heard."

Her eyes widened. Her lips parted slightly in invitation.

And so there was only one thing to do. He lowered his head and brushed his lips against hers. Then, finding no argument, he kissed her again, finally wrapping his arms around her shoulders and holding her close.

So close that it felt like their clothes melded together and their bodies were almost meshed. To his surprise, Lydia wasn't the least bit hesitant. Within seconds, her hands were around his neck and she pressed closer.

He parted his lips, half waiting for her to pull away. She didn't.

Finally, when he realized that his hands were starting to roam, he knew things had to end.

Abruptly, he lifted his head.

Lydia, looking flustered, stepped away.

"You okay?" he asked.

She stared back at him, her lips were still parted. But there was no fear or regret or pain in her expression.

No, instead, she looked more beautiful than ever.

And right then, right there, he knew that she'd been what he'd been missing all his life.

Especially when she nodded.

"Shame we picked today to tromp around in the Millers' field," Mose said over his shoulder. "We're going to look like we've been mud wrestling, don'tcha think?"

Luke stumbled as his buddy's words hit him like the back end of a piece of plywood. "Mose, since when have you been thinking about mud wrestling? And do I even want to know the answer?"

"Oh, Luke. Stop being such a prude. I was flipping the channels on the television the other day and came across a mud wrestling event that was taking place before the start of a monster car rally."

"Oh, brother. I'm sure you did. And I guess you decided to stay on that channel and watch it?"

"It was mighty entertaining. Even some women got into the act."

Luke stumbled, splashing more mud against his leg. "Mose, really?"

"Oh, come now. It was all in fun. And it's not like I'm fixing to go find a woman to wrestle with."

"I hope not."

Mose grinned. "I'm just making conversation. Where do you think they get the mud from?" He picked up a coated boot. "Maybe from here." He whistled low. "You know, now that I think about it, we could have our own mud rally here . . ."

He was now officially shocked. "I can't believe you're saying this."

With a somewhat evil grin over his shoulder, Mose laughed.

"Are you sure you've been patrolling the evil, dark streets of Cincinnati? Because at times I wonder if you really went to Mayberry."

"I've been in Cincy. And news flash, nobody mud wrestles there."

"They might do less bad things if they had more fun, eh?"

Luke couldn't help but agree as he tromped on. Earlier that morning, he'd called Mose and told him he'd wanted to take another look at the spot where they'd discovered Perry's body.

He didn't have a good reason for the excursion except that he kept running into walls in the investigation and he had the real need for some fresh air and the company of the one person in Crittenden County who wasn't going to lie to him.

"Well, here we are," Mose announced a few minutes later. First pointing to a row of wood and stones, he said, "This is where Abby Anderson and her girlfriends were sitting. Then, the story goes that Abby went running after her backpack and found it pretty much resting on top of poor Perry's body."

Only Mose could describe it like that.

"What did they touch?"

"Not Perry, for sure!" Mose exclaimed, once again giving into his penchant for dark humor. "When we got here, the backpack was still resting on the brambles that surrounded the body." He scratched his head, then stepped forward. "As much as I could tell, the girls didn't get much farther than right here. They got close enough to understand what they found, then backed right up."

Visualizing the scene, imagining the girls he'd known back in high school, Luke nodded. "I don't know any girl who wouldn't have done the same."

"Me neither."

Luke walked to the edge of the well and peered down. Looking for clues, though he knew the search would most likely be futile. "Who went down the shaft?" he finally asked.

"The medical examiner and two rookies, I think." Mose grimaced. "Gathering Perry's body was no easy task, I tell you."

Though he'd seen plenty of death, his stomach still clenched. "No, I mean afterward. Who went down and collected samples? Was it you?"

"Um, actually . . . I don't know if anyone went down the well."

Luke turned to his friend sharply. "What are you saying?"

"I'm saying that I messed up," he said after a moment. "We were in such a hurry to get the body up, well, I guess we didn't investigate any further once the body got loaded to the ambulance." He paused again. "It's no excuse, but it's just me here, you know? It's just me and other things happened and I forgot."

It was obvious that Mose's information had been hard to admit. But Luke was starting to realize just how much pressure and stress would result from living the life of a small-town country sheriff. There was little support and precious few resources.

Mose shook his head. "What's happened to me? Have I gotten stupid?"

"No." But just the same, Luke didn't offer any support. If no one had returned to hunt for evidence around the site of the body, then a serious oversight had been made and the responsibility rested firmly on Mose's shoulders. "You got a camera in your car?"

"Yep. I'll go get it. Then, I'll climb on in and collect evidence."

Luke didn't volunteer to take his place. He knew Mose

needed to do the hard work in order to feel better about his mistakes, plus with his bum knee . . . "And I'll take notes."

What wasn't said was that in all likelihood, anything that they did find was likely unusable for evidence. Too much time had passed. A good defense attorney could argue that anyone could have tampered with the area. After all, crime scene tape seemed to only keep people out in the movies.

Moments later, Mose came loping up with a new expression of determination on his face. Still not meeting his eye, the man handed Luke a notebook, took off his ball cap, hung the camera around his neck, and put on a head lamp. Finally, he knelt by the entrance of the dry well.

Luke wasn't sure if Mose was drawing strength or praying. Maybe he was doing a little bit of both. "You okay with doing this?" he asked after a minute.

"More than okay." Raising his chin, he at last looked Luke in the eye. "But that said, if I get stuck in here, don't you hesitate to pull me out."

Luke patted his bum leg. "I'll do my best to get help."

Mose's answer was tossing his keys Luke's way. "You might need these after all."

And then, with the agility of a teen, he began his descent.

This time, it was Luke who was the one who closed his eyes and prayed.

Chapter 21

"I never thought Perry and Lydia made all that great of a couple. No one in our circle of friends did."

WALKER ANDERSON

Still holding her hands, still feeling her soft breath against his skin, Walker spoke. "I need to get back to work. We've been out here way too long."

When Lydia half flinched, he knew he'd made a major mistake. She might have been Amish, but she acted like any other girl he knew. He had to be careful of his words in case they were taken the wrong way.

As they headed back to the store, she lagged behind him. As they continued, he bit his lip and wished he could do over the last twenty minutes. If he could, he wouldn't have taken her into the woods in front of half the town. He sure wouldn't have kissed her.

And if he had kissed her, well, the first thing he would have said afterward wouldn't have been that he had to get back to work.

Once they were out from the privacy of the wooded trail

and the store was back in sight, Lydia quickened her step and returned to his side.

And that was when he realized she wasn't asking questions about when they were going to see each other again. She wasn't like some girls, girls so eager to push him into a relationship he wasn't ready for.

Which, perversely, made him want to start talking about anything besides that kiss. Clearing his throat, he said, "What's new with you and your parents? Are they still wanting you to forget that you're adopted?"

"I think so. But, they have told me the name of the home, and let me look up the contact information. I'm ready for some answers."

"What do you think you'll find out?"

She shrugged. "I've already discovered that everyone involved at the Sweet Angels Home signs forms granting something called an 'open adoption'. I found that information in their ad in the phone book."

"What's open adoption?"

"From what I can figure out, it means that everybody can keep in touch if they want. So, you know, there wouldn't be any secrets." She rolled her eyes. "I guess they wanted to be the only ones keeping secrets."

"When are you going to call the agency?"

"When I get up the nerve."

"Well, when you get up the nerve, and if you do set up a meeting, I'd like to take you."

"Why?"

"Why not? I mean, unless you have plans to go with anyone else?"

"I don't have plans with anyone else."

"I have my truck, so it would be easy for you just to go with me. And I'd be fine sitting in on it, or waiting for you."

Looking as startled as a frightened doe, she looked closely at him. "Really? You'd do that?"

He shrugged. "We're . . . friends, right?"

"Oh yes. Right."

By this time, they were standing in the front of the store. Walker could hear Mr. Schrock's voice carrying through the partly open door. "When do you want to go?"

"Can you stop by my house sometime tomorrow? I'll try to work up the nerve to call this afternoon."

He smiled, glad she was going to let herself move forward instead of being frozen with worry. "I can do that."

"And Walker?"

"Yeah?"

"I just want you to know . . . you're not the first boy I've kissed."

"I figured that."

Her voice turned sassy. "So I don't want you to think I'm going to get all dreamy-eyed around you and start thinking that the two of us are something we aren't."

"Good. Because, you know, I'm not looking for a girl-friend."

"I'm not looking for a boyfriend. Not at all."

"Glad to hear it." Of course, if he was so glad, why was he feeling more than a little jealous? She bit her lip, his eyes followed. "I'm going now. Bye."

He raised a hand and walked to the door. Made sure he didn't look back at her.

And swallowed hard before he greeted Mr. Schrock and whatever else was waiting for him.

* * *

An hour before, her father had lit a fire; the room was so cozy now, and one by one, all of the Plank siblings settled in the room. Reuben was reading a farm journal, Lydia playing Trouble with Becky and Petey. Her mother was mending yet another pair of Petey's pants, and her father had a book open.

Lydia knew there was going to be no better time to do what she had to do.

"Hey," she said. "I have some news."

Reuben looked up. "Some new boy is gonna come calling?"

"Ha, ha." Nervously, she tried to imagine an easy, casual way to give her announcement. But of course there wasn't a way to tell this easily. "I know some of you have heard things . . ." She glared at Becky. "But I thought it was time to have it all out in the open."

The room had gone so silent, it seemed as if the shock had pulled out all of the air from the room. Petey frowned. "What are you talkin' about, Lydia?"

She looked at her parents for help, but only saw heartbreak on her mother's face and displeasure on her father's. "Mamm and Daed told me that they adopted me from a children's home in Paducah. And tomorrow, I'm going to visit it to see if I can learn about who my birth parents are."

"What's a children's home?" Petey asked.

"A place for children whose parents don't want them," Reuben stated.

As mother closed her eyes, her father glowered. "Reuben, that ain't so, sometimes something happens to a parent and they aren't able to take care of their children. They get sick or die."

Becky's eyes widened. Looked scared. "Why were you there? And how did Mamm and Daed know to come get you?"

Reuben folded the paper and raised his voice. "And how come we never heard about it?"

Lydia felt a small bit of satisfaction hearing the same questions out of her siblings' mouths that she'd thought a dozen times, especially since Becky and Reuben were keeping their mouths shut about overhearing the earlier conversation.

But as she glanced toward her parents, she saw anger in their eyes. Her mom's eyes were filled with tears as she looked out the window.

Her father stood up and pointed to the doorway. "You all may leave now. We will discuss this later."

"Daed, we might as well talk about this now," Reuben said. "It's not like it doesn't affect us."

"Reuben, you go out. And take your brother and sister with you."

Just as Lydia got to her feet, too, her father pressed his hand on her shoulder. "You may stay here, Lydia."

She stood fuming. Even though it had been uncomfortable, her parents should have allowed her to talk to her siblings about this. Out in the open.

When the room was cleared, her father spoke. "You shouldn't have done that."

"I had no choice. We're talking about my life. I don't want who I am to be some closely guarded secret. Not anymore."

"You are breaking my heart, Lydia," her mother said through a wash of tears. "Never in my wildest dreams did I ever imagine you would react this way when your father and I told you the news. I can't believe you told them all that you are going to visit that place."

"Mamm, you told me I could contact the adoption home."

"But I never thought you really would!"

Lydia glanced her father's way.

His eyes were solemn when they met her gaze. "This search you've begun . . . you canna stop it?"

"I didn't say that. But I think I need to do it." It was so much easier to stay focused on her father instead of her mother's tears. "I'm not going down this path just to make you upset."

"We still are, however."

"I still love you both. You know that."

"I know that, daughter. Of course I know that," he said softly.

"If you love us so much, why do you need to know who birthed you?" her mother asked from behind a curtain of tissues. "Why does it make a difference?"

"Because these people are part of who I am."

"*Nee.* You are Lydia Plank. You are our child. That is all you need to know."

"Maybe when I *was* a child," she agreed. "But I am no longer a child. I'm a grown woman, and I deserve to know why I was given up for adoption. I need to know who these people were. Only when I know what really happened will I be able to know what to do next."

"I don't want you to leave us."

Incredulous, Lydia said, "Mamm, you don't truly think I'm going to go find my birth mother and suddenly want to be with her instead of you?"

A flash of guilt formed in her mother's eyes before she blinked. "I don't know what you're going to do."

All the self-pity she'd been clutching evaporated. In her parents' faces, she saw raw vulnerability. Truth was, Lydia was a little nervous, too. She didn't know what she was about to discover, or how she would deal with things when she did. But more than all the doubts that warred inside her was the complete sense that God was on her side. Only He could have given her parents the strength to tell her the truth—and He had been with them *and* her birth parents all those years ago.

She felt sure that He had brought Walker into her life at just at this moment, too. Otherwise, it all seemed too far-fetched that an English boy who she'd known only in the slightest of ways would suddenly become so very important to her at this moment in her life.

And though she'd always sought to listen to her parents and take their advice, at the moment He was whispering in her ear, telling her that this was the time to do what she needed to do.

"Mamm, Daed, tomorrow, I'm going to go to the adoption agency and maybe even to the courthouse—wherever I need to go in order to discover the truth about my past. Walker said he'd come with me."

"Why do you need that English boy to go?" her mother asked, her tone accusing.

"We're friends. I've told you that."

"Accompanying you to the adoption agency sounds like he's more than that."

Here was her chance. "I think God is behind all of this, Mamm. I think He must have felt the time was right for us all to discover some truths. With His help, that detective will soon learn who killed Perry. And I'll know more about my past."

"And what about that *boo*—? That boy?" her father asked. His tone seemed to convey everything he thought—basically that she was being foolish, and that the person she was spending time with was foolish, too.

"He's not a boy, Daed. He's a man, and he's making his

own decisions, with God's help, just as I am." Recalling their kiss, but even more than that, recalling the complete sense of peace she'd felt in his company, she smiled slightly. "I like him."

Her parents exchanged glances. "Like him, how?"

For a moment, she was tempted to gloss over her feelings. To evade their piercing looks and searching expressions. But she was done acting like a child. "I like him as I've never liked another man. I think I might even be falling in love with him," she added, somehow managing to surprise both her parents and herself with that one remark.

Her mother opened her mouth, closed it quickly, then looked like she was fighting her own struggles to valiantly keep more sharp retorts to herself.

Her father watched his wife attempt to stifle her tongue and chuckled. "Lydia, dear, you are mighty wise. If I ever had any doubts as to if our Lord kept his sights on us, that he was working by our side to guide us, what just happened has surely made all my misgivings disappear. Only God would be able to stifle your mother's tongue at a moment like this."

Lydia felt her eyes prick with tears. Here she'd defied their wishes about keeping her adoption and her birth mother a secret from the rest of the kids, about Walker, and even about visiting the adoption agency. But instead of pushing her away, her father was making jokes. Suddenly hopeful, she looked to her mom.

Who, after sending a look of irritation her husband's way, sighed. "*Jah*. God is *gut*. And as for your feelings for this Walker . . ."

"Yes?"

Her mother shrugged. "Well, I suppose it is out of my hands."

"I didn't mean to do any of this . . ."

Her mother glanced upward to the sky. "But someone else did, *jah?*" Opening her arms, she motioned Lydia forward. "I know you're a woman and all, and that I didn't actually bring you into this world . . . But do you still have a hug for me?"

"Always," she said, hugging her mother tight. "Of that, you should never doubt. I love you, Mamm. I love both of you."

"I don't want to lose you, Lydia," she whispered.

"You haven't lost me, Mamm. I promise you that." And with that promise, some of the tension that had surrounded the three of them dissipated.

After kissing her cheek, her father turned to the window. "Ah, it looks like Walker is here. You'd best go see him."

"Okay."

"Lydia?"

She paused. "Yes, Mamm?"

"Ask Walker if he'd like some oatmeal cookies, if you'd like. I made them fresh this morning."

Her mother's peace offering made the tears that she'd been holding back break through. With tears running down her face, she felt pure relief—mixed with pure happiness as she caught sight of Walker again. It hit her hard. "I'll do that. I'll ask him about the cookies right now."

She scampered out of the room, through the front door, and down the steps. "Walker?"

He stopped. Smiled at her brightly. "Hey, Lydia."

"Would you . . . would you like some cookies? My *mamm* made them fresh today."

He stilled, looked at her, looked beyond her to where he, and Lydia, realized her parents stood, watching. And then he nodded—just as much for her as for them. "Cookies sound great. Thank you, Mrs. Plank."

"You . . . you are most welcome, Walker," her mother replied graciously.

Glancing toward her father, he caught her eye and winked.

Suddenly, everything in her world felt just right. Maybe even better than that.

Chapter 22

"I never could understand why Perry thought something was missing from his life. Until recently, that is. Now I understand completely."

LYDIA PLANK

"I guess you get a lot of visitors like me," Lydia sputtered. "Visits from people who had been adopted?"

Mortified by how nervous she sounded, Lydia half waited to be laughed at.

But instead of grinning, Marianne, the director of the Sweet Angels Home only looked at her with compassion. "We get our fair share of visitors," she said gently. "Some of them are folks who want to know about their past."

As Lydia exhaled, Marianne leaned back in her chair, looking from Lydia to Walker. "Fact is, I've given up trying to guess why some people come back to learn about their birth parents and why some never do. Though, of course, some never see the need to visit here. Some people's parents have shared all the details about their birth parents and the circumstances of their birth from an early age."

The woman's last statement had a vague question at the

end of it. As Walker shifted beside her, Lydia knew it was time to dive in. "I never knew I was adopted until recently. I'm afraid I know practically nothing about my birth parents."

The director took off her glasses and peered a little closer at Lydia. "From the beginning, our organization's motto has been to make the relationship between birth parents and adoptive ones as strong as possible. Though some families don't choose to share a lot of details, most have been committed to transparency."

Lydia wasn't sure what transparency meant, but she knew that her circumstances were very different from what the woman was describing. "I'm afraid that hasn't been the situation for me."

"Our center has always been committed to open adoption, when all parties are comfortable with continuing a relationship in some form, or comfortable with a relationship in the future. But twenty years ago, when your adoption went through, might have been before we made that commitment."

She was, it seemed, about to say more when another woman appeared at her office door. "I'm sorry, but may I borrow you for one moment?"

The director got to her feet. "I'll be right back. Please excuse me."

When they were alone, the tension in the room seemed to grow.

Lydia felt uneasy. She wished with all her heart that her parents hadn't kept their secret for so long. Things would have been much easier for everyone involved if they'd embraced the truth and been honest with her from the start.

From the moment Walker had picked her up, she had felt agitated. Her parents, though trying to put on a brave front, looked devastated.

And while Walker was trying to be supportive, Lydia felt a new barrier between them as well. Though she wasn't brave enough to ask, she was concerned that he was regretting his offer to take her. What she was getting into was painful, difficult, and personal. Perhaps it was too much for a friendship as new as theirs?

"I'm sorry I dragged you here," she whispered. "It was unfair of me to make you do this."

"Don't worry about it. I'm glad I came."

"Truly?"

"Definitely. There's no way I'd want you to go through this by yourself." Taking her hand, he squeezed gently. "Just sit tight and keep being brave. Then we'll get the answers we came for."

"You make it sound easy."

"It's not. I know it's not. But we don't need to make it harder than it has to be."

"Walker, you are smarter than you look."

He chuckled, wiping away the tension in the room as effectively as if he had an eraser in hand. "I get that all the time."

She was still smiling at him when Marianne returned.

"Ah," she said. "Lydia, you've got some color in your cheeks now. I'm glad about that. For a moment there, I thought you were going to faint on me."

"I do feel better," Lydia admitted. "Though, I still am not sure what to do now."

"How about I go retrieve your file and then we'll look at it together? Perhaps it will make some things clearer."

"That sounds great," Walker said.

Bracing her hands on her desk, she paused. "I feel like I should warn you that sometimes people find answers they weren't ready for. Do you think you're prepared for the details of your story?"

Lydia glanced at Walker. His smile was gone, but his gaze made her feel just as secure. Without a word he was letting her know that he was going to stay by her side no matter what the outcome.

No matter if she'd been born Amish or English . . . or even from another country. She was still going to mean the same to him.

That acceptance was worth more than gold to her.

"I'm sure this is what I want."

"Alrighty, then." Marianne stood up and motioned for the two of them to follow her out of the room. "There's a meeting room just down the stairs by the front door. There's coffee and tea and water there, and usually a plate of cookies. Why don't you two go there and relax for a few minutes? It will take me about a half an hour to get your records."

Another half hour? The wait was surely going to drive her crazy!

Luckily, though, Walker seemed to have a far better presence of mind. "Thank you. We'll be waiting."

Walker held her hand as they walked down the stairs, remaining silent, letting her take time to process what was happening.

Knowing the truth, even if it wasn't easy or helpful or good, was the only option. It was difficult to go forward in her life if she kept looking back.

When they got to the sitting room, Walker walked right to the small table where a pair of Thermoses and a couple of rows of soft drinks and water bottles were waiting. "What do you want?"

"Nothing."

"You sure?" He picked up a water for himself.

"I am sure." She was so nervous, even the thought of swallowing water made her feel ill.

After taking a long drink, and an even longer glance her way, Walker took a seat and texted someone on his phone.

She folded her arms over her chest and tried to look calm.

Then, as the clock overhead ticked slowly, she gave up and tried to just breathe.

Time went by slowly.

After thirty minutes Marianne hadn't returned. Walker finally spoke. "You all right, Lydia?"

"Oh, sure."

"Really?"

"*Nee*. But I wanted this, and I will get answers eventually." She looked worriedly at the closed door, then at the clock. "Why do you think it's taking so long?"

"No telling."

"What if she can't find my records? What if there's a problem?"

"I doubt that's what happened. You know how things go. I bet she got called to the phone or something. She seems pretty busy."

"I suppose." But still, every minute that passed felt like two hours.

After another fifteen minutes, she blurted, "Walker, what if she found out something terrible?"

"Then we'll deal with it. But no matter what, we'll find out the truth, right? That's why we're here."

Lydia bit her lip and tried not to tap her foot.

Walker must have noticed her uneasiness. He held out his hand. "Want my hand?"

"You think that will fix things?"

His lips curved up slightly. "No, but it might make waiting easier."

She slid her palm into his and enjoyed the way his covered hers completely. Making her feel protected, like part of a set. Seeking to lighten the mood, she joked, "Of course, this doesn't mean there's anything going on between us."

"Good. Because, you know, I'm not looking for a girl-friend."

"And I'm still not looking for a boyfriend." She almost smiled.

"Glad we're clear on that." He was prevented from saying anything else when the door opened and Marianne stepped through.

"I'm sorry it took me so long," she said. "I had a bit of a problem looking for your paperwork."

Oh, but she'd known that something was wrong. "Why?"

"Your situation, I mean, the way your adoption was handled . . . it went a little different than most here."

"Why is that?" Lydia didn't like to think that she'd started life in a mysterious way.

Marianne exhaled. "Because there were extenuating circumstances about the woman who gave birth to you." She paused again.

"Can you just tell us?" Walker asked. "Lydia's about to go crazy."

"I just want to know the truth."

"I understand." Sitting down, Marianne handed Lydia a folder. "Your mother was in poor health when she delivered you. She had a disease, multiple sclerosis. From what the records say, she'd been warned to not have children."

"Multiple Sclerosis? What's that?"

"M.S. affects the ability of nerve cells in the brain and

spinal cord to communicate with each other effectively. Severe cases can be debilitating."

Lydia felt completely unnerved. Never had she imagined that her real mother had had medical problems. "What happened to her?"

"After she gave birth to you, from what I understand, her health took a turn for the worse. She and her husband were worried that she wouldn't ever be able to take care of a baby, let alone herself. She knew she wasn't going to be able to walk, or do much, I suppose."

"So that's why they gave me up?"

Marianne looked at her solemnly. "I can't speak for them, but it looks like they gave you up because they knew you'd never really have a mother if you stayed with your birth mom. Records say she passed away just six months after giving birth to you."

"Oh, my goodness!" Lydia felt a deep stab of pain in her heart. How could it hurt so much to lose someone she didn't even know?

The director sighed, then continued, obviously taking care to keep her voice professional and clinical. "In addition, your father was worried that he wouldn't be able to take care of a baby when he was mourning his wife. They were older, you see."

Lydia shook her head. She had imagined a teen pregnancy. Or a mother on drugs. Or a hundred different scenarios. Not this.

"Were my parents Amish or English?" she asked.

Marianne smiled slightly. "I'm afraid I didn't read that far. But everything you need to know is in that folder. Take as much time as you two need to read through everything. When you're ready to leave, please leave the folder with the receptionist." After a pause, she held out her hand. "Good luck to you, dear. And may God be with you."

Lydia shook her hand. "Thank you. And thank you for this."

When they were alone, Lydia sat next to Walker on the couch and read through the faded paperwork by his side. Her birth mother had been forty-five years old. Not too terribly old to have a baby now, but twenty years ago it would have been out of the ordinary.

They'd lived in Erie, Pennsylvania.

And under religious affiliation, it was blank.

With a sense of doom, Lydia felt more befuddled than ever before.

Now she understood what the director had been trying to say. Expectations rarely ever matched the reality. Perry taught her that.

If only she'd remembered.

"Detective, would you still care for breakfast this morning?" Frannie asked.

He'd slept late after being up most of the evening, going through all the notes from the investigation.

And now, of course, his ever-present host was checking up on him. Again. And looking at him like he was a child in need of discipline. "Did you save me anything?"

"I did. Nothing too much. Just fruit and a bagel. And a turkey sandwich for later."

"That's all, huh?" He smiled, suddenly glad she'd been keeping tabs on him. "Frannie, I swear, you're like the sister I never had."

Her brow furrowed. "Surely not. It's simply that I'm starting to understand what you like."

"Do you have a moment to sit with me?"

"I have to work, Mr. Reynolds."

"I know. But I need to speak with you about something."

Gingerly, Frannie approached the table and sat across from him. "Is there a problem?"

"Maybe." With effort, Luke finally asked the question he'd been meaning to, but did his best to try to sound as frank and nonjudgmental as he could. "Frannie, you never told me that you knew Perry Borntrager."

"You never asked."

"That's hardly fair. You know I'm here to investigate his death. You've deliberately been keeping information from me," he added, finally giving up on his hope to stay calm, cool, and collected. "Were you seeing him?"

"For a time, I suppose I was."

"And what happened?"

"We discovered that we didn't suit."

"How did you decide that? What happened?"

She paled. "What happened between Perry and me did not bring about his death."

"I didn't mean to insinuate that. But can you let me know when you became involved?"

"Officer, I don't think it's important—"

"Frannie, please," he snapped. "It's important to the investigation. When did you see him last?"

She swallowed hard. "On December thirtieth."

Finally, they were getting somewhere! "Where were you?"

"At the Schrocks' store. He was in the front, walking with his sister. I didn't speak to him much, though," she said quickly. "None of us did."

He stilled. " 'None of us'? Who was there?"

She looked down at her hands. "Lydia Plank, Walker Anderson, Jacob, of course."

"Jacob?"

"Jacob Schrock." After a pause, she said, "Jacob, then Perry and Deborah, his sister. My friend Beth. And me."

Luke struggled to hide his surprise. So many people had seen Perry the day before New Year's and Frannie was the first one to tell him about it? "What did Perry say? What did you say to him?"

She looked away. "I don't remember."

"Frannie, I'm not playing a game."

Her eyes looked troubled. "I didn't think you were. I just have no more information for you. I'm afraid I cannot help you anymore, Luke." And with that, she turned away from him and walked to the kitchen.

Though he wasn't invited to follow, he did. Then tried another tack. "Don't you want to make sure justice is served for Perry?"

"It already has been served. Perry is gone, and he's having to visit with St. Peter up at the gates of heaven for his sins. God doesn't need my help in that area."

"I do, though . . ."

"Please excuse me. I've got to go get another room ready."

"We're not finished with this conversation."

"Yes, we are. You might be a paying guest, but you're still a guest in my home. Don't forget that."

"Then I think it's time I stayed someplace else."

"Truly?" She turned on her heel, looking so taken aback and disappointed, he almost changed his mind. But now that he realized that she, too, had been one of the last people to see Perry, he needed to maintain some space from her.

He couldn't pretend her evasiveness was okay. "I'll get my things and leave within the hour."

"Where will you go?"

He didn't know. "It doesn't matter. I'll find someplace. Look—I understand that you're afraid. You're either afraid of something you've done or something you know."

Her cheeks flushed as her lips parted. After she swallowed, she said, "Will I see you again?"

"Oh, I'll be seeing you. Don't worry about that."

Chapter 23

"Why does anyone do what they do? Only the Lord knows for sure. Besides, it's better to make new mistakes than to repeat old ones."

AARON SCHROCK

As they pulled out of the parking lot, the enormity of what had just happened hit her. Lydia felt completely crushed. "This is everything I feared would happen, Walker. I didn't think it was possible, but I feel even worse than I did before."

"I know it's hard to hear, but at least now you know your birth parents obviously cared a lot about you, Lydia. It's understandable why your dad was worried about raising you by himself."

"I just hoped that I'd get better news, that's all."

"What would have been good news?"

She bit her lip, then spoke. "I don't know. I guess I wanted to know whether my parents were Amish. I had half-convinced myself that if the papers said 'Methodist' or 'Baptist,' my decision would be made. I'd known whether I was supposed to be Amish or not."

He darted a look her way. "You'd consider being English if your birth parents were that way?"

"Yes."

He chuckled. "Well, I guess you're stuck living like the rest of us then. You're going to have to figure things out on your own."

She frowned. "I thought you understood how I felt."

"I understand that you were hurt by your parents keeping secrets from you. And, I understand why you want to know more about your past."

"But you don't understand my need to know their religion?"

"I do . . . but then I don't, too. A person's faith is a personal thing, right? I don't know if knowing what your birth parents believed would make your decisions right now any easier."

"Walker, I thought you were on my side."

"I thought you should find out about your birth parents," he corrected. "But that doesn't mean I'm not going to give you my opinion."

"I see."

It was obvious she was irritated with him. Well, he was starting to feel irritated, too. Over the past few weeks, he'd listened to her complain and worry. Today, he'd taken time off school to drive her to the agency and had spent the last few hours trying to be supportive. But instead of being grateful, she was finding something new to be upset about.

"Lydia, I think you should make the choice about being Amish or English on your own."

"I don't think there's much of a decision to make anymore."

"Why do you say that?"

"If I was born Amish and was raised Amish, then I'm going to need to stay Amish. But if I'm going to not leave the order, then that means that we shouldn't spend any more time together."

"Are you saying I was your backup plan?" He didn't even try to hide his contempt for her reasoning.

"No. I mean, not exactly. It's just that if I was going to be English, then we might have a chance. But if I'm going to stay Amish, then we don't."

Walker gripped the steering wheel hard as her words sunk in. "Wow. I never thought our friendship was going to depend on a piece of paper. You should have warned me. If I'd had known, I would have been more stressed out."

"You are being deliberately cruel."

His temper flared. "No, Lydia. That would be you. I had no idea I was only going to be in your life on a trial basis, just in case you had use for me. I thought we were friends no matter what."

"We are friends."

"I don't think so. We were going to be friends—or maybe even something more—if it worked out. If it was easy for you."

Her blue eyes darkened with unshed tears. "You know that wasn't what I meant. You know how hard it's been these past weeks, realizing that Perry hadn't run off to St. Louis, that he's been dead in the ground and I didn't even wonder where he'd been."

"Everyone's been thinking that," he said, exasperated. "Haven't you realized that?"

"But we were sweethearts."

"You hadn't even seen him in weeks, right? I mean besides the night we all saw him at Schrock's store."

"I saw him the day after, too. On New Year's Eve," she blurted.

He almost pulled over. Then, thankful that he needed to slow down for a stoplight, he gathered his emotions as best he could. "I know what we said about keeping this quiet, but I didn't know you saw him on your own. Maybe you saw something important. Lydia, you better tell Detective Reynolds."

"I didn't 'see' anything, Luke." Her voice sounded near tears. "And if I tell him, he'll suspect me. I might have been the last person to talk to him."

"If you didn't kill him, someone else did."

"If I didn't kill him?" Pain mixed with guilt in her eyes. "After you drop me off, I don't want to see you again."

He was so fed up with her—so hurt that their kiss, their walks, their talks hadn't meant as much to her as they did to him—he gave it right back to her. "Great, because when I drop you off, I hope I never do."

"Perry only broke my heart when he got mixed up in things he never should have. What's your excuse?"

Her accusations were too much. "Don't you ever compare me to him again. Perry was a loser, Lydia." After hesitating, he said, "Perry was a drug user and a dealer. He lied and cheated and hurt more people than we'll probably ever know. I am nothing like him."

Lydia said nothing, though tears slid down her cheeks.

Walker did his best to pretend that he didn't notice.

It was a lot harder to pretend he didn't care.

When Walker finally pulled into her driveway, Lydia couldn't open the door fast enough. However, she paused to do the right thing. "Thank you for taking me to the agency."

He didn't even look at her. "I don't want your thanks."

"All right, then." She swallowed hard. "Goodbye, Walker."

He said nothing, only looked behind him, then reversed. Leaving only a trail of dust in his wake.

As she watched the dust settle, she felt like sinking to the ground as well. In the span of a few hours, she felt like she'd just lost everything important in her life.

The front door opened behind her.

"Daughter, you're back early."

For the first time in a while, Lydia turned to her mother's voice with a true feeling of eagerness. "Yes, Mamm."

"Look at you! You're crying." Her mother sat down on the top step and motioned her close. "Come talk to me. Did you go to the adoption agency?"

"I did."

"And . . . did you find what you were looking for?"

"I discovered my birth mother gave birth to me even though she'd been advised to never have children. She had a disease. Multiple Sclerosis."

Her mother pressed a hand to her chest. "I didn't know that."

"She died soon after having me, and her husband knew he couldn't raise me alone." Lydia braced herself for another wave of pain to hit her hard. But instead of despair, she felt almost at peace.

Although the truth wasn't what she'd hoped for, at least she knew where she came from. That was something, at least.

"I bet the memories might have been too hard for him to bear," her mother said after a few moments. "He must have loved his wife very much."

"I guess he did. He gave me up."

Her mother's chin lifted. "Your birth father let the agency find a better place for you. Your father loved you enough to give you to us, to two people who wanted you so much. Lydia, I should have found out the truth years ago and been open with you. It would have been easier on all of us."

"When you adopted me, you had another baby on the way. I guess it was too late to change you mind?"

Wrapping an arm around her shoulders, she said, "It wasn't too late. Lydia, we wanted you. Your birth parents' selfless actions were to our benefit. And for that, I will always be grateful."

Her mother's honest words made a lump form in her throat. "I still don't know if my birth parents were Amish or English," she blurted. "I just assumed it would say in the file."

"Ah. And that bothers you?"

The pain made talking difficult. *"Jah."*

"And . . . what did Walker say?"

Her mother's question caught her off guard. Since when did her mother care about what an *Englischer* boy thought? "I'm afraid we fought on the way home."

"Why?" she asked quickly. But before Lydia could catch her breath, her mother held up a hand. "Sorry. I mean, would you like to tell me what happened?"

"I told him that I had only intended to see him more if I had been born English. Because then it would make it seem like jumping the fence and being English would be okay."

Her mother visibly schooled her features. "Ah. So . . . so you're not going to leave our faith?"

"I guess not," she said slowly. Realizing even as she spoke that she wasn't sure how things were going to be resolved.

"Ah."

"But you still wish you could see Walker?"

She turned toward her mother. Her mother had put into words feelings she didn't even realize were there.

"Walker will never be Amish, will he?"

"No." Lydia sighed, looking at her black tennis shoes and

suddenly wishing she was barefoot. "He's never going to be Amish, and I don't think he's ever going to understand me or how confused I feel."

"People change, child. Opinions change too—these past few weeks have taught us that."

"We told each other goodbye, Mamm." Remembering the complete feeling of loss she felt, and how the dust from his tires flew up in the air and then settled again, looking for all the world like Walker and his truck had never even been there, Lydia slumped. "And worse, now I'm back where I was. Without a sweetheart."

"You're young, dear. It will happen." She stood up. "I don't know why I'm saying this, but perhaps it would be a good idea for you to do some thinking about your feelings for this Walker."

"Why?"

"Maybe there's more to him than just being an *Englischer*. Maybe there's more to each of us than just our specific faith. Our God guides all of us, yes? For a little while, I think I had forgotten that."

She turned and opened the door.

"Mamm?"

"Yes?"

"I need to call the detective and tell him something about Perry."

Her expression sharpened. "Hasn't he heard all you know?"

"I'm afraid not. But Mamm, as soon as I tell him, I'm going to go back to work at the greenhouse. I think I should return to my normal routine."

"Your help will be appreciated, but there is no hurry. You were right to ask for time off."

Opening up her purse, Lydia found the detective's card, and holding it in one hand, she left her purse on the steps and walked down the road to the phone shanty.

Suddenly her secrets didn't seem to matter all that much anymore. She was alone again, with only her memories and regrets for company.

She couldn't help it if Detective Reynolds thought she was a suspect. Or if he started to think she was a bad person because she'd kept secrets.

All that really mattered now was that she could live with herself every day. If she could do that, it might be enough.

"Reynolds," Luke blurted into the phone as he climbed the dark stairs to the attic in Mose's house. His friend was a pig.

It was night and day from the pretty, lemon-smelling oil and wood of Frannie's B & B.

"Detective? Detective Reynolds? Is that you?"

Gripping the phone harder, he tried to place the voice. "Is this Lydia Plank?"

"Jah." Over the line, her voice sounded thin and wary.

And Luke leaned his head against the wall, frustrated with himself.

"It's me. Hey, I'm sorry I answered like I did. I had something on my mind."

"I hope it wasn't anything too terrible."

As he located the light switch, he grimaced at his bare surroundings. Things definitely looked better in the dark. "It's nothing at all. Now what can I help you with?" he asked as he walked toward the child's sized desk and chair in the corner of the room.

"I need to talk to you about Perry again, if you have time."

Luke gripped the pencil he'd just picked up. There was

a hint of steel in Lydia Plank's voice. It sounded harsh and determined. New.

Maybe this was just the information that he'd been waiting for. "Can we do it over the phone?" He pulled open his notebook and scratched out today's date and time. He was tired of waiting. Tired of talking and talking. Just once he'd like one of the residents of Crittenden County to give him news in a straightforward way.

"Uh, I'd rather not. What I have to tell you is private. I'd rather not discuss it from a phone booth on the street."

"I completely understand." He straightened. "Where and when do you want to meet?"

"Can you come to my house this evening? We can talk there. Whenever you have time."

He looked at his watch and mentally calculated how long it would take him to finish moving in, shower off the dust and grime, grab something to eat, then get to her place. "One hour? Can I see you in one hour?"

A sigh of relief met his offer. "I'll be waiting. Thank you."

She hung up, leaving Luke to wonder if he was finally getting the break he'd been hoping for. If so, that meant he might only have to spend one night in Mose's dirty attic.

At the most, two nights.

Looking around at the old toys in sacks, at the old furniture that all looked broken or too unstable to use, he smiled.

He could solve the case and move back to his apartment and take full advantage of his air-conditioning. And his shower.

Yep, in no time, he could be back where he belonged. Where he needed to belong.

He was so happy about that, he decided to not even bother unpacking. He'd take wrinkles over dust and bugs any day.

Chapter 24

"Just because a boy don't meet everyone's expectations . . . it don't mean he deserved to get hit on the head and shoved in a well."

DEPUTY SHERIFF MOSE KRAMER

Luke found Lydia Plank sitting on a wooden bench in her family's rose garden. The fact that they'd sat there before together didn't escape him. Of course, the last time they'd sat together, he'd been the one full of questions and she'd been the one evading. She'd hardly looked at him, either.

Now things were different. Instead of looking shuttered and evasive, her whole expression was one of pure openness. From her wide eyes that looked directly at him, to the soft smile of welcome she gave him.

Even her stiff posture had lessened. And the two glasses and pitcher of lemonade beside her gave him no doubt that she was more than ready to make him feel at ease.

But instead of doing that, Luke felt his whole body go on alert. What had happened to bring about such a transformation?

"Lovely evening," he said as he approached. "For once the rain stopped."

"Hello, Detective. I thought you might be thirsty?"

"Lemonade sounds great. Thank you." He took the proffered glass, then sat down and waited. They were done with small talk and conversation, and they both knew it.

After a fortifying sip, Lydia set her glass down and took a deep breath. "Detective, I have something to tell you."

He took out a pad of paper and a pencil. He didn't really need it; he was good at memorizing information. But he figured it would set her more at ease. "I'm ready."

She closed her eyes briefly, opened them, then spoke in a rush. "I'm afraid I lied to you about when I last saw Perry."

"Ah."

"I saw him just a few days before he disappeared. And on New Year's Eve, too," she added in a rush. As soon as she was done speaking, she exhaled, picked up her glass with a shaking hand. Then set it back down.

"I see."

"Are you mad that I lied to you before?"

What could he say? He'd known from the beginning that she was keeping information back. But telling her that wasn't going to do either of them any good. "I'm not mad. I'm glad you told me now."

"I had wanted to tell you, but I was afraid, you see. I didn't want you to suspect me any more than you did."

Luke felt curiously deflated. He'd been hoping for more information. For something earth shattering.

But maybe there was more to the story?

He picked up his glass and sipped slowly, buying them both some time. When she sipped too, he smiled to himself. The way she was breathing so unsteadily made him worry about her. The last thing either of them needed was for her to hyperventilate or faint.

When she put her glass down, he spoke. "Why did you lie about when you saw him last?"

"Because it made me uncomfortable. I felt like I was betraying a confidence." She paused. Shook her head. "No, it was like I was betraying myself."

Betraying herself?

He took another sip of lemonade. It was obviously homemade; the tart, sour sting of fresh lemon juice hadn't mixed completely with the ice water and sugar. The result was tasty and made waiting for Lydia to gather her thoughts bearable.

"See, Detective Reynolds, when I last saw Perry, it was at a store in Marion."

"At Schrock's?"

"No. A group of us all saw him in front of Schrock's on the thirtieth, but we all kind of ignored him." She looked away from Luke, her eyes scanning the horizon. "Perry had kind of looked like he wanted to talk to us, but he'd burned so many bridges we turned away from him. On New Year's Eve, I saw him at the grocery store on South Main Street. He was sitting on a park bench at the edge of the parking lot."

"Alone?"

She nodded. "I saw him when I drove my buggy in, and decided to walk over to see him. He looked kind of forlorn, you see. And I was feeling guilty about how nobody had talked to him the day before." She looked over Luke's shoulder, like she was remembering a scene from long ago. "Used to be, Perry had been one of the crowd."

Luke wrote a couple of notes down. "So you walked over to him because you were worried . . ."

"I was. And I wasn't hurt or mad anymore. I walked over because I wanted to see for myself how he was doing. It had been so long since we'd talked."

"And you thought he'd tell you how he was?"

"Maybe not everything, but yes, I did think he would talk to me." Lines formed around her mouth as she frowned. "There were a lot of rumors about what he was doing . . ."

"About drug deals?"

"Jah." She bit her lip. "About a lot of things. He didn't look good, detective. He was pale and had lost weight. When I asked him if he was okay, he said he wasn't."

He took another sip, waited. Then gently nudged again. "Lydia, why wasn't Perry okay?"

"He was seeing another woman, I don't know who. She'd made him upset." She paused. "I think he was worried about other things, too. I don't think he was fancying his new English friends. It seemed they wanted more money from him. They wanted more money than he had."

"Do you have their names?" Luke forced himself to sound detached. Calm. He didn't want his excitement to scare her from telling him everything she knew.

"I do not. I didn't want to know their names, I'm afraid." Pretty blue eyes met his again. "To be honest with you, Detective, I didn't want to know anything more about Perry. Breaking things off with him had been hard for me. I didn't want to get involved in his life all over again."

"Then what happened?"

She bit her lip. "He asked me if I would have him back if he changed. Again."

"Again?"

"If he considered joining the church again." She waved a hand, obviously at a loss of how to describe the conversation. "If, you know, he went back to acting more like he used to. More the way I'd hoped he'd stay."

"And what did you say?"

"I told him no." Her voice held all the confusion and all the pain that he guessed was in her heart. "I told Perry that I knew who I was, that I knew who I wanted to be . . . and that I had no patience for a man who was confused about his life. I fear I was terribly full of myself and rather mean to him." Sliding a finger around the rim of the glass, she added, "I didn't think it was possible for him to make amends, which is wrong, I know. All of us can repent and ask forgiveness, don't you think?"

Luke slowly nodded.

"*Jah* . . . that is what the Bible teaches us."

"You told Perry this after you approached him? Even though you just told me you didn't want to make Perry mad or distrustful?"

"It doesn't make sense, does it?" she asked. "I can't explain myself except to say that I was feeling two different things . . . worry for a friend, but still hurting as a girlfriend."

"I see."

"Do you? See, that is why I've never shared the information, Detective. I didn't keep this a secret because I wanted to shield Perry. It was because I wanted to shield myself. Back then, on that day, I was so sure that I would always be right and he would always be wrong. Instead of caring about someone who was clearly in trouble, I wanted to keep myself from feeling more pain."

Sitting up straighter, she continued. "But lately I've realized that people can change. Oh, not like Perry of course, but incidents can happen. Or secrets can be told that change absolutely everything you thought to be true . . ." She paused. "I've told you everything now. I am sorry, Detective. I hope I haven't disrupted your search too much."

"What matters is that you finally did tell me everything you know. That helps a lot."

She got to her feet as well. "Detective, what do you do if you aren't sure how to pick up your feet and start walking? I seem to feel like I'm frozen in place right now. If you don't mind me asking, that is."

He shrugged, then pressed a hand to his stomach. "If all else fails, I trust my gut. And then I start walking, because we all have to go somewhere, right? It's pretty impossible to stay in one place for long." He waved then, and turned toward his vehicle, but not before catching a glimpse of Lydia sitting back down.

Luke wasn't sure, but he had a feeling she might be there for a very long time.

That, of course, was just a guess.

It had been a while since she'd eaten breakfast with Walker. "What are you doing up so early?" Abby asked as she walked to the cabinets and pulled out a box of Rice Krispies and a bowl.

He looked up from his own bowl of cereal; his was Cheerios. "Couldn't sleep."

After grabbing a spoon from a drawer, she looked his way. "Milk still out?"

"Yep." He lifted the gallon container. "Juice is here, too."

Once she got her cereal, she retrieved a glass and sat to his right. In the just the same spot she'd always sat with him. For years and years.

"Do you think we'll ever switch cereals? Mom and Dad switch all the time. I never liked anything but Rice Krispies."

He flashed a smile. "I was the same way with Cheerios."

Three bites later, Walker was finishing up his juice. "You ready for school?"

"Yep."

"Nervous?"

"Not so much. I've been thinking about something Grandma Francis said about weeding."

"What was that?"

"She told me to try to get rid of some of the garbage I've been carrying, and look around and appreciate what I have."

Intrigued, Walker leaned back in his chair. "Really?"

"Well, she didn't say 'garbage,' she said 'weeds.' But it was the same thing. She told me that only God needed to worry about my plans for the rest of my life. And in the meantime, I should try to learn something at school."

Walker's bark of laughter lifted her spirits. She smiled back at him. "Grandma Francis is a pistol, don't you think? I'm surprised Grandpa puts up with her."

He smiled her way. "She's not for sissies, that's for sure. She's never been worried about speaking her mind." Scooting out his chair, he rinsed out his bowl, then poured himself a cup of coffee. "Good luck today. Maybe with a new, Grandma Francis, attitude, things will be better for you."

"I hope so." Looking at Walker more closely, Abby decided that there was something off about him. "So, what are you doing today?"

"Same thing I'm always doing. Work and school."

"Will you see Lydia?"

He looked away, studying his coffee cup long and hard. "I don't think so. We might not see each other for a while."

"Because she's Amish and you're not?"

"Basically." He sipped again. "She's right. I feel the same

way. I don't want to be in a relationship that doesn't have a future. What's the point, right?"

"But the point it that you really like her and she really likes you back."

He stilled. "Do you think so?"

There was such hope on his face she smiled as brightly as she could. "Lydia stared at you when she didn't think you were looking."

He blinked, sipped his coffee, then turned around, shrugging. "It's over now."

"It doesn't have to be, does it?"

Instead of answering her, he grabbed his cell phone and checked the screen. "So, you want a ride to school?"

"So I don't have to walk all around the Millers' farm? Definitely."

"Go get your stuff. I'll be out at the truck."

Ten minutes later, Abby stepped out of his truck and waved goodbye, smiling at a story he told her about one of college friends.

Still thinking about her brother, Abby almost ran into another girl by the main door. When their bodies connected, her lunch fell to the ground.

"Hey!" she said.

When Abby glanced at her again, her heart sank. Way to go, she thought. She not only ran into another girl, but it was a cheerleader. "I'm so sorry. I wasn't watching where I was going."

"Obviously. You were smiling like crazy. No one can be that happy to be here."

"Oh. My brother just dropped me off. He was telling me a story." Feeling dumb, because who else in high school actually talked about their brothers? She bent down, grabbed her lunch sack, then stepped to the side. "I'm sorry again, Valerie."

"Wait." Valerie looked her over. "You're Abby Anderson, right?"

Abby nodded and tensed. Waiting for the inevitable comment or question that always came, something about finding a dead body.

"Aren't you in my American History class? Second Block, Hernandez?"

She blinked as her mind wrapped around the unexpected question. "Yeah."

"Did you understand the homework?"

Slowly, she let down her defenses. "Kind of."

"Do you mind if I show you what I did and you can tell me if I did it right? I wasn't sure how she wanted us to set up that graph."

Abby couldn't believe it. Here was a perfectly nice girl, Valerie James—a cheerleader, no less—and she wanted to talk to her about homework?

"Sure. Anytime."

"How about now?"

"Now?"

Valerie pointed to the clock mounted on the wall above their heads. "We've got, like, twenty minutes before first bell. Is that okay?"

"Sure." Next thing Abby knew, she was walking side by side with Valerie in the halls. Smiling as all kinds of people walked by.

More than a couple of people smiled back. Two said hi.

That's when Abby realized that today might just be the best day ever.

Chapter 25

"Some say a fool can't ever be trusted. I prefer to say that a fool can't ever be trusted twice."

AARON SCHROCK

Maybe it was time for a new job. It was becoming obvious that these days people were coming into Schrock's only to get rodent updates.

It was also becoming obvious that everyone—Mr. Schrock included—thought it was in Walker's job description to provide those updates.

"Walker, have you found all the guinea pigs yet?" Yet another person asked.

"Nope."

"How many are missing?"

"I'm not sure," he replied. Yet again. After listening for squeaks and hearing nothing, he got down on his knees and straightened an arrangement of leashes and other dog and cat items.

"Oh, Walker? Anything new with the pigs?"

Straightening, he bit back a groan. Maybe if he didn't reply the lady would go find Mr. Schrock?

"Walker? Did you hear me?"

"Yes, ma'am." With effort, he pasted a smile on his face. "Hey, Mrs. Miller. Uh, no. I don't think all the guinea pigs have been rounded up yet."

Just thinking about all their failed attempts made him frown. The pigs on the loose were surprisingly destructive and sneaky. And vocal! When the store was empty, they loved to chirp and chat to each other.

Though they were plenty quiet now.

She looked around the floor with distaste. "Maybe you should set a trap."

"I think that's what the snakes were for." He now knew for a fact that mousetraps didn't interest those pigs in the slightest.

"I wouldn't downplay the use of a good steel trap, Walker. Guinea Pigs are cute and furry, but they're going to raise a ruckus, mark my words."

"Yes, Ma'am." He kept his other thoughts to himself, because it really wouldn't be a good idea for him to talk badly about his boss.

But things had gotten out of hand. But one or two of the pigs were still on the loose, and had become a constant source of amusement for all the customers.

It was getting pretty old, working at a place that everyone made fun of. And a place that was like an overgrown circus. Too much was going on, way more than three rings' worth. What he needed was a nice, calm job. One that kept him busy but was predictable.

Racking his brain, he tried to think of something that fit the bill.

He thought about it while checking out two men who'd

come in for hardware supplies—and while he checked out Mrs. Miller and handed her her packed box of goods.

He was watching her leave, and thinking about maybe applying for a job at the university's student center, when his boss came back inside.

"Mrs. Miller get her eggs okay?" Mr. Schrock asked.

"Yep. Everything else, too."

The shop owner watched her through the glass in the door. "She's lookin' better, don'tcha think? For a while, she was looking mighty glum."

"It was probably hard, having Perry's body found on her land and all."

"Even though Mose and that fancy-pants detective seem to have decided long ago that Perry's death wasn't Perry's fault."

"Well, Perry was murdered. Someone must have had a pretty good reason to want him dead."

"True." Mr. Schrock looked at him for a long minute, then brushed his hands over the front of his trousers. "But no one really knows the why of it, do they?"

Walker figured his boss had a point, but he kept his silence.

"Well, now. You're going to be here another three hours, right?"

"Yes, sir. Do you have anything special for me to do?"

"How about you clean and straighten up things for a bit? With all the commotion that's been going on, things have gotten a bit out of sorts."

"I can do that. Sure."

"*Gut.*" He started to turn away, then stopped. "You being here is a blessing, Walker. I don't know what I would have done without you these past few weeks, especially with Jacob gone to Lexington. I probably don't tell you that enough."

Suddenly, guilt overwhelmed him. He knew had to say something. Knew he had to tell the whole truth. "Mr. Schrock, I never told you, but I quit because I saw Perry steal from you. I saw him take a twenty-dollar bill out of your cash box."

The older man paused. "I know."

Walker couldn't have been more shocked. "You did?" Now he felt even worse about the whole situation. "I'm really sorry. I know I should have tried to stop him."

"You were frightened, weren't you?"

Too embarrassed to speak, Walker nodded.

Mr. Schrock reached out and squeezed his shoulder. "It's okay, Walker. I knew Perry was up to no good, too. But I took my time firing him." His voice barely above a whisper, he said, "I kept hoping he would decide to stop all that. Or that I would realize that he wasn't doing things I suspected him of doing."

"He only got worse, though."

Mr. Schrock nodded. "That is true."

"I'm sorry I never told you. You know, before."

"You don't need to be sorry. What matters is you told me, *jah*?"

"Yes." And Walker realized Mr. Schrock was right. It did feel better to get the truth out between them.

Seeking to lighten the mood, he said, "Mr. Schrock, you ever get tired of everything being so crazy in here?"

"Not at all." Looking mildly offended, he said, "Besides, things ain't that crazy."

"Something is always going on. I mean, really." Walker stopped himself from naming examples. Because it was pretty obvious that guinea pigs and snakes were just the tip of the iceberg.

But that didn't stop his boss from frowning deeply. "You, Walker, sound like my wife."

Feeling hopeful, he said, "What does Mrs. Schrock say?"

"About what you'd think. She seems to think my life would be easier if I didn't have such foolhardy schemes." He leaned forward, capturing Walker in a piercing gaze. "But I've enjoyed the commotion, if you want to know the truth."

"Why?"

"Because it's kept me young. And laughing. I've gotten a lot of enjoyment from the guinea pig hunt, I can tell ya that."

"But maybe something else—"

But Mr. Schrock wasn't listening. His voice had warmed and he was looking off in the distance with a fond expression. "The way I figure it, I've only got one life to live. It might as well be exciting, you know? The last thing in the world I'd ever want is to stand here being bored." His lips turned up. "And have you seen how crowded it's been lately? Business is up."

That was news to Walker. "I wasn't under the impression that people were buying anything. I thought they only came to look and talk."

"That's because you're not the owner, Walker," his boss said with more than a touch of pride. "People are happy to stop by, pick up a few things so their gawking won't seem too rude, and take a peek at the action. It's exciting, that's what it is."

"Maybe," Walker replied.

Mr. Schrock shrugged. "I'd rather have excitement than know what I'm getting into every day. Wouldn't you agree that it's better to be surprised by what life gives you instead of planning everything? After all, we all need to enjoy today; it won't come back."

"That would be good, if I didn't like plans."

"Ach." Mr. Schrock's expression turned knowing. "Now we're getting somewhere. You've been thinking about Lydia Plank, ain't so?"

"A little bit."

"That Lydia, she's always been a favorite of mine. I had hoped she and Jacob would court, but they didn't suit."

Walker winced. He hated even thinking about Lydia being with any other guy. "Lydia and Jacob are pretty different."

The older man chuckled. "Some might say the same thing about you and Lydia, pup."

Even though he hadn't planned on getting the opinion of his boss, Walker couldn't resist a little free advice. "So, you think I need to step back and give Lydia space and time to figure out what she needs?"

"That's what I would do, but you should do it only if you care for her." His eyes twinkled. "And we both know you do."

Obviously his boss had been keeping a pretty close watch on everything that had been going on. "I care, but I don't know if I should."

"Seems to me that a person can't help their feelings." He winked. "I mean, take Mrs. Schrock. She still loves me and I've been practically bringing every creature from Noah's ark into our shop."

Walker chuckled. "You may have a point."

"I know I'm right about this. Just give Lydia time, Walker. Besides, you've got other things to work out."

"Such as?"

"Well . . . I know you've been upset about Perry Borntrager." He held up a hand when he saw that Walker was about to protest. "It's not a secret that we've all been upset about what happened to him, Walker. I know I am."

"I wish Sheriff Kramer would solve the case. Then Detective Reynolds could go back to Ohio, and the rest of us could go on with our lives. Waiting to find out who killed Perry is making everyone on edge."

"I think that city detective is doing the best he can." Leaning forward, he quipped. "Guess what, I heard the detective's been busy."

"Oh, yeah?"

"Um-hum. Heard he's found a few more leads." Mr. Schrock shrugged. "That's just hearsay, of course. All I do know is that if anyone in Crittenden County knows something about Perry that they haven't told the police, I hope they step forward. The detective can't do his job without knowing all the facts."

And just like that, the mood in the store changed. Walker became even more aware of the secrets he'd been keeping. "Actually—"

"Nope. Don't you be telling *me*. Talk to the detective, son."

"You think so? Even if he tells other people? And if the news gets out, and it might hurt some people along the way?"

Mr. Schrock studied him for a long moment. "Seems to me that trying to stop the truth from rising to the surface is a thankless task. People already are hurting, even people who didn't know who Perry was. And the longer that city detective is here, the longer everything will go on. No, we need to rip the bandage off the secrets, so to speak. Get everything out in the open."

The visual his boss was creating made Walker wince. "Mr. Schrock, that's pretty disgusting."

"Murder ain't pretty, son. Hasn't anyone ever told ya that?"

After his boss walked away, Walker pulled out his cell phone and texted the detective, asking for a meeting.

He tried to pretend he had a good reason for having the man's name in his directory.

Tried to pretend that he didn't feel a huge sense of relief when Detective Reynolds texted back that he'd be over within an hour.

Now all he had to do was hope no more animals were going to ruin his day for another sixty minutes.

Or that anyone would come in and ask about the wayward guinea pigs.

But that, of course, was probably too much to ask for.

Luke figured there was something in the air. What else could be encouraging these kids to finally start divulging secrets when pretty much everything he'd been saying for the last week or two had been falling on deaf ears?

When he opened the main door to the country store, he now knew enough to shut it firmly behind him and wait a minute. His muscles were tense and all of his senses were on alert, ready to be attacked by hens on the loose.

Mr. Schrock looked at him curiously. "Afternoon, Detective. What might you be you doing?"

"Preparing myself for flying poultry."

The shop owner scowled. "The hens are penned up today."

"Is there anything else on the loose? I feel like I now need to pause when entering, just to see what else might be exploding or running around."

"Well, we've got a few runaway guinea pigs, but unless you're a stalk of celery, I'd say you've got nothing to fear. So, did you come to gawk or buy?"

Feeling vaguely embarrassed, Luke shook his head. "Neither. I came to speak with Walker, if he's still here?"

"He's here." The store owner looked him over in the kind

of way that made Luke want to double-check that he hadn't spilled something on his shirt. "Why don't you have a seat over by the parking lot? There're some benches out there. I'll have Walker bring you some iced tea."

There was an edge to the man's tone, one that brooked no argument. That was fine. He'd happily play the game if it meant that he could get out of Crittenden County sooner than later.

"I'll be out there waiting."

He sat down on one of the benches. Moments later, a buggy parked near him. Almost immediately, an Amish woman slowly got out, secured her horse to a hitching post, then walked right by him, never once looking to meet his gaze.

Was she shy, or keeping her distance because he was English?

Or, perhaps it was because he was still a stranger to everyone.

Or maybe it was because everyone knew he was there to ask too many questions and pry into secrets.

But for whatever the reason, Luke found himself wondering, just for a moment, what it would feel like to finally feel like he belonged.

Less than five minutes later, Walker strode out to meet him, two plastic cups filled to the brim with tea in his hands.

Luke stood up to take one from him. "Thanks."

"No problem. Thank you for meeting with me."

Walker looked more nervous than he'd ever been. He'd set his glass on the ground by his feet and was gripping the edge of the bench so hard that it looked like he was afraid he'd collapse if he relaxed.

Luke took pity on him and prodded him on. "Want to go

ahead and tell me your news? Sometimes it's easier to get it over with."

The muscles in his cheeks tightened. "Perry was stealing money out of the cash drawer at the store," he blurted.

"Ah." After waiting two beats, he said, "And you never told your boss?"

Walker shook his head. "Perry said if I told he'd make sure Mr. Schrock would hear that we did it together."

"So what did you do?"

"I quit." After darting a look his way, Walker rested his elbows on his knees. "I figured no one would believe me. Perry was taking quite a bit of money, and it was just me and Jacob and Perry who had access to the cash drawer. I was the only one not Amish."

"Hmm."

"I know I should have done something better than that. I know quitting was pretty spineless."

Luke sipped his tea and carefully plotted his next words. To him, this was what detective work was all about. It wasn't car chases and shoot-outs and stake-outs. It was being able to ask questions that got answers. It was a talent for discovering the truth, no matter how hard the truth was to admit.

"Did you ever see Perry after you quit?"

Walker stared at him hard. "No."

"Sure about that?" He stretched his legs out. "Maybe you saw him by chance? Maybe he wanted more money . . ."

"I never saw him again. I turned to all my English friends and college and tried to make sure I was never around here."

"Do you think Mr. Schrock ever knew about the thefts? I bet he missed the money. Did he ever question you?"

"Not then. But it turns out that he knew." He shrugged, looking haunted. "Neither of us said anything, though." Looking once again at his knees, at his hands that were clenched together in front of him, he shook his head. "I really messed up, though. I should have said something to somebody."

"What do you think would have happened if you had?"

Luke didn't ask the question lightly. There was a certain wistfulness and despair in the boy's voice that conveyed that there were many unresolved hurts in his heart.

"I don't know."

"Time's up for saying I don't know." Determined to get some answers, Luke pushed harder. "Think, Walker, and tell me."

Pure hurt entered the boy's eyes. "If I had told, maybe Sheriff Kramer might have been called. And while I might have been blamed, too, maybe Perry would've gotten caught." His voice cracked. "And then maybe he would've changed."

"And?"

"And he'd still be alive, okay?" His voice turned hoarse as he angrily swiped a tear on his cheek. "If I hadn't been such a pansy, he would still be alive. Detective Reynolds, Perry's death is completely my fault."

To his surprise, Luke felt a lump in his throat, too.

"Perry's death isn't your fault."

"Yeah, right."

"I don't know what God had planned, but I feel certain that if you had told, Perry might have lashed out at you. It seems to me he was in a pretty desperate state of mind before he went missing. And believe me, you aren't the only person in the county to think that Perry had jumped the fence and left on his own accord."

Slowly Walker stared at him. "Yeah?"

There was such hope and wonder in the boy's voice that Luke was tempted to smile. Instead, he nodded slowly.

"Yeah. I didn't know Perry Borntrager, but I know dealers and theives and addicts. That path is a dangerous one, and once a person is sliding down that path, everything that's right and wrong gets skewed and twisted. I'm not saying that holding back information was the right thing to do. But I will say that I don't think you alone could have changed the direction of Perry's life."

Walker blinked hard, then grabbed the glass and drank half the tea. When he visibly calmed himself, he looked back his way. "What happens now?"

"Now? I'll keep digging. And you . . . you relax for a bit. When I need more information, I'll find you."

"And in the meantime?"

"In the meantime, live your life, Walker. You're a good man." Luke stood up then, grabbed his plastic cup of tea, and walked to his truck.

Nothing was settled. Nothing was solved.

But he was finally getting a clearer picture; people were finally talking to him, and he had a few ideas of who he was going to interview next.

It wasn't a lot, but it was something. And right that moment, it was enough to raise his hopes that Perry's murderer would be brought to justice.

Chapter 26

"The first time I met Perry, he was trying to put four or five squirming, yowling kittens in a cage Mr. Schrock had put out. Customers were everywhere; a couple of them complaining about something.

I stood there, frozen.

"Here. Take two, English," he'd said with a grin, thrusting a pair of the hissing cats at me. "No way am I going to do this job by myself."

See, that's kind of how Perry had been. He was at his best when things weren't going good. It was only when things were quiet that he seemed uneasy."

WALKER ANDERSON

"Go on home, Walker Anderson. You look like you've been run over by an ornery ox. I'm thinking you need to relax a bit."

"Thanks, Mr. Schrock." Walker felt like something far bigger than an ox had run him over. The way he was feeling, it seemed the damage had been caused by something more along the lines of a Mack truck. "I'll be back tomorrow, early."

"You come when you're supposed to. No earlier."

"Yes, sir."

He took the long way home. He needed time to compose himself before he saw anyone in his family. The way he was now, his mom was going to take one look at him and begin a monster interrogation.

He drove by the high school, drove by a group of shops and the library. Thought about how for most of his life, he'd taken the town for granted. Nothing much had ever changed.

Then, it seemed, all at once, everything had changed. Now Miller's field wasn't just the Millers' anymore, it was where Perry's body had been hidden. And Schrock's store just wasn't where he worked—it was the place where they'd all ignored Perry the day before he went missing.

Though he hated to think about it, his mind drifted back to that night. He'd stopped by Schrock's to say hi to Jacob, and to get an idea if Mr. Schrock would maybe hire him again. Jacob had been standing out on the front porch, chatting with Lydia and Frannie Eicher. Frannie's friend Beth had been there, too. When he'd arrived, it had almost been like a party . . . everyone was talking about Christmas and discussing plans for New Year's Eve.

Sitting in one of the rocking chairs next to Lydia, Walker was listening to Jacob tell a story about his father.

They laughed and joked around.

And then Deborah Borntrager showed up. The girls stiffened, but were nice enough to Deborah. But once Perry came out of the shadows, leaning against the railing, the mood changed again.

He looked bad. He'd lost a good thirty pounds, and his skin was broken out, and the glow that was usually a permanent fixture in his eyes was gone.

"Hey," he said. "Never thought I'd see all of you in one place."

All of them froze. The girls looked away. Jacob turned his back to Perry. Just like they'd never been friends at all. Suddenly, Walker was the only person facing Perry. "Hey, Perry," he said. "How are you?"

"I'm screwed, that's how I am." He gripped the railing. Almost like he needed the support. Lowering his voice, he slurred, "Hey, Walker, how 'bout I join y'all?" He almost smiled. "We could talk about old times."

Walker didn't want Perry anywhere near. "You better not." Hastily, he came up with a lame excuse. "Mr. Schrock will get mad, you know."

"Oh. Well, want to go hang out with me? We don't have to do anything. Just sit." He waved a hand. "Catch up. I . . . I could use a friend right now. I'm deep in some bad stuff . . ."

"I better not."

"No? Oh. Oh, yeah. Sure." He walked off, leaving Deborah.

When he was out of sight, Jacob laughed nervously. Minutes later, Frannie, Beth, and Lydia left, taking Deborah with them.

"Want to get a Coke or something?" Jacob asked.

"Nah . . . I'd better get on home," he said.

But he hadn't gone straight home. He'd driven for hours. Thinking about Perry needing a friend.

And thinking about how he'd refused to be one.

Walker shook his head, coming back to the moment. As he drove past the park, he saw her. A long figure, swinging on the old rusty swing set that had seen better days around 1980.

Against his better judgment, he pulled into the parking lot.

Lydia's head popped up when she spied him. But to his relief, she didn't run away. Instead, she stayed where she was and looked at him with wide eyes as he walked toward her.

His mind went blank.

And then, when she smiled, everything he wanted to say came rushing forth. Just like it had been on the tip of his tongue all along.

"Lydia, we need to talk."

"About what?" Her voice sounded hesitant. But her eyes . . . they looked hopeful.

He took that to be a promising sign.

"Us."

"Oh? What about us?"

He noticed she wasn't smiling, but she wasn't looking wary or scared, either. No, instead she was kind of looking at him in a whimsical way, like he was telling her a story that she was unexpectedly interested in.

He sat down on the child's swing two over from her. "I think you were wrong when you said we didn't belong together."

"You do?"

"Yep. Lydia, see . . . I think we have a future."

Her eyes widened. "Really? Even if I'm Amish and you are not?"

"Even so. Though we come from different worlds, I still want to be with you."

Her mouth dropped open like she was trying to find the perfect words. Finally she said, "Did something happen? I thought we were mad at each other."

He grinned. "I don't want to stay mad. Do you?"

She shook her head. "As soon as I cooled down, I wanted to apologize. I should have . . . I mean, you've been such a good friend to me."

He looked at her sideways—afraid to hope that she wanted more. But just as afraid to not tell her what he was thinking. "I want to be more than your good friend, Lydia."

The seconds that passed while she visibly gathered her courage felt like the longest minutes of his life.

Then finally, she spoke. "I want us to be more than friends, too. All I know is that I like you a lot. I like you, and I like being with you. That's enough for me."

"We don't have to decide anything about our future right now. Not if you don't want to." Walker gazed at her face. "I think we've both learned that it's important to take it one day at a time." He smiled. Thought about how brave she was. Thought about how she'd dealt with everything that had been thrown at her lately. She lost a boyfriend, then found out he'd been murdered. Then discovered she was adopted. And now, she was being brave enough to date him. To grow closer. To be his friend.

"But I will let you in on a little secret . . ." He paused. Could he really tell her how he was feeling? If she was being so brave, he should show some courage too. "I'll have you know that I've recently fallen in love myself."

"Is that right?" One perfect brow lifted. "With anyone I know?" There was a new lift to her voice. A warmth, a surety that he'd heard before.

That tone made him smile, right in tune with the way his pulse was racing. "You know her. You know her very well, as a matter of fact."

"Oh?"

"Uh-huh. See, she's a great girl. Really great."

"Girl?"

"Girl, woman, whatever," he said over a chuckle. "See, the thing is, she's not perfect. But she's pretty much perfect for me."

"You really think so?"

"Yep." More softly, he said, "Here's something else about

her. She's pretty. Really pretty. But what's more important than that is the way she carries herself. She's graceful and sweet and strong." He paused, then looked her way. "Fact is, that Lydia Plank is pretty much the strongest woman I've ever met. Before I knew it, I'd fallen in love with her. Full on. Head over heels."

She turned and looked at him, too. "What are you going to do about that?"

He got to his feet and walked the three steps, even though it felt like three miles. Stopped in front of her. "I thought I'd let her know how I felt. Finally."

She got to her feet. Her hands looked like they were shaking. Was that the reason she was still gripping the chains of the swing?

"And then?" she murmured.

Carefully, he pulled her hands from the chains and wrapped them securely into his own. Linked their fingers. "And then, after I told Lydia this news, I thought I'd take her hands . . . then pull her closer. Into my arms." He did just that. Guided her closer. Close enough to notice how luminescent her eyes looked.

"And after that?"

"And after that? I don't know. I guess I'll have to stand and wait and see what she thinks about what I have to say."

She nibbled on her bottom lip. Seemed to think about his words for about two seconds.

Then stared at him and smiled. "Well, here's what I'm thinking is going to happen—"

"Yeah?"

"It's just a guess, mind you?"

"What?"

"I have a feeling that when Lydia Plank hears that speech,

why, she's going to loop her hands around your neck"— she paused, doing just that—"and then she's going to say that she loves you right back."

His heart felt like it was about to explode. "Do you have any idea if she's going to maybe kiss me then?"

"You really want to know?"

He nodded. Tongue-tied again.

She flashed a smile before she rose on her tip toes and kissed him, full on the lips, right there in the middle of the park.

In plain view of the parking lot and the street and the group of preschoolers that had just come running over to the jungle gym.

And when they finally stopped in order to catch their breath, Walker held her close.

And he realized that they didn't have all their troubles figured out right that moment. Perry's murder was still a mystery. So was their future.

But for now, knowing they had each other, right there, right then . . . well, it was enough.

And if they had love, they didn't need to know what would happen in the future. All they needed was a desire to tackle it together.

That much he knew to be true.

Dear Reader,

A couple of years ago, when I was researching areas for the Families of Honor series, I came across an Amish community nestled in rural western Kentucky. The community was rather small. The whole area was rather secluded. And there was a creek that ran through the middle of it called Crooked Creek. I knew I wanted to visit there—at least through a book!

A year passed. I ultimately set the Families of Honor books in northern Ohio. But I still couldn't forget about Crittenden County. And as writers often do . . . I had an idea. I decided to write a trilogy of books about a man who died, and how his death affected a whole lot of people, both Amish and English. After somewhat nervously asking my editor what she thought about me writing a series of romances set in the middle of a murder investigation, I began the series.

Writing *Missing*, the first book of The Secrets of Crittenden County series, has been especially gratifying. I've loved the challenge of writing about a mysterious death all while showing that hope and God's grace can be present anywhere. It's been hard and scary and challenging. I've enjoyed getting to know the folks of my fictitious Crittenden County, most of all Mr. Schrock and his never-ending array of bad sales ideas. I also enjoyed writing about Lydia and Walker—two people thrown into circumstances beyond their control but who somehow end up better for it.

I hope you enjoyed the book.

Thank you, as always, for taking a journey with me to another town. I hope you will find that your visit to Crittenden County was time well spent. And I sincerely hope that you will continue the series with *THE SEARCH*. I promise, more secrets will be revealed!

With blessings and my thanks,

Shelley Shepard Gray

Please "friend" me on Facebook, visit me at my website, or write to me at:

Shelley Shepard Gray,
10663 Loveland, Madeira Rd. #167,
Loveland, OH 45140

Questions for Discussion

1.   Many of the characters in the novel deal with the idea of *change*, like the ripple effect of water. Can you think of any instance when one decision caused a ripple effect in your life, or for your family?

2.   Some of the people in Crittenden County felt guilty for not worrying more about Perry when he went missing. Do you think this guilt is deserved? Could Perry's death have been prevented?

3.   Lydia wonders how the new knowledge about her birth parents will influence the rest of her life. What do you think? Is she overreacting to her parents' news?

4.   I enjoyed writing about Walker and Abby's relationship. Who in your family are you particularly close to? How has that relationship helped you during a time of crisis?

5. Abby's Grandma Francis talks to Abby about "weeding" out the unnecessary problems in her life. What in your life could use some weeding?

6. How has Walker proven that he is the man for Lydia? What do you think needs to happen next for their relationship to move forward?

7. I found the following Psalm to be particularly inspiring for the writing of this book:

"I will call to you whenever I'm in trouble, and you will answer me." (Psalm 86:7)

What does the Psalm mean to you?

8. I thought the Amish saying "It is better to make new mistakes than to repeat old ones" was particularly apt for *Missing*. Does the saying have any meaning for you?

Turn the page for an exciting preview of
Shelley Shepard Gray's next book,

The Search

On sale June 2012

THE SEARCH

The Secrets of Crittenden County
Book Two

Prologue

December 10

Perry Borntrager was on drugs again.

Frannie Eicher had suspected it when she first spied his glazed expression, then had known it for sure when she heard his slurred words. Now, here she was, alone with him in the outskirts of the Millers' property. Not a soul knew where she was, or that once again she was meeting him in secret in a place where they weren't supposed to be at all.

Oh, she was sure he wouldn't hurt her. Perry wasn't dangerous. But knowing that they were completely alone, that no one would hear if she cried out for help, was unsettling.

Especially since at the moment Perry wasn't acting like himself.

The Perry she'd known all her life had been patient. Methodical. A man who was easy to get along with, a steady kind of man.

That was not the case anymore.

"Glad you finally made it." His voice was snide, clipped.

"I'm sorry I'm late," she said. "I had a terrible time getting out of the inn, everyone wanted 'just one more thing'." Frannie smiled sheepishly. Then waited, half hoping he'd take her bait and ask about her cherished bed-and-breakfast.

He didn't.

"It didn't matter if you came on time or not. Nothing would change my feelings. I hate it here. I always have." A low laugh erupted from his chest. "But you knew that, right?" He was walking in a zigzag way. Almost as if he was having trouble placing his feet just so on the uneven ground beneath them.

"You hate being here on the Millers' farm?" she joked as she struggled to keep up with his awkward pace.

He didn't realize she was kidding. *"Jah,"* he said over his shoulder as they approached the abandoned well on the edge of the property. "The Millers' farm, Marion, Critten-den County. Kentucky . . ." His voice grew louder. More hostile. "What's the difference, anyway? I hate it all."

She stopped a few feet away from him—where it was safe—though she reminded herself that he would never hurt her. "If you don't like it here, what are you going to do?"

"Get away when I can."

She shouldn't have been shocked, but she was. "And go where?"

"I don't know. Anywhere. Someplace else." Slumping against the stacked rocks that surrounded the top of the well, he looked at her contemptuously. "What about you, Frannie? Don't you want to get away?" The cold air made his breath appear like little puffs in the sky. It also served as a reminder about how cold she was.

And how much colder their relationship had become.

She felt his gaze skim her whole body, as if he was looking at her from the top of her black bonnet covering her *kapp* to the toe of her black tennis shoe, and she'd come up wanting.

"I've never thought about leaving here," she said hesitantly. "Crittenden County is home. Besides, I just took over the Yellow Bird Inn." Unable to stop herself, she added, "I refinished the wood floors, you know, and it looks so pretty . . ."

Perry merely stared.

She swallowed. "Um. I . . . I could never leave it."

"You could never leave it." His blank stare turned deriding. "That inn ain't nothing special."

She'd spent the last month helping two men paint the outside a wonderful, buttery yellow. The yellow color went so much better with the name of the inn than the white and black paint ever did. The Yellow Bird Inn needed yellow paint, surely.

Because it was a special place. And very special to her. "One day it might be."

He spit on the ground. "It's not going to make any money. No one comes here unless they have to."

She fought to keep her expression neutral. As if he hadn't hurt her feelings. "My aunt seemed to do all right with it. And some people have come to visit and stay." Lifting her chin, she said, "Why, just the other day an English couple all the way from Indianapolis said they'd tell their church friends about my B&B."

His voice turned darker. "The only reason the English come here is look at the Amish."

"They come for the scenery and the greenhouses, too." She bit her lip. "We are blessed to live in such a pretty place, you know. Why, we are surrounded by trees and hills and valleys."

He laughed softly. "Frannie, you need to get your head out of the clouds. The English come here to gawk. To take our pictures with their camera phones." His voice deepened.

"You're not going to make any money, Frannie. You ought to leave that place."

"And do what?"

His mouth opened, then shut again quickly. As if he was having trouble forming his thoughts.

She waited. As she stood there, her toes began to burn from the cold ground. Her eyes watered from the brisk wind.

And once again she wished Perry would get away from those people who supplied him with the drugs that made him unrecognizable to her . . . to all his friends.

"The guys I've been working with, they've promised me big things," Perry finally said, his voice strained tight with emotion. "You . . . you could come with me. If you changed."

Frannie knew the men he'd been working with were *Englischers*. *Englischers* of the worst sort. They weren't local. They only came to their area with the intent of causing trouble, of encouraging more people to take the drugs Perry was now so fond of.

"I don't want to change, Perry." Feeling her way through the conversation, she looked beyond him, looked into the dense, lush woods on the outskirts of the Millers' property. "I like it here. And I like how I am."

And though she didn't want to be prideful, she felt disappointed that he didn't see her attributes. Most boys had found her light blue eyes and auburn hair pleasing. Most people found her efforts to continue her aunt's bed-and-breakfast to be commendable.

It was obvious he did not.

"You are stuck in an old boarding house in the middle of a county down on its luck."

"Perhaps." She smiled slightly, determined not to let him

see how nervous she was becoming. "I guess I'm still the same Frannie I've always been."

For a moment, his gaze softened. Just like he, too, remembered how they'd once played tag in each other's yard after church. How they'd been friends before he'd ever courted Lydia. Before he'd finally looked her way with new eyes, finally saw her as though he hadn't realized that she'd been there all along, just waiting for him.

"You aren't the same. Just like me, you're different than the way you used to be. Change always happens. It can't be helped."

"I suppose you're right." She bit her lip. How much did she want to say when he was in this condition?

But how much did she dare keep inside? Didn't her heart mean anything? Didn't her soul and conscience count just as much?

"Perry, I don't want you to move away. And I don't like the men you've been keeping company with. I wish you'd rethink your decisions." She ached to tell him more, to beg him to seek help.

But his thunderous response stopped all that.

"What are you? My mother?"

"Of course not," she said quickly.

His gaze darkened. "I don't need another mother, Frannie. One nagging woman in my life is more than enough."

"I know. I mean, I know that, Perry. I'm only offering my opinion. That's all."

"Don't."

There was a new anger in his voice, and she knew she'd put it there. It was time to go. Perry had chosen his path and he certainly wasn't going to change it for her.

Perhaps he wasn't even able to make the changes for himself. Maybe the drugs weren't ever going to loosen their grip on him.

She stepped backward. "I'm going to go back home now."

"Alone?"

"*Jah.* I . . . I think it's best. I mean, I don't think we have much more to say to each other."

He stared at her for a long moment, then held up his hand. "Hold on. I . . . I brought something for you." He fumbled in a pocket in his coat, pulled out a pair of sunglasses. "These are for you."

"You brought me sunglasses?" She couldn't imagine a more peculiar gift. Especially on such a cloudy, wintery day.

"Yeah. They're nice, ain't so? Expensive, too. Cameron, one of my friends from St. Louis, picked them up for me. He got two pairs." He threw off the comment, just as if she were no more important to him than an afterthought.

She was becoming even more confused. He'd brought her men's sunglasses, given to him from one of his drug dealing friends? "Whatever would I do with them?"

"Wear them, of course." Crooking a finger, he motioned her closer. "Come here and try them on."

They were only sunglasses. Though it wasn't in the norm for Amish to wear sunglasses, it wasn't unheard of, either.

But these sunglasses looked expensive. And looked so worldly. These screamed English and were built for a man's face, not her own.

They seemed to stand for everything she was not.

And right then and there, she knew she couldn't accept them. Couldn't touch them.

All they would do was symbolize everything that was wrong with them. With her. With Perry.

"No. I don't want them, Perry."

"You're not even going to try them on? Not even going to touch them?" He held the glasses by one of the handles. "What's wrong, Frannie? Afraid you're going to get tainted?" His voice was loud now. Loud enough to reverberate around them.

But still not loud enough for others to overhear.

She stepped farther back. "I just don't want them. You should keep them."

His eyes narrowed. Then, with one swift motion, he tossed the glasses with an arc.

Frannie followed their path with a lump in her throat. "Perry! You shouldn't have done that."

"If you don't want them, I don't, either. We'll leave them for the Millers. Maybe their cows or something can use them." He grinned as if he'd made some joke. "Go, Frannie. Go on, now."

"Perry, don't be like this. Maybe we can get you some help . . ."

"I don't need *help*, Frannie. And I don't need you. Just go. And let's hope we never see each other ever again."

She turned. And ran.

And realized as she heard his laugh behind her that finally . . . finally they once more had something in common.

She, too, hoped she'd never see him again.

But of course, she doubted she would ever be that lucky.

BOOKS BY
SHELLEY SHEPARD GRAY

THE SECRETS OF CRITTENDEN COUNTY

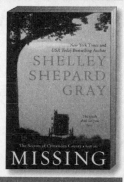

MISSING
978-0-06-208970-0 (paperback)

The peaceful Amish community of Crittenden is thrown into chaos when one of their members is found dead at the bottom of a well. As the town copes with their loss and deals with an outside police investigation, two people who knew the victim discover strength in a most unlikely companionship that offers solace, understanding, and the promise of something more.

FAMILIES OF HONOR

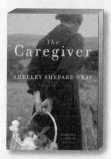

THE CAREGIVER
978-0-06-202061-1 (paperback)

A chance encounter changes the lives of a young widow and a broken-hearted man. While they try to forget each other, neither can disregard the bond they briefly shared.

THE PROTECTOR
978-0-06-202062-8 (paperback)

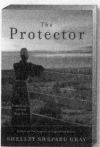

Ella Troyer feels bitterness towards the man who bought her family's farm once her father passed away. What she does not know is that he secretly hopes Ella will occupy the house again . . . as his wife.

THE SURVIVOR
978-0-06-202063-5 (paperback)

In the final book in the Families of Honor series, young Amish woman Mattie Troyer has healed from the cancer that nearly took her life . . . but can she find the man who can mend her lonely heart?

SISTERS OF THE HEART

HIDDEN
978-0-06-147445-3
(paperback)

WANTED
978-0-06-147446-0
(paperback)

FORGIVEN
978-0-06-147447-7
(paperback)

GRACE
978-0-06-199096-0
(paperback)

SEASONS OF SUGARCREEK

WINTER'S AWAKENING
978-0-06-185222-0
(paperback)

AUTUMN'S PROMISE
978-0-06-185237-4
(paperback)

SPRING'S RENEWAL
978-0-06-185236-7
(paperback)

CHRISTMAS IN SUGARCREEK
978-0-06-208976-2
(hardcover)

**Visit www.ShelleyShepardGray.com and find Shelley
on Facebook for the latest news on her books!**

Available wherever books are sold, or call 1-800-331-3761 to order.